Thomas Christopher Greene was born and raised in Worcester, Massachusetts. He graduated from Hobart College and the MFA in Writing Program at Vermont College. His first novel, *Mirror Lake*, was published in 2003. He currently lives and works in Vermont. Tom can be found at www.thomaschristophergreene.com

AFTER THE RAIN

On the idyllic banks of the Dog River, in the lush green countryside of Vermont, Charlie has built a life for himself. He's happy enough running the family restaurant, and his only real regret is the absence of his brother, Owen. Once close, Owen and Charlie have not seen each other for years now — the ties of brotherhood were torn apart by their father's strange legacy — and a trail of postcards is all that is left. Charlie's is a solitary existence until he hires Claire to assist him in the restaurant. They begin a passionate affair and, in Claire, Charlie feels he has found his reason for living. But when Owen returns it seems suddenly that the past is destined to threaten both brothers' future . . .

Books by Thomas Christopher Greene
Published by The House of Ulverscroft:

MIRROR LAKE

THOMAS CHRISTOPHER GREENE

AFTER THE RAIN

Complete and Unabridged

CHARNWOOD
Leicester

First published in Great Britain in 2004 by
Century
The Random House Group Limited
London

First Charnwood Edition
published 2005
by arrangement with
Century
The Random House Group Limited
London

British Library CIP Data

Green, Thomas Christopher, *1968 –*
After the rain.—Large print ed.—
Charnwood library series
1. Brothers—Fiction 2. Vermont—Fiction
3. Large type books
I. Title
813.6 [F]

ISBN 1–84395–867–8

Published by
F. A. Thorpe (Publishing)
Anstey, Leicestershire

Set by Words & Graphics Ltd.
Anstey, Leicestershire
Printed and bound in Great Britain by
T. J. International Ltd., Padstow, Cornwall

This book is printed on acid-free paper

The author gratefully acknowledges permission from
Daniel D. Greene to reprint the song
'I'll Never Be Long Gone' which was released by
The Butterflies of Love, copyright
© LLC Big Bower Music and Daniel D. Green

FOR TIA

Bury me in the trunk of your car.
I won't be ready to sleep.

I'll drive underground,
follow your footsteps around town,
until I track you down.

Vanishing and reappearing,
I'll never be long gone.

Bury me wherever you are.
I don't want to have to search that far.

I know a place where we could go,
where it always snows,
but it's never cold there.

Vanishing and reappearing,
I'll never be long gone.

THE BUTTERFLIES OF LOVE,
I'll Never Be Long Gone

BOOK I

1

The last day of Charles Bender's life, he closed the restaurant, Charlotte's, for the first time since the birth of his second child, Owen, seventeen years before. This was in September. It was a beautiful Vermont day, high clouds floating in a clear blue sky, a warm sun for the season and the first of the fall leaves beginning to change, hints of red and yellow and purple among the deep green of the forest of Eden.

Charles had spent the morning at the restaurant calling those who had reservations for this evening, old friends many of them, some of whom had made their plans weeks in advance. Charlotte's was on a back dirt road in a converted one-room schoolhouse but it had a reputation that belied both its size and its location.

He had also called the waitresses, women who, for the most part, had been with him from the beginning, and told them to take the night off. A few questioned him, wanted to know if everything were okay, but most said little, for Charles was widely liked but was also a man who did not invite questioning easily. Next he called his two sons at home and told them not to bother coming into the kitchen today, that he was closing Charlotte's for the night. He told them they would eat at home because it was something they never did and because he wanted

3

to. They, too, did not ask any questions for the same reason the waitresses did not, and for the same reason the customers did not. They loved their father very much and they respected him. But they had learned as children to accept his motivations for what they were. When he finished talking to them, he asked to speak to their mother, the small restaurant's namesake, Charlotte herself. He told her he was making a family dinner. In her voice he heard traces of concern but he did not worry about it, for he knew that she, too, would not ask. Long ago, Charlotte had learned to trust his instincts, to give in to what he wanted, and know that at heart he was a gentle man who tried to do the right thing.

After he made his calls, he took one last long walk around the place. He lingered in the large kitchen he had built with the help of a few friends some twenty years before. The large kitchen with the wooden farm table in the middle, the commercial stove and indoor grill along one wall. A walk-in on the opposite wall. It was a room he loved like no other. He loved the stove the best, how when you stood in front of it you could look out the windows to the flood-plain and to where the Dog River ran through the forest of poplars and spruce and birch behind. He had been in other commercial kitchens and found them to be soulless places. Factories for food. Gleaming stainless steel and never any windows. While he knew that beauty could be created in such a place, he always wondered why it should. Why not cook somewhere that gave you inspiration? That tied you to what you found important? The forest and the soil and the water. The earth itself. For this he had the windows, and he had the back porch, where on many nights when service slowed he would sit and smoke and look into the dark, look at the deep forest, listen to the night sounds, the different sounds of the river during every season, the sounds of peepers in the spring, the deep abiding quiet of winter.

Charles left the kitchen and walked into the dining room. He smiled when he entered it and looked around as if seeing it with virgin eyes, remembering what it was like when he first bought it. Here, in this room, he thought, is where you see the schoolhouse it once was. You see it in the old wide-plank floorboards painted gunmetal gray. You see it in the large windows that look out the front to the Old County Road, and then beyond it to a narrow valley with steep forested escarpments on either side, the Peak of Hunger Mountain rising above it all. You see it in the original chalkboard that runs along the wall next to the kitchen door. The chalkboard that once held arithmetic lessons for a forgotten generation of Eden children, that now was used to write the daily menu. You see it, as well, in the pot-bellied woodstove that dominates the corner opposite the small bar, used now more for ambience than for heat, yet lit nonetheless when the temperature drops, aged and cracked ash burning hard and fast in the firebox on winter days.

Charles stood in the middle of the room and

drank it all in, the small tables, the ladder-backed chairs, the tangerine walls. If it were a normal evening, in just a few hours the voices of the diners would fill the room, soft jazz in the background, and he would be in the kitchen firing sixty entrées over four hours. He knew tonight it would be empty. And though he would not be here to see it, he fully expected that, on other evenings not so different from this one, nothing would change, that it would go on. Go on in his image. He counted on it, in fact.

Outside, Charles hung the Closed sign on the handle of the large schoolhouse door. He stopped and took in his surroundings, the grassy floodplain, the river, the green forest starting to show its color, the bluish rocky peaks of the Worcester Range beyond the valley with its steep forest walls. Hunger Mountain.

He lighted a cigarette and he looked at the blue sky above. He watched the swiftly moving clouds, white and puffy, a shade of gray on the earthward side, catching the first shadows of the evening, hinting at the rain to come. But for now the breeze when it blew was warm on his arms. It was a perfect day. A perfect Vermont day.

★　★　★

Of the two boys, Charles Bender Jr., known to all as Charlie, was more his father's son. He was almost six feet four, as tall as Charles, and while on this day he still had a full head of brown hair, you could see where it was starting to recede on his forehead and you could see that it was

6

thinning. He had his father's pale blue eyes, a robin's egg blue, and while you might not think him handsome, there was a strength about him, a presence, that echoed his father. By contrast, his brother, Owen, the younger of the two Bender boys, had the good fortune to physically resemble his mother. Charlotte was the kind of beauty seldom seen in Eden, a tall, willowy blonde who turned heads in a northern town of this size. Owen had her fair hair, and her sharp green eyes, and he was tall, too, though not as tall as his brother, closer to six feet two, and slender. He had his mother's features, her small nose, her high cheekbones, and you might have thought him a pretty boy if it were not for the saving grace of his jaw, which suggested his father, strong and angular, and had the effect of making his whole face masculine.

On the night their father closed the restaurant, the two boys knew something was happening. They knew this was not simply another family dinner. Yet it remained unarticulated between them. For if they were to talk about it they might have guessed what it was, and neither of them wanted to admit what they saw, and what they knew their mother saw, and perhaps others as well: their father was dying. And while both of the boys were too young to know anything worth knowing about dying, they thought they knew it when they saw it, and they were at an age when to give it words would have given the thought, the idea, credence.

The truth was that Charles Bender, since he was in his early teens, had been a heavy smoker.

He loved to smoke. He loved everything about it. He loved the feel of the thin cigarette in his hands, the inhaling of the smoke into his lungs, the contemplative mood that smoking put him in. Regardless of what you think of smoking, if you have ever tried it, you know it can supply a certain comfort. He especially liked smoking at the end of a busy night, preferably in the summer when it was warm, when he could sit on the back porch of Charlotte's and listen to the clink of dishes being washed, dishes on which he had delivered the best food he could deliver; and listen, too, to the river and the woods and know that the day behind him was a day richly lived; a day in which he had done all he could to slow the dark gathering around him while he smoked, as if that were possible in the first place, as if that were not simply some illusion designed to give men an inkling of a significance they did not possess.

About six months before the night he closed the restaurant, though, Charles had developed a persistent cough. A cough that started low in his chest and in the mornings was especially bad; a hack that hurt him more than he let on. One morning in the spring, he had coughed so hard that he broke a rib, though he did not tell anyone. His son, Charlie, came out the back of Charlotte's and found his father sitting on the steps, half bent over, clutching his side. When he saw his son, Charles said, 'I'm okay.'

'You sure?' said Charlie.

His father nodded. 'Go back inside.'

And Charlie did as he was told, though he

went right to the dining room where his mother was, where she stood looking over that evening's reservations. He told her what he had seen and he said, 'He needs to go to a doctor, Mom.'

'You know your father.'

'We should do something.'

The boy watched his mother sigh, look at him for a moment, then take her hand and run it through his brown hair. 'He won't do it, Charlie, you know that. He's a stubborn man and he hates doctors.'

Charlie let it go though it ate at him. There were times when he could not forget about it and then there were times when late at night he would lie in bed and stare at the ceiling, the moonlight coming through the window and illuminating a slice of bed, a slice of floor, and he would think about life after his father was gone. Sometimes he talked about it with Owen, though it was always Owen who brought it up, and Charlie, being the elder, felt the need to protect him from a truth he knew his brother already understood.

On the night their father closed Charlotte's, the two boys sat with their mother at the kitchen table in the old farmhouse on Signal Ridge and they watched their father cook. Their father who looked older than his years with his heavily weathered face, his blue eyes staring out from beneath his wrinkled brow; their father who despite his age and his health still looked capable of real vigor with his muscled arms, veins like tines running from his wrists to his elbows.

He started by opening a bottle of wine from

9

the cellar, a white Bordeaux that the boys knew came from the part of the cellar they were not to touch. He poured each of them a glass and he talked about the wine, why it was the color of straw, how this suggested its age, and he instructed them to let it linger in their mouths before they swallowed. It was grassy wine but rounded and Charlie had not fully developed a taste for it, but he knew why it was good.

While they sipped their wine, Charles scrubbed a dozen oysters in the sink with a stiff brush, and when they were cleaned to his satisfaction he placed them on the grill and they could see the steam rising off them. When the oysters opened, Charles removed them with tongs to a plate covered with rock salt. He dropped a teaspoonful of his best meat reduction on each oyster and brought them over.

'Taste the salt, the sea,' he said.

They were hot, but the contrast of the salty oyster liquor and the richness of the meat glaze kept the flavor on their tongues until they took a swallow of the wine and had another. Next he made a salad of dandelion greens from the garden, dried cherries, and duck confit they had helped him make months earlier by stewing duck legs in their own fat and hanging them in the barn to dry before storing them in jars protected by the same fat they had been stewed in.

He showed them how to make the dressing, a warm ginger balsamic vinaigrette, and while both boys had worked side by side with him for years, had eaten his food since they were children, they knew he was doing something special tonight. When they had finished the salads he went to the fridge and said he had a surprise, and they stood and followed him.

'What is it?' Owen said when their father removed something the size of a football wrapped in a towel.

'The real thing,' Charles said as he took it out. 'Foie gras.'

The boys looked at the grayish-brown liver with the red veins running through its two lobes.

'Doesn't look like much,' said Charlie.

'Wait till you taste it,' their father said. 'I had it brought from Canada. From France. It's illegal here, unless it comes in a can, but we won't tell anyone, will we, boys?'

They smiled. Charles cut thin slices from one lobe and with a paring knife he deftly removed a long vein. He heated a cast iron skillet until it started to smoke and he dropped the slices into it and quickly flipped them.

'It's almost all fat,' he said. 'If you cook it even a second too long, it melts into nothing.'

They ate the foie gras on pieces of brown toast, and it was like nothing they had ever eaten before, rich and soft, buttery, with only a hint of the livery taste they had expected.

Next Charles opened a red Bordeaux, almost thirty years old, and it was soft and round and tasted like the earth itself. 'The vines that grow these grapes,' he said, 'go back to Caesar. Think about that. Caesar. Of course they probably weren't as good at making the wine then. But still. Enjoy it.'

The boys and Charlotte sipped the wine, and

11

Charlie, looking at his father, saw in his movements, his enthusiasm, a happiness he had not seen in a while, a lightness about him, and he knew he was doing what he loved, working in the kitchen and teaching, sharing his knowledge of food, something that for him transcended everything else. In that moment Charlie decided to put aside his fears, the things he could not control, his wondering about why this dinner, why tonight; by so doing he hoped to fall into the moment, the taste of the food, the beautiful wine that was going to his head.

They ate a chateaubriand roasted with wild mushrooms, cooked medium rare and sliced on the bias. Charles served it with a brandy sauce. They ate green beans blanched and then sautéed in brown butter. They ate cubed potatoes slowly cooked in duck fat. And when they thought they could eat no more, their father brought out roasted hazelnuts and chocolates and a bottle of port so old the label was completely illegible.

After, they would say it was the greatest meal they had ever had, and they knew they would never have one greater. While they ate, they talked and they joked and they laughed as a family. They told stories that they all knew by heart but never grew tired of hearing. While all of them may have suspected it, only one of them knew for sure that this was the last time they would ever be together.

★　★　★

After dinner the two boys cleaned up. From the living room they heard the stereo and on the turntable the sounds of Etta James drifted in to where they washed dishes and scrubbed pans. Their parents were dancing. It had been a long time since they danced but the boys remembered what it looked like: an archetypal scene of childhood, their parents twirling each other around the room after a night of heavy drinking, their father dipping their mother toward the floor, her mock-shrieks as he did so, the look of bliss on her face when she rose up back toward him and he took her into his strong arms, brought her to him, and they began to move again, fluid and knowing of each other, moving like people who had a history of moving together.

Now, taking turns washing and drying, the boys were both happy about the dancing and now and again they would smile at each other and shake their heads and laugh. At one point Charlie caught sight of them cutting across the door frame, his father with one hand on the small of his mother's back, his other holding her hand in his. His father had a wide grin on his face and his blue eyes were locked onto hers and they were oblivious to Charlie watching, to the clink of the dishes in the sink, to anything beyond the small orbit in which they moved while they danced. It was a sight that Charlie would remember in the days that followed; one that he would see in his mind and use as comfort, one that he hung on to in those moments when he needed a way to see his father other than how he would come, inevitably, to see him.

When they finished the dishes, the two boys stood in the door frame of the living room and they watched their parents dance. Charlie was feeling the effects of the wine and the port and he could tell Owen was as well. Seeing this in their faces, their father looked over at them and smiled as he spun Charlotte on his hand, brought her to him. 'My two boys a little drunk?' he said.

'Leave them alone,' their mother said.

'Yeah,' said Owen. 'You should talk, Pop.'

The song came to an end and their father went to the turntable and lifted the needle off the record and it scratched slightly as he did so. He signaled to the two boys. 'Join me,' he said, and then to Charlotte, 'I won't be long. Wait up for me.'

Charlie and Owen followed their father out on to the porch. The air had cooled and the night sky was black and without moon. Over the mountains the stars were heavy and bright. The woods that started at the end of the pasture in front of them were full of night sounds, crickets and the cry of a whippoorwill. Their father lighted a cigarette with the quick motion of a man who had been lighting cigarettes his whole life. They watched him inhale and then waited for the raggedy cough that followed.

'Sit,' he said, motioning to the white wooden bench against the wall of the porch. The boys did as they were told, sitting down, looking up at their tall father who in the dim light towered

14

over them, his gravelly voice sounding as if it came from farther away, from out in the field.

'Indulge me for a moment,' he said. 'What I have to say is important.' He paused, dragged hard on his cigarette, tossed it spinning out into the yard, its cherry tip visible in the air before disappearing out into the blackness. He quickly lit another. 'I know I can be an old pain in the ass,' he said.

'Dad,' said Charlie.

'Let me say this, Charlie, okay? I know I can be an old pain in the ass. And you are good boys, both of you. You are. You have worked hard and you have made me proud. And you need to know that. It's not a good life growing up in a restaurant. Other kids get to screw around on weekends and you guys have to work. And you never bitch about it. And for that I'm grateful. Now, whatever happens to me — '

'Nothing's going to happen to you,' Owen said quickly.

'Things happen to all of us,' their father said. 'We can't control that. All we can control is how we respond to them when they do. And we can control what we value. For me that has always been food, and wine, and the land and the water that gives us both. You've heard all this before.' He chuckled slightly. 'More times than you'd probably like. Let me say this though: there is nothing more important than a good meal. Don't forget that.'

'We know this,' Charlie said. 'And you're calling us drunk.'

Their father inhaled deeply. 'Well, I know.

15

Maybe I am. Let me just say one more thing here and then I'm going up to bed. You boys need to make your own path. You don't have to do what I did. Not that I have not had a good life, I have. I wouldn't change one damn bit of it. But remember that. Carve your own path. Follow your instincts. They are the most important thing you have. Your intuition. It is as important in life as it is in cooking.'

'Is that it?' said Owen.

'Yes,' their father said. 'That's it. Now I'm going in. Sleep well, boys.'

Charles Bender tossed his last cigarette of the night out into the field and went for the door to the house. Before he did, though, he stopped for a quick moment, and in the dark he squeezed first Charlie's shoulder and then Owen's and they felt his strong hand and then he was gone.

'What the fuck was that all about?' Owen said when he had left.

'The booze?'

'I guess so.'

'What do you want to do?'

'I don't know. I'm not tired. A little buzzed. But I could smoke one in the barn.'

'Me too,' said Charlie.

The two boys stood and they left the porch for the yard, the star-filled sky above them. Even though it was fall, they could feel the grass dewy on their boots as they went. Charlie reached the barn door first and he opened the large doors and though there were lights in here, they did not need them for they knew their way well enough. They walked across the hard earthen

16

floor and in the dark Charlie felt for the wooden ladder, and when he found it he pulled himself up and behind him he heard Owen on the rungs too. The floor of the hayloft was soft in places but they knew these too and they moved along the ones that were supported by beams until they reached the upstairs doors and these they swung open to the night sky. They sat down on the edge with their feet dangling over the yard and from here they could see the house and the dark mountains and the hills of Eden, all of it dimly lit by starlight. The light in their parents' room had gone out and the only electric light came from the kitchen and this lit a rectangle of yard next to the house.

'You want me to roll?' Owen said.

'Sure,' said Charlie and he took the bag out of his pocket and handed it and the papers to his younger brother. Owen took one paper out of the stack and held it between his fingers and filled it with a ribbon of the green pot, then quickly twisted it, brought it to his lips and licked the seal with his tongue. He handed the rolled joint to Charlie and Charlie lighted it and inhaled deeply. They sat there smoking the joint and looking out over the hills and they did not speak. Charlie felt the marijuana go to his head and he relaxed into the high. In the distance they heard the sound of a truck shifting through the switchbacks on nearby Spruce Mountain. The breeze picked up and the air it blew was cold, suggesting in its breath the winter to come. Above the star-filled sky was still clear though off to the west they could see the first heavy black

17

clouds moving in, obscuring the horizon to their left. They smoked the joint until it was nothing more than a tiny nub that began to burn their fingertips. Owen took the roach and stashed it with the others on a rafter behind the door. When he sat down again he leaned back on his elbows and said, 'Yep,' and they both laughed at this like it was the funniest thing they had ever heard. Then they sat again in silence. They were brothers and they knew each other better than they had ever known anybody, and when you are like this you can sit in silence and not speak and it is the most comfortable thing in the world.

*   ★   ★   ★

That night while they slept the heavy clouds from the west crossed the mountains and into Eden, and with them came the rain, a cold, driving rain that fell in sheets and rattled the twelve-pane windows in the bedroom the two boys shared in the old farmhouse. Charlie slept fitfully with alcohol and pot-fueled dreams and at one point the rain was falling so hard it woke him, and he rose up on to his elbows and watched it streaming down the windows and the light outside was gray and subdued with dawn. He was able to fall back asleep but he tossed and turned and sometime that morning he woke suddenly, sensing his mother before he even heard her, before she opened the door to their room, and then she was there and he knew from the look on her face that something was wrong, that something was terribly wrong.

'Mom,' he said, 'what is it?'

'It's your father, Charlie. He went into the woods.'

Charlie sat up, rubbed his eyes; ran a hand through his hair. 'So?'

'He had a gun.'

'I don't get it.'

'Hunting season is two months away, Charlie. I'm worried he might — '

Charlie's head was pounding from the previous evening's alcohol but he needed to stand and he did, rising quickly and feeling light-headed. 'I'll get him,' he said and by now their voices had woken Owen and he was looking at them with the slight daze of recent sleep.

'What's up?' Owen said.

'Get dressed,' said Charlie.

'What's going on?'

'Just get dressed. Hurry.'

Charlotte left the room and Charlie heard her footsteps going down the stairs. He slipped on a pair of jeans and a T-shirt, and outside he could see that it was still raining, though not with the fury it had during the night. Owen climbed out of bed and followed Charlie's lead, sliding into his jeans, pulling a shirt over his head.

'My fucking head,' Owen said.

'I know,' said Charlie. 'Let's go.'

'What is this?'

'It's Dad,' he said. 'He took his rifle into the woods.'

Owen caught the look in Charlie's eyes and he did not ask anything further. A few minutes later

19

they were out the front door, the screen slapping shut behind them, their mother moving out of the kitchen to watch them go, two boys cutting across the wet pasture on a gray, rainy fall day to find their father in the woods.

They were children of Eden and they knew these forests and hills even better than their father did. He had been taking the two of them deer hunting since they were old enough to shoot a gun, and Charlie got his first spikehorn when he was eight, Owen a year later. He still remembered seeing the deer from the stand they had built, how it moved and shimmered like water between the trees, how his father told him when to pull the trigger, how the animal collapsed to the forest floor when he did. He remembered how he cried when he stood over the carcass, the life having already seeped out of it. How his father lighted a cigarette at that moment and put his hand on the back of his neck, told him it was good to cry, it showed he respected the killing. And he remembered how he felt better when venison was on the menu at Charlotte's and his father proudly told anyone who would listen that it was Charlie's venison.

Now, Owen entered the forest of tamarack, spruce and maple first, at the only clear opening, an old logging road. The boys did not speak, for they figured their father would most likely have gone to the stand; it was the only logical destination. They went as fast as they could, a half-run down the sloping old logging road, stopping to climb over fallen trees. The road was narrow and led them away from the house and around the side of the ridge. The tree cover was heavy here and they could no longer feel the rain though their shirts were soaked through from the run across the wet field. Soon the road came to an end and in front of them was the thick forest, sloping sharply away from them, other hills visible through the trees, some of them partially obscured by a rising mist. Their experienced eyes picked up the deer run that started to their right, little more than a break between trees, wide enough for one man to pass through. They took this and it was narrow and the forest fell away steeply on their left and the going was slow. The run led them along the spine of the hill and they knew that shortly it would intersect with another, wider run that would lead them to the stand in the large oak. They had both seen the footprints in the wet mud beneath their feet; sloshing footprints from their father's boots that had half filled with water, though it was hard to tell how long ago he had made them.

Soon they hit a stretch where they could move quicker, the run widening a bit, when they heard it. A sound like no other, a sound they knew intimately. Its report echoed off the hills and back to them and Charlie said, 'Fuck,' and they began to run as fast as they could, recklessly moving downhill, their hands in front of them in case they tumbled.

They reached the intersection of the larger run and they could sprint here, side by side, their breath coming hard and fast as they went. When they reached the small clearing where the stand was, they saw it, the stand, but there was no sign of their father. They stood breathing heavily next to the tree, and with no canopy above them now the soft cool rain soaked their hair.

Charlie scanned the small meadow with his eyes and then he saw his father, and in the half-second he looked over at his brother, he knew he had seen him too. He was directly across from them, slumped against a tree on the ground.

'Oh, Jesus,' Owen said.

When they reached him, he almost looked normal, as if he had decided to rest. But there was a burnt smell in the air and no amount of rain could conceal the fact that the back half of their father's head was no longer there. That there was a mass of blood-matted hair and then nothing.

Charlie heard his brother's sobs and inside him there was a pain like he had never felt before. He sank to his knees. Sank to the muddy ground. There was a ringing in his ears and he became aware of the spinning of the earth beneath him. A not so subtle turning and churning. He wanted nothing more at that moment than to find something to hang on to, something to make it stop.

2

They took turns carrying him out of the woods on their backs. They held his arms down along theirs and they looked like old pictures they had seen of Indian men dancing with bear carcasses on. They looked like men lugging a heavy cross.

It was uphill the whole way and their father was a big man but they did not care, both of them wanting to carry him for the pain of it made the pain they felt within themselves easier to handle. While one carried the other walked in front, pushing branches out of the way so that they could pass.

They managed to get him up to the house, and as they approached the porch their mother came out the screen door and Charlie, who was in front now, his brother behind him with their father slung over him, caught her eyes, and he understood that she had known already that this was what they would find. He wondered why she had sent them anyway and part of him wanted to hate her for it, wanted to blame her; but most of him knew that this was one of those things where blame made no sense, where anger was as useless as this incessant rain in the fall, rain that could not help anything, for the short growing season had already passed them and all it could accomplish was a softening of the beauty that this time of year, if they were lucky, could bring, when the leaves turned a myriad of colors, when the hills were full of gold and reds and purples.

They laid their father on the porch. The boys were in charge now. Owen ran to the kitchen and made the call and Charlie went to his mother, and he took her into his arms and he held her. She was sobbing so hard she was having trouble breathing and he wanted desperately for her to be strong but he understood that this was not possible. He wanted to hold her until she could not cry any more. Her tears were wet on his shoulder and she seemed small in his arms. He held her tight. 'It's okay,' he said. 'It's okay.' He said it over and over and he wanted to believe it. But at the same time he knew their father was their rock, what they leaned on, what defined them, and he knew that he could not, not now, wish anything away. What was, was, and all they could do was try to handle it. No more, no less.

The rest of that day was a blur. The ambulance came and took Charles Bender away. Some friends of the family showed up, people who meant well; and somehow Owen and Charlie and Charlotte managed to eat trays of lasagne and other food they normally did not like. The decanter of Scotch on the bureau in the living room was not an answer, but it helped. Eventually the rain stopped and the mist rose out of the valleys and engulfed the old farmhouse. The late-afternoon sun struggled to fight through and at its strongest was little more than a diffused orange above the mountains, the color of an egg yolk. Night came. They were grateful for the dark as it showed a change in time. Time was what they needed. That was what everyone said. For Charlie, it couldn't come fast enough.

⋆ ⋆ ⋆

They buried Charles Bender two days later. Buried him on a cool fall day when the sun moved in and out of high clouds. They buried him in the cemetery on a sloping hill above the town of Eden, a cemetery with gravestones that dated back to the mid-1800s, gravestones with names barely legible, babies next to mothers, mothers next to fathers. Gravestones bent back in their plots, sad gravestones, small and ill-kempt. All of the important names of Eden were there: Morse, Beckett, Singleton, Fiske, Walden.

The plot Charlotte picked was near the top of the hill, near where the forest started, and from it you could see, if your eyes were good, Charlotte's itself. You could see it by tracing the Dog River where it ran through the trees, where the river straightened out on that stretch by the Old County Road. You could make out the roof of the former schoolhouse and you could see the river running past it and you could see where it fitted into the world around it; where it fitted into the mountains in the distance, into the thick forest, where it stood in the dramatic landscape that was Eden.

From the truck in front of the gates, Charlie could see that the funeral home people had already arrived. He saw the black hearse parked up amongst the stones, near their father's final resting place. Charlie was behind the wheel of the truck, his mother in the seat next to him, Owen leaning over the bench behind. They all wore dark sunglasses and they sat as if the sitting would make what they were about to do go away, but they all knew better. The boys were waiting for their mother. They knew they were on her schedule and they were grateful for it. They were grateful for her grief for in an odd way it mediated their own, dulled it; made it possible for them to focus on something beyond what haunted them after discovering their father dead in the woods.

In a lone bare tree near the hearse on the hill above them, one of the funeral home men startled the murder of crows that had roosted there and at once they all flew off its branches and into the sky, black birds moving for a moment in a kind of formation before breaking apart, swooping over the land in pieces of black, their cries coming through the closed windows of the pickup.

Their mother said, 'Let's go.'

Charlie opened his door and Charlotte opened hers and Owen climbed over the bench seat and exited out of Charlie's side. They walked together through the wrought-iron gates of the cemetery and then up the paved path that cut through it. On the treeless hillside the wind blew strong and ruffled their clothes as they went.

At the graveside, the funeral director, a kind man named Crane, asked them if they wanted to say anything and they did not and nodded no and he did not respond but looked at the two men on either side of the shiny oak coffin, and while they watched, Charles Bender was lowered into the loamy earth.

Charlotte looked away when the boys fulfilled tradition by scooping out handfuls of dirt and throwing them on to the shiny wood of the coffin, the granules of dirt sliding off it and running down the sides. When the men began shoveling in the hole, the three of them turned and began to walk back down the drive, the two boys standing on either side of their mother, locking arms, as if supporting her, which they were doing, but supporting themselves as well.

Once in the pickup, Charlie went to turn the key to start the engine when his mother said, 'Wait.'

She said, 'There is something I have to tell you.'

Charlie turned and looked at her. Her gaze was straight ahead and she did not make eye contact with either of the boys. Her expression was impassive. 'Your father,' she began. 'Well, you know. He could be difficult.'

'Mom, get to the point,' Owen said.

'He left a note,' she said.

'What do you mean?' said Charlie. 'How long have you — '

Charlotte Bender sighed. 'I found it the morning that he went into the woods. It was on my bedside table. I thought about not giving it to you because I didn't want you to see it the wrong way. But then I decided it was not for me to judge. You were old enough to see for yourselves.'

She reached into the side pocket of her

27

cardigan sweater and she took out a folded piece of paper. Charlie snatched it from her fingers and quickly opened it. His eyes absorbed what it said, and he understood instantly why his mother had thought about not sharing it.

It read: *Charlie, take care of my two Charlottes. I love you all.*

'Let me see,' Owen said.

'Owen, it's bullshit,' Charlie said.

Owen took the note from him and read it. Charlie watched him through the rearview mirror. He saw his brother take it in, what it meant, that their father had intended for Charlie to take over the restaurant. That there was no place for Owen here any more. Because he wore sunglasses, Charlie could not tell if his eyes were wet, but he did see his brother steel himself, the muscles around his mouth tightening against any tears that might come.

'Let's go,' said Owen. 'There are people waiting.'

'It's bullshit,' Charlie said. 'We can do whatever the hell we want, you know that.'

Charlie looked to his mother for support but she offered him nothing. She continued to gaze out the window at the trees. He looked back again at his brother, searching in his eyes for understanding, for acknowledgement, but Owen was looking back up the hill at the grave, at the hearse that was beginning to move, the work up there done.

★ ★ ★

28

They drove in the pickup down the back roads of Eden to Charlotte's. It was cold enough outside to have the heat on in the truck and it was warm as they went. The late-afternoon sun hung low and fat above the mountains. There was a light breeze and the first fallen leaves blew in front of the tires on the hard dirt road. The dirt was darkened from the heavy rain of the previous week. They did not pass any cars and Charlie drove fast. Normally Charlotte would have said something about his driving but this time she stared blank-faced out the window to her right at the passing woods. Charlie was dwelling on the note and he wondered if Owen was as well, and he wished someone would say something, anything, and when he thought he should, his brother shattered the silence from the back by saying, 'Who all is going to be here?'

Charlie saw his mother shrug. She said, 'Friends of your father's. He had a lot of friends. Not close friends of course, but people who knew him.'

'Acquaintances?' Owen said.

'Something like that,' his mother said. 'The waitresses of course. Probably some of the farmers.'

'What do we need to do?' said Charlie.

'I don't know,' Charlotte said, and then paused for a moment before saying, 'Be strong.'

When they reached the Old County Road, the river was on their right, and they could see it next to the road, slow-moving water, and it followed the road until it reached the bend before the restaurant, at which point it curved back into the trees away from them.

Charlie pulled into the parking lot. It was full of cars and pickup trucks like the one they drove. When they stepped out, they could hear the soft flow of the river behind Charlotte's and they could hear a car heading their way on the road, the distinctive muted sound of tires on the hard dirt.

Together, as they had done leaving the cemetery, they walked toward the old schoolhouse, the restaurant their father had built, and they walked arm in arm, Charlotte between her two tall sons. They still wore their sunglasses and when they reached the solid wooden door that led into the dining room they did not take them off, though they paused for a moment, as if collecting their shared breath, and then Charlie moved forward and brought the latch of the handle down and pushed the door open.

The dining-room tables had been removed and the room was full of people. Most of the talking stopped when they entered and heads turned, but then, as if conscious of the silence, people awkwardly picked up their conversations and tried not to stare. Charlie made out the waitresses, huddled near the bar, and he saw young Joe Collins, the dishwasher, and he saw some of the regular customers and the men who brought the beef and the pork and the lamb. He saw the organic vegetable farmers, bearded men in their thirties who relied on people like his father with their beliefs about food for their business. With them were women he had not seen before, Vermont women with their dark hair streaked naturally with gray, women who probably taught school or did some other work that allowed the farm to run and allowed them to have children and keep a pottery studio out in their barn.

'I need a drink,' said Owen.

'Ditto,' said Charlie.

'Mom?' said Owen.

'Vodka,' she said.

Owen left them and went to the bar. Some of the waitresses moved toward them and they were full of condolences, and Charlie watched their lips when they talked but he barely heard what they had to say. It had only been a few days but he was already of the mind that there were only certain things that people could say in situations like this and he thought he had already heard them all. He saw his mother hugging these women, and how they hugged her back; and his mother was the model of graciousness and if he had anger toward her through this ordeal it dissipated by watching her handle herself. Charlotte had lived long enough to know her role and when the situation warranted it, and Charlie was grateful when a moment later his brother was back with their drinks, his mother's vodka on ice and amber liquid for the two of them.

'What is it?' Charlie said.

'Bourbon,' said Owen.

'Good.'

Charlotte spoke first. She took one long sip of her drink and then put it down on the windowsill. Everyone in the old classroom-turned-dining-room faced her as she talked and she was tall and blonde and beautiful, and as she talked she kept swiping at the long strands of hair that fell over her angular face. She surprised Charlie with the forthrightness of her remarks and he admired her for what she said.

She said, 'I want to thank you all for being here. My husband would have really enjoyed this. All of you filling this space with drinks in your hands.' She smiled. 'He loved this room,' and as she said this, she extended her hands outward to take it all in. 'He really loved this room. I remember when he first showed it to me, and it was all rundown and he said he wanted to make it into a restaurant. I thought he was crazy.' A pause, some light laughter. 'But he was right, as he was about so many things. My Charles,' she said, 'did things his own way. He was a visionary, I think. I really do. He saw an old schoolhouse and thought that people would learn to love it as he did. And they have. I mean, look at us. How many meals have we shared together here? Here on this road next to the river. God, how he loved this place. And I want to tell you something. Charles may have done things his own way, but he did them right. There was no cutting corners with that man. He wanted the best of everything and he knew what the best was and he wanted to pass it on. To me, to his boys, and to all of you. He did that. He did. But Charles lived life on his own terms. He could be difficult, and those of you who worked for him I don't expect you to acknowledge that, not now anyway. That is not what we are here for. But he could. We all saw it. We live in a small town. When Charles brought me here from New York that was clear right away. How small this place was. How beautiful. And in a small town there are no secrets. There can't be. It's not possible. And so I want to say this. And I want my sons especially to hear it though I think they know it.'

Charlotte reached out then, reached out to both Charlie and Owen, and she put a hand on each of their shoulders and they leaned slightly into their smaller mother. She continued, 'Charles died the way he chose to live. You can call it what you want. You can whisper about it however you will. And that is your right. I won't take it away — I can't take it away. But it was on his own terms. And that is all I mean to say about that.'

When she finished speaking, the room was so silent you could hear when people shifted their weight from one foot to the other. First she turned to Owen and he hugged her hard, and then she turned to Charlie and he did the same. When she faced the room again, Charlie raised his glass and said, 'To my father. To Charles Bender.'

And so on a fall afternoon when the dying sun slanted its last light through the large schoolhouse windows and on to the wide floorboards, patrons and workers and vendors, customers, all who had been touched by Charlotte's, drank for the man who had brought them here when he was alive, and brought them here again after he was gone. Despite the pain his wife and his sons might have felt, they knew if Charles were watching he would draw a measure of appreciation from it, from a vision realised, whatever the hardship that led to it.

★   ★   ★

Charlotte's stayed closed for a little more than two weeks after the memorial service. It was Charlie's decision and he made it because he needed time to get his head around the idea that the restaurant he had known since he was a child was now his. And he needed time to grieve. He spent many hours alone out in the barn, sitting on the edge of the hayloft as he often did at night with Owen, and while he sat out here he thought about things. It was easier for him here, away from the house, where his brother and his mother and he had taken to moving around each other like ghosts. Owen watched television all day and his mother barely left her bedroom, coming down to throw dinner together, returning upstairs with a big glass of vodka and not coming out until the morning.

Sitting on the edge of the hayloft, looking out over the hills that grew in color with each passing day, Charlie thought about his father. About his vision, his dream. And as he thought about it, it helped ease the pain he felt, for he realised that despite how it had ended, his mother was right: what his father had set out to do, he did, and not many people in this life could say that.

In the fall of 1962, two years before Charlie

was born, Charles and Charlotte Bender were newly married and living in New York City. Charles had come from the upper peninsula of Michigan and he had always loved the outdoors. He had grown up hunting and fishing. He had gone to the city for college and this was where he met Charlotte. They fell in love and were married. Charlotte finished school but it was not for Charles and he dropped out. He began to work in restaurants, and in their neighborhood they fell in with a group of artists and theatre people and on many nights they would entertain them at their small apartment, Charles cooking for everyone. Nights when they stayed up late and drank and smoked and talked about art and poetry and food. They were at the center of the universe. It was a heady time and they were young and in love and for Charlotte there was no place she wanted to be more than the city, with its colorful people and busy streets. For Charles, though, there was always something missing and until he joined a few of his friends on a hunting trip to northern Vermont he did not know exactly what it was.

One of the New York friends had a deer camp on the fringe of Eden, Vermont, and the moment he saw this small northern town, with its views of the mountains and its rolling highlands, Charles Bender fell in love.

On the second day of his trip, they were driving down the Old County Road when Charles saw the old schoolhouse next to the river. Stuck in the grass by the road was a simple sign that said: *For sale by owner.* Charles turned to Sam Marsh, one of his friends from the city, and said, 'Stop.'

They pulled over, and much to his friend's dismay spent two hours walking around the land, looking into the windows of the rundown old school building, staring down the steep valley toward Hunger Mountain. It was a beautiful fall day, peak foliage, and the grass of the floodplain was the brightest of greens. Later Charles would say that a gentle calm had come over him, and he knew that he was home.

That afternoon he called the number on the sign and without consulting Charlotte or anyone else he bought the place on the spot for a song. 'What are you going to do with it?' Sam Marsh asked him.

'Live here,' said Charles.

They hunted for two more days and they did not get any deer but for Charles that was okay. There would be lots of time for deer hunting. On their return trip he phoned Charlotte from a pay phone at a gas station and he told her that he had bought an old schoolhouse, in the most beautiful place she had ever seen, on the edge of a river with views of the hills and the mountains and no other houses visible from it. He told her to start packing, that while the weather was still warm he wanted to move and begin renovations right away. It will take some work, he said, but this is where we are meant to be.

When Charlotte caught her breath she said, 'You're lucky I don't divorce you right now.'

The following week, Charlotte and Charles arrived back in Eden and when she saw the schoolhouse she did not see the beauty that Charles saw; she did not feel its magic the way he did; she did not fall in love with the river and the hills full of color. She cried. She tried to stop but she could not and as much as he hoped they were tears of joy he knew her well enough to know better. 'What the hell am I going to do here?' she said. 'Tell me that. There is nothing for me here.'

They stayed that night at the inn at Eden and they ate dinner in its old wood-paneled restaurant. Over a bottle of wine they could hardly afford, Charles made his case for the move. He told her they could build a life here richer than any they could have in the city. He said that she should just watch: their friends from the city would realise the wisdom of their decision and follow them. He talked about the cost of living, and anything else he could think of. Finally he told her about what it would be like for their children to grow up in the beauty and safety of the woods, building forts among the trees, skipping over stone walls, swimming in the river on summer afternoons. He cajoled and he pleaded and she said nothing until later that night when they lay together after making love, and she conceded he was probably right about the children. And she said, 'I'll move here with you, but not to that schoolhouse.'

And so they found the old farmhouse on Signal Ridge. It, too, was rundown, and had belonged to a single man in his nineties who had died there, but it was large and cheap and had nice land. They had to buy it full of the old man's stuff, and they spent the first several weeks there cleaning it out. Now that the decision was made to be in Eden, Charlotte threw herself into the work of making house and this pleased Charles greatly, and many of their friends from New York made the journey and helped them out.

One Saturday night in early October when much of the gang from the city had made the trip to help them put a coat of paint on the old clapboards, they had finished dinner and were sitting on the porch smoking and looking out at the last vestiges of sun in the sky, streaks of purple above the hills. Charlotte brought up the fact that Charles still had to sell the schoolhouse.

She said, 'I'm afraid we're stuck with that elephant.'

Sam Marsh, Charles's closest friend, said, 'Why not keep it?'

'And do what?' Charlotte said.

'Open a restaurant.'

Initially this elicited laughter from everyone on the porch, but as they began to talk, Charles began to see it, how it would work, and they stayed up until three in the morning talking about little else, and Charlotte gave Sam a hard time for suggesting it, but in her husband's eyes she saw the fire of certainty she had seen that night at the inn. And she knew not to get in the way of this, that it was something he needed to do. And when, a year later, the schoolhouse had been repainted, and a kitchen had been built on the back, and he showed her the handmade sign with her name in large script, she knew that this was why they were here, why they had come to Vermont, and that sometimes if you put yourself in a position to know something it comes along and reveals itself to you.

Almost twenty years later, their son, Charlie, sat on the edge of the hayloft with his feet dangling above the yard and he thought about all the stories he had heard his parents tell about those early days. About coming to Eden, the impulsiveness of his father. And he thought back to one of his earliest memories: watching his father on the floodplain behind Charlotte's slaughtering chickens with an axe. He saw his father as he had looked then, tall and strong, wearing a cap cocked on one side of his head, a cigarette dangling from his lips; he saw his strong forearms, his foot pressing down on the chicken, holding it in place; he saw the axe rise high in the air and come down, severing the head, and then the comic dance of the chicken when his father released it, moving in small circles until it could not move any more and fell like an empty bag to the ground. It was a sight that as a child had scared the hell out of him. It had filled him with awe for his father. Looking out across the hills at the fading light, he realised that some things might have changed, but that was not one of them.

⋆ ⋆ ⋆

Charlotte left first. After dinner one night during those two weeks she told the boys she needed to talk to them. They sat in the living room, in front

39

of the first wood fire of the season. Outside it was cold and dark. The days were growing shorter and they were deep into fall now.

'I've been doing some thinking,' she said. 'A lot of thinking actually. Tomorrow I'm going to New York.'

'For how long?' said Charlie.

'I don't know yet. Probably for good.'

Owen looked away. 'Just like that, huh?'

'There's nothing for me here now. In some ways there never was. This was always your father's love. Eden. The restaurant. Now it's yours. As far as I'm concerned the house belongs to both of you now. I want to be in the city. I have friends there. Things for me to do.'

'What are you going to do for money?' said Charlie. 'Where will you stay?'

'I can stay with the Marshes to start. Until I find a place. And I have plenty of savings. We saved quite a bit for both of you to go to college and you've been clear that you have no interest in that. It's not what I would want for you, but I understand it.'

'Well, I don't understand this,' said Owen.

'I don't want to be the old lady on the hill,' Charlotte said. 'It's your turn. Your turn to run Charlotte's, if you choose to.'

'Charlie's turn, you mean,' Owen said.

'That's not fair, Owen,' said Charlie. 'I don't want it this way. We should do this together.'

'No,' said Owen, 'it doesn't work that way.'

'I don't see why. I don't. Because of a note he left?'

'Let's not get into it,' Owen said. 'It is what it is, all right?'

'Fine,' said Charlie and he turned away from his brother. As he did so, it occurred to him that by inheriting the restaurant, if that was indeed what had happened, he might be the one that lost out. Owen could indeed carve his own path as their father had instructed them to do. Charlie, on the other hand, was destined to follow his father's. And while he might have chosen to do so anyway, the fact that he was not given the option became remarkably clear to him and he thought about saying so but decided not to. There are times, Charlie thought, when you say what you think. And then there are others when you are better off keeping your thoughts to yourself.

That night Charlie took a bottle of wine out to the barn and he sat and watched the stars. Charlotte retired early and Owen watched television. Charlie was aware of a frost growing between him and his brother and he did not want it to happen. He understood how Owen felt but he did not know how to solve it. Now that his mother was leaving, he was worried that things between them would fall apart completely.

The next morning the two boys drove their mother to the train station in Montpelier where she would take the Vermonter to New York. She left them with numbers where they could reach her and she said she would call and that they would be together again at the holidays. And Charlie knew she was not coming back. That she would always be his mother but that her time in

41

Eden had come to an end. In the days that followed the first snowflakes moved through the air. And while it was still too early for them to stick to the earth, Charlie knew that winter was coming, and for the first time in his life he would move into it, into the snow and the cold and even the crystal-clear days when the sky was the palest of blues, as something other than a child.

3

In November, Charlotte had been gone for over a month, and the restaurant had been open for three weeks, things finally beginning to return to normal, when Owen followed his mother's lead and left Eden.

That morning, Charlie was in the kitchen of the restaurant. Outside it was a cold, gray November day, the near leafless landscape devoid of color, the low sky looking like snow though none was called for. He had begun the prep work for that day, slicing onions, dicing cloves of garlic, washing greens in the big sink. It was the bread-and-butter work of this business and Charlie liked it. It was meditative work, the slap of the knife blade against the maple block, the breaking down of ingredients, the creation of the mise en place.

Since they had reopened, Owen had joined him every morning, prepping in the kitchen, and at night, while Charlie worked the line, Owen ran the front end. They did not talk about it but secretly Charlie hoped that this détente between them would last, that maybe they had come to an understanding that would allow them to move forward together as it seemed to Charlie that they should.

When the kitchen door swung open and his brother came in, Charlie knew what it meant. Slung over his shoulder was a duffle bag and the look on his face spoke volumes.

Charlie looked at him. 'What's this?'

'I'm out of here,' said Owen. 'It's time.'

With the back of his knife, Charlie slid the skin off another onion and then made quick work of it, tossed the small dice into a bowl with the others. 'Where you going?'

'Boston, I think. Maybe the cape. I wouldn't mind being on the ocean.'

'I hear it's lovely in November,' Charlie said.

Owen smiled. 'Can you give me a lift to the bus station?'

'Do you need to do this?'

'I do.'

Charlie looked at his handsome brother. 'First Mom and now you.'

'First Dad, you mean,' said Owen. 'This is your life, Charlie. Not mine. I need to find mine.'

Charlie nodded. 'Okay,' he said. 'Hang on a second.'

Charlie wiped his hands on a towel and went into the dining room. He knelt down behind the bar. Under here was a small safe and he opened it and took out the cash they had received from the past few days. He did not bother counting it but simply took the stack of bills and then closed the safe. He stood and turned and looked at Owen.

'I can't,' Owen said.

'You have to.'

'I'm serious, I don't want it.'

'I'm not giving you a choice,' said Charlie and he handed him the money.

Owen took it from his hand, then put the pile of bills down on top of the bar. 'No thanks, I said.'

'Why does it have to be like this?' said Charlie.

'I don't need your money, Charlie. I need a ride. And if I had another way, I wouldn't ask for that either.'

Under the leaden-gray sky they drove on the back roads of Eden to the paved road that led to the rural route that would take them to Montpelier. They drove in silence and Charlie could feel his brother's anger without him saying anything. Charlie wanted to tell him that it was not his fault, none of this, that if he wanted to blame somebody then he should blame the old man. After all, they were simply following the path he had set out for them.

In the last year of his life, Charles Bender had done something for his two sons that Charlie now fully understood, and though he had never mentioned it to Owen, he assumed his brother understood it as well. When it became clear that the two boys had no interest in college, Charles began to teach them to cook. Oh, they had always helped prep and knew the basics of working the line. But he had never before stopped the flow of the work in the busy kitchen to mentor them, to show them the foundation they needed to know if they had any intention of making a living as he had.

In the mornings he would present them with what he called blind baskets. Each boy was handed a wicker basket covered by a towel. When they removed the towel, they had forty

45

minutes to create from scratch an entrée out of the ingredients that lay within.

Every time they did it, they were each given the same ingredients. That first time, the basket contained a whole chicken, a pint of heavy cream, a handful of morels, a bunch of tarragon. They could use any staples they wanted from the pantry. Charlie worked from one end of the large wooden table and Owen from the other. Charlie had a knack for this; he saw what he would do the instant he lifted the towel, the direction the dish should take laid out in front of him as clear as a road. For Owen, it did not come as easily and it showed.

For the first meal Charlie quickly broke down the chicken as he had been taught, into eight stewing pieces, and these he seared until they were brown in a large skillet. Next he braised them with white wine and when they were almost cooked through he added the cream and the morels and the tarragon. It was a classic and simple preparation and when his father tasted it he said that it was just what it should be, which for Charles Bender was the highest praise he could give.

As for Owen, he took the chicken and roasted it whole, stuffed with the morels and the tarragon. He used the cream in a gravy he made for the finished chicken. It was a good effort and the taste was fine but their father wasted no time in explaining why Charlie's work was stronger.

They executed the baskets three or four times a week. And while Owen sometimes nailed it, mostly he struggled, while Charlie seemed to move easily into it, as if he had been born to this. It was only later, after his father's death and on the night of the memorial service when Charlotte had shared his note, that Charlie realised what it was his father was up to. He was preparing for his succession. He knew that he was dying and that there was nothing he could do about it except to ensure that his legacy — his vision — remained intact. To do so, he was testing his two boys, to see which one had the mettle to become their father. Charlie had emerged from that test, and now, driving down Route 15, passing old farms in the pickup truck, he prepared in his mind to say goodbye to his brother. He tried not to think about how long it would be before they would see each other again. And as he thought about it, he realised that the events of this morning were preordained, preordained by a man who was no longer with them.

★ ★ ★

At the bus station in Montpelier, little more than a white trailer next to the railroad tracks, the bus had not yet arrived. The two brothers stood outside and kept their hands in their pockets against the cold. In front of them they could see the golden dome of the statehouse and behind it a hill full of leafless trees rose up against the dark sky. Standing here, they fell into a familiar rhythm, as if there was nothing between them, and they small-talked about the restaurant, about the winter to come, about girls they had

47

known in high school. They talked as if this were some weekend trip Owen was about to take, as if in a few days they would stand in this same place before getting back into the truck for the drive to Eden. They talked as if their lives had not been altered in the past months, as if they were two brothers as close as brothers could be; sitting on the edge of the hayloft, their feet dangling, smoking a joint under the stars.

In time the bus pulled in and passengers stepped out into the cold and waited for the driver to open the side compartments so they could get their bags.

'Well, this is it,' Owen said, reaching down for his duffle bag.

'Please let me know where you are,' said Charlie.

Owen nodded. Charlie saw that his eyes were moist but he did not say anything about it. This is hard on him too, he thought. He just does not want me to know it.

'Give me a hug,' said Charlie.

And they embraced then, awkwardly, the embrace of siblings at a parting, Charlie patting Owen on the back as he held him. Charlie wanted to cry at the uncertainty of it all but he did not want his brother to see this. Instead, when they pulled away from one another, he gave him a big smile, touched his shoulder for a moment. Owen returned the smile and then turned away from Charlie, handed his ticket to the driver, and walked up the steps into the bus.

Charlie waited until the bus pulled out of the parking lot and turned left across the river and over the iron trestle bridge. He watched the bus move toward the highway until he lost sight of it behind a large brick building. Then he climbed back into the cab of his truck and drove under the steely-gray sky back to Eden. It had come to this. He was the only one.

★   ★   ★

The son was now the father. That winter Charlie gave himself completely to the restaurant, arriving in the morning when it was still dark, leaving after midnight. He worked as if the work itself was enough to heal the past. During dinner service he was like a man possessed, sauces bubbling on the stoves, fish being seared in hot pans, meats needing to be turned at precise intervals on the grill. In truth, it was too much work now for one; unlike his father, he did not have two boys who could help. But Charlie loved the cooking, loved the heat of the moment when six entrées were going at once on the line, when the waitresses could not hustle the food out fast enough for his liking.

Most nights he was so bone-tired that back at the farmhouse on Signal Ridge pouring himself a glass of brandy was nothing more than a ritual: he would barely have a sip before he was snoring in the large armchair in front of the television. Sometimes he would spend the entire night here, and other times he would wake in the deep blue of early morning and struggle upstairs to his bed.

Sundays, the only day the restaurant was closed, were hard for him now. Before, when his

49

father was alive, he looked forward to Sundays, a time when he would not have to work. Now he wandered around the house, wondering what to do with himself.

He began to take long walks on those quiet afternoons. Regardless of the weather, he would put on his boots and head out the long driveway to the miles of dirt road that cut through the woods of Eden. Sometimes he'd walk through heavy snow, the limbs of the evergreens that leaned over the roads weighted down. Other times the brilliant sunshine in the winter sky almost blinded him with its reflection off the snowy fields. Either way he trudged along until it tired him out, and then he returned home to the woodstove and to a simple dinner he made for himself, the one night he did not cook for others.

But mostly, he worked.

One afternoon at Charlotte's he decided to clean out the old pantry and he was hard at it when he heard laughter from just out the porch door, where Althea and Peg were smoking cigarettes. It was a job that had not been done in ages, and there were jars of spices as old as he was. He was standing on a stool, rifling through old boxes, when he heard their laughter and it occurred to him that it was directed toward him. He got off the stool, went to the door, looked at the two older women smoking in the cold, put his hands on his hips and with mock anger said, 'What?'

'Honey,' Althea said in her smoky voice. 'You need to get laid.'

And when she said it, the two women broke

into peals of laughter, and Charlie couldn't help but laugh himself.

'What makes you think I'm not — ' he began to say.

'You don't have time,' Althea said. 'You never leave here. If you were getting laid, trust me, we'd know about it.'

'That's nice,' Charlie said, and then he went back inside and he could hear them laughing and he knew it was good-natured and meant to be, but that when you got right down to it, they were right.

There had been girlfriends in high school. A trip to Quebec where both he and Owen paid to lose their virginity when they were fifteen and fourteen years old. In truth, he had never been comfortable around women. He was always aware of his size, his height, and he was given to shyness. Owen, by contrast, was not only comfortable talking to women but also attracted them with his good looks; from the time he was a boy, girls and even older women were drawn to him, to the prettiness of his eyes, the sharpness of his features.

Yes, Charlie thought, Althea was right. He needed a woman. But this was Eden, and that was easier said than done. Most of the girls he knew had left for college and it was not like he was in a position to meet people, unless they came into the restaurant on one of those occasions when he ventured out front, or he hired them to wait tables, which would require one of the waitresses who had been there since the beginning to leave. Charlie knew this was unlikely, and he did not dwell on it, though somewhere within he understood that there was something missing from his life, and he did not yet know how to find it.

★ ★ ★

Once a month, on a Sunday evening when he was home, Charlie heard from his mother. She called him around dinner time and they would talk for almost an hour, and he told her about the restaurant and about the house and she always acted as if nothing interested her more. As he talked, though, he sensed her distance, but he could not help but tell her about his life for she was his mother and the life was his, regardless of the fact that it was a world she had left behind, almost as if it never happened, as if she had never come from New York all those years ago with a man who had a dream she believed in. The fact was they were much more comfortable when they talked about her life. How she was enjoying the city; all her old friends in the village who had her over for dinner; what it was like to walk down the city streets in winter, the snow falling in the gray sky, clinging to the trees on the street, covering things underfoot for such a short time before it was swept away. So different from Eden, she said. People everywhere, people from all over the world. And the food, Charlie, she told him, the food. Your father, she said, loved Eden because he could cook what came from the land and the rivers around him. And she said she understood that. But, she told

Charlie, New York by comparison is the world's supermarket. You would not believe what you can find here.

For his part, Charlie always listened to her. But he was his father's son and what she told him had little appeal: it was not something he thought about in any real way. Sure, he was too young to be set in his ways, but Eden was what he knew and while he did not think about it in terms so stark, he knew that it was all he would ever know.

While Charlie talked to his mother once a month, the winter passed with no word from Owen. Charlotte knew, naturally, about his leaving and sometimes when they talked they speculated about it and where he was, and often when it was discussed they were reduced to clichés, the 'no news is good news' refrain.

In late March, the first signs of spring came to Eden. The days grew steadily warmer, and while it would occasionally still snow, most of the snowpack had begun to melt, the river running high. In time the first snowdrops fought through the soil, tiny flowers covering the floodplain. Small buds began to appear on the trees, and here and there one of the deciduous trees would bloom a sudden pale green, almost gold. Above in the sky at night, lying in bed at the old farmhouse, Charlie would hear the geese on their flight north, high above in a V in the dark, a steady honking that made him smile to hear it.

This was Charlie's favorite time of year. The days were getting longer, the summer still to come, the year long and in front of him and full of promise. Winter was now squarely at his back. Some nights at the restaurant it was warm enough to open the windows and the soft breeze moved through the kitchen and the dining room, and when there was a break in the clatter of the kitchen he could hear the peepers in the marsh, the steady breathing of the woods. New life all around him and this was Eden and you could not help but feel it.

On Sunday mornings, as his father had taught him to, he foraged in the woods near the river for the wild ramps that grew here for only a few short weeks, and at Charlotte's he threw these on the grill with a touch of olive oil, salt and pepper and their oniony flavor was the perfect accompaniment for grilled meats. He also stopped on the sides of the road and amid the ferns he found the first fiddleheads of the season and these he would deep-fry as a side dish. There were also the first wild mushrooms of the year, chanterelles and oysters and pheasants. These he harvested on long hikes in the woods and turned them into stocks and stuffing and roasted them with pine nuts, garlic and rosemary. He smothered the spring lamb raised by a farmer out in Glover with their woody flavor.

Then, one sunny morning in May, when Charlie checked the mail in the box out by the road at the farmhouse on Signal Ridge, in addition to the usual bills and catalogs, there was a postcard. He felt his heart leap in his chest for he knew who it was from before he even had a chance to absorb the picture on the front which showed Rio de Janeiro from the air, with the

54

word *Rio* written in broad script across the photo. He turned it over. There was the familiar handwriting of his younger brother and it told him what he wanted to know. Owen had joined the Merchant Marines and was working as a chef on a freighter. 'Cooking sloppy Joes, if you can believe it,' he wrote. 'The ocean is endless, blue for ever, but the sunsets are the coolest thing you've ever seen. The ports are nice. Three months at sea, three off. Owen.'

Charlie stood there with the woods all around him and read the postcard over and over. His hand shook slightly as he did, and after the third time he began to laugh out loud.

★ ★ ★

They came at three- and-four-month intervals for the next five years. From all over the world. Panama. The Azores. Corsica. London. Rotterdam. Places that Charlie could scarcely imagine, though in his mind he often pictured his handsome brother walking the streets of strange cities teeming with people, eating in small cafés, sleeping in motels where the sound of foreign voices reached his room. They were two brothers separated now by the size of the world and its broad expanse of oceans. But they were fulfilling the prophecies that had been handed to them, handed to them in the woods of Eden on a fall day when the rain fell in torrents and wiped away much of what they had come to rely on, to believe in.

4

They say that different people deal with the passing of time differently. In Eden, Vermont, for instance, it is a commonly shared belief that time can be slowed if you live deliberately. If you stop and watch sunsets; if you spend time sitting on porches listening to the woods. If you give in to the reality of the seasons. The truth of the fall and the winter and the spring and the summer. And the two other seasons that are celebrated here: stick season, the time when the leaves have fallen off the trees and the snow has not yet arrived. And, of course, mud season, usually happening in late March or early April, when the dirt roads give up a winter's worth of icepack and driving becomes nearly impossible because the roads are full of deep grooves and in some places are as soft as quicksand.

For many of the people of Eden, those who live in cities like Boston or New York or Los Angeles, those who commute on busy highways and work eighty hours a week, are chasing some fantastic ghost that is difficult to comprehend. Life is short, an Edenite might argue, why rush through it?

Charlie Bender, like his father before him, loved Eden and its woods and valleys and rivers, but he was closer in temperament and drive to his city brethren. The first five years that Charlotte's was his and his alone, he was often at work by nine in the morning and did not leave until after midnight. On one level his hard work paid off. The restaurant had never been more successful, and though there was little population to speak of, to eat at Charlotte's on a Monday you needed to call three weeks in advance. Many of the regulars, even those who considered it heresy to say it out loud, had come to the conclusion that Charlie Jr. was a better chef than his old man.

To be fair, he was a similar cook to his father. They both believed in taking the best ingredients and treating them simply. 'Just don't fuck it up,' his father used to say all the time. 'You're given a great piece of fish, a trout out of the river for four hours, and the last thing you should do is dress it to a point where you don't even know if you're eating trout any more.'

The difference was that Charles Sr. had done things the same way for so long, simple regional cooking, French and Italian country cooking, that if you were prone to be critical you might say that the food was incredible, but that it never changed. The coq au vin of twenty years ago was the same coq au vin still on the menu. And while there is a lot to be said for keeping true to a vision, sometimes subtle changes lead to improvement.

So, during those years when Charlie first had the restaurant, he began to introduce some small changes his father would not have thought of. Things he would practice on himself on those Sundays when he did not need to leave the house on Signal Ridge. Ideas he picked up from books, from television. Using Japanese wasabi to give heat to a salad of wild-crafted greens. Braising poussin in soy and star anise the way they do in China. Marinating strips of lamb leg in Moroccan spices, the flavor of cinnamon blending with the gaminess of the meat to become almost indiscernible, a low note of sweet smokiness.

The result of all this was that Charlie did not have a life outside the restaurant. By the time he was twenty-five, he looked easily ten years older. His hair was receding, and his clear blue eyes had developed small bags underneath them. He did not sleep enough. There was no time for women. All he did was cook and work and dream of cooking and work. He noticed the world around him less and less. He paid no attention to the river behind the restaurant, the river with its thousand lives every year, constantly moving and shaping in new directions. Summer sunsets over Hunger Mountain when the whole sky turned pink, then blood-red, then faded to a deep purple until the stars emerged and the darkness came. Winter snowstorms when the snow piled high against the house. Spring rain. All of it was out of focus to him. He could only see the food in front of him, what he was creating and the precision of the plates as they left the kitchen. He could only see the new dishes that haunted his dreams, ideas he wanted to put into practice. Some that worked out, others that did not. He could only see the work, and while there was beauty in that, all beauty needs context. Charlie's father had understood that, and Charlie used to. In a short span of time, he no longer did.

* * *

Then, one morning in late January, during the year that Charlie turned twenty-six, he was leaving the house to go to Charlotte's for the day when it happened.

Oftentimes in the last week of January in Vermont there is a thaw. The deepest of cold for a few days gives way to temperatures that reach the forties and fifties and the sun for the first time in months feels warm on your face. The roads go soft, some of the snow melts. This was the case this year, and the morning that Charlie walked out his door, they had had several days in a row of warmer weather. The snow on the roof of the old farmhouse had been melting, and water had been falling in a stream from the eaves on to the front granite steps that led to the door. During the night, though, as the temperature dipped into the teens, that same water had formed into clear black ice, and when Charlie stepped onto it, his feet went out from underneath him and for a moment he was completely airborne, before landing in a heap on the now-clear stone path that led to the driveway.

He lay there in shock. The pain shot from his elbow to his wrist and he knew without anyone telling him that his arm was broken. He rolled half on his side and it hurt so much he cried out. He managed to get himself up by leaning on his other arm and then slowly using his feet for leverage until he could stand. He drove one-armed to the nearest hospital, three towns away, and there they confirmed what he knew. He had a clean fracture of his radius, and they put his arm in a plaster cast. Charlie Bender was more than capable around the kitchen, but with one arm no one could put out sixty dinners a night. It would be four to six weeks before he would be at full strength. He needed help.

And so it was that Charlotte's closed for yet a second time during his tenure. Fortunately, it was in the midst of winter and not summer, when the seasonal people came down from their camp houses and bought the expensive wines to go with their food. But it was money lost nonetheless and Charlie might have been more morose about it than he was if he had not taken his new cast as a clue that he should hire someone else. That he should find someone to help him in the kitchen. He did not expect that they would do so much more.

★ ★ ★

Her name was Claire Apple. She was the third interview he conducted, and from looking at her résumé he had no interest in hiring her, for she was a culinary school graduate and Charlie shared with his father a bias against the formal training that this education provided. 'Cooking is about intuition, about feel,' Charles Bender once said. 'How can you teach that in school?' But Charlie interviewed her because the first two

60

chefs who had come in, both middle-aged men, had experience in fancy kitchens but had failed to impress him with how they cooked. For people with a depth of experience they were timid, did not cook with the ease of men who understood food. They moved awkwardly around the space, too aware of the young owner and his gaze. Charlie knew they wouldn't work and so he asked Claire to come in.

The day she walked into Charlotte's was in early February, and it was in some ways a typical Vermont winter day: slightly overcast, a light snow falling on to the dirt roads and settling into the branches of the spruce trees. It was cold but there was no wind so the cold was bearable. Charlie was in the kitchen when he heard her at the front door, her voice, a voice he would come to know even better than his own, a strong, confident voice, deep for a woman. She called hello.

Charlie went to the door and opened it and he got his first look at Claire Apple.

She was a beautiful woman. Sometimes it took people a while to realise how beautiful she actually was. It was not the fleeting, conventional beauty of the movie star or the model. She was the kind of woman that might not strike you as remarkable on first glance. But the more you looked at her, the more you were in her presence, the more you came to see the subtlety that was her beauty. She looked like a woman in an El Greco painting. Her face slightly long, her petite nose slightly off-center; but her eyes were the richest shade of black, slightly almond in shape but large. Her skin was clear and pale in the winter. She was full-lipped, and her hair was the color of her eyes and was tied with a barrette behind her head. She did not wear makeup and did not need to. She stood about five foot six, and she was not slender but ran more to curvy; and carried herself like someone completely comfortable with who she was and who did not care for a minute how others viewed her.

'I'm Claire,' she said when he answered the door.

'Charlie,' he said, 'Charlie Bender,' reaching out and shaking her hand. 'Come in, please.'

Charlie stepped aside and let her pass. As he closed the door, he noticed there was a slight tremor in his hand not covered by the cast, and his initial thought was: I can never hire her. I cannot work with this woman. He did not know her but he knew, in the amount of time it took for him to open a door, that she scared him, that he was suddenly incapable of being himself. And this was happening in the one place in the world he was most comfortable. He took a deep breath.

'This is the dining room,' he said.

Claire walked around, her eyes taking in the tangerine walls, the simple wooden tables, the small bar, the woodstove in the corner lit up from the fire he had started before she arrived, the chalkboard wiped bare since there was no service.

'I love it,' Claire said, and when she said it he knew she meant it. He watched her walk around and when she reached the black-and-white family pictures that ran along one wall she stopped and studied them.

'This your family?' she said.

'Yes,' said Charlie. 'My father started the restaurant.'

Claire nodded and Charlie moved closer to her. 'This is him, I take it?'

'Yes,' said Charlie.

'Your mother here?'

'Yes, that's Charlotte herself.'

'And who's this?' She pointed to Owen.

'My younger brother,' said Charlie, and waited for her to comment on his good looks. Most people who did not know him who saw that picture did. But she did not say anything like that, and instead turned and said, 'Looks like a nice family.'

'Thanks,' said Charlie. 'Should we get started?'

'Ready when you are,' said Claire.

★   ★   ★

Charlie led Claire into the kitchen. A gray light from the overcast day came through the windows. He showed her around quickly and then he gave her the test he had given to the others.

Charlie said, 'My father always said that you could tell how good a restaurant was by how well they roasted a chicken. In other words, if you do the little things right, everything else should follow. So I am asking everyone who interviews to take the time to roast a chicken. Are you game?'

'Sure,' said Claire. 'I'm ready.'

Charlie set her up at the wooden table, much as his father used to do with the two boys and the blind baskets. From the walk-in he brought her the chicken, a free-range a farmer had raised for him down in Rochester.

'Feel free to use the pantry, anything you need. There are fresh herbs on the windowsill there. Anything else, just ask.'

'Okay,' said Claire and she smiled at him. He told himself not to get his hopes up. This wasn't going to work. Charlie pulled up a stool and rested his broken arm on the wooden table. He sat because he was tall and did not want to appear to be hovering. He was maybe four feet from where she was set up and he watched her every move, as he had with the others, though he was more self-conscious with her, because she was a woman and because she was beautiful and because he felt awkward around her, as if he were the one being interviewed and not her.

Claire took the bird and in the sink she washed it inside and out and then dried it. She laid it on the table. Next she chopped onions and lemons into small dice and from the plant growing on the windowsill she took several sprigs of rosemary. Some of these she left intact while with the others she separated the needles from the branches and rough-chopped them and added them to the small bowl in which she had placed the onions and lemons. She anointed this mixture with olive oil and stuffed the cavity of the bird with it.

She rubbed the whole chicken with olive oil,

64

seasoned it with salt and pepper, and Charlie loved the way she used the salt, the most important thing in the kitchen, the way she measured it without thinking with her thumb and index finger; the way she worked intuitively with it, the way she scattered it across the skin with a confidence that suggested she went by what her heart told her; that she needed no guidance.

'Is your grill on?' Claire asked.

'Yes,' Charlie said and she went to it, laid the bird on it, skillfully turning it several times to give it the grill marks and the smoky flavor, and then removed it to one of the old frying pans, bent and black with age. She turned the oven to 425 and then began to work on her side dishes.

From the pantry she grabbed a large red potato and Charlie watched as she cut this into a half-inch dice. She julienned a carrot and she tossed both the carrot and the potato around the chicken.

'Stock?' she asked.

'In the cooler,' said Charlie, 'those plastic jugs when you walk in.'

In a moment she was back, and she poured a little of the good chicken stock around the bird, and added a little brandy from the bottle above the stove as well, and then when the oven had reached temperature, she placed the pan inside on the middle rack.

'What do you have for vegetables? *Haricots verts?*'

'Yeah,' said Charlie. 'There's some green beans in the fridge.'

Claire went to the small fridge against the far wall and from it she took a handful of the green beans, frenched them, and then quickly blanched them in boiling salty water, letting them cool in an ice bath, bringing out their color.

'How long will your chicken roast?' Charlie asked.

'Twenty-three minutes.'

'That's rather exact, don't you think?'

'I could be wrong,' said Claire. 'But I gave it a good grilling and it's a small bird and a hot oven.'

'Okay,' said Charlie, 'we have some time then. Do you have questions about the job?'

'I do,' said Claire, coming toward him. She veered away and took the other stool that was against the wall and brought it over next to Charlie. While she did so, he thought about her body beneath her clothes. She pulled the stool within a foot of him and sat down and she looked at him with her dark eyes and he had to look away for a quick moment, feigning disinterest.

'What are you looking for?' Claire said.

Charlie thought about this. The truth was that he was looking for her. There was no question. He had been in her presence for all of thirty minutes, and all of a sudden he was aware of his heart, of the blood running like a stream through his veins, of its steady pumping. He was aware of his hands folded on his lap. Aware of the slight fidgeting of his boots against the base of the stool. She made him uneasy and comfortable at the same time. But mostly she made him feel

66

present in a way that made him realise that he had not been for a long time; that despite how hard he worked he had been going through the motions, serious and dedicated, yes, but also somehow absent.

Charlie looked her in the eyes. Dark and large and practically without any white. Absolutely lovely. 'I'm looking for someone who can hold their own in this kitchen. It gets busy. And we don't have the support that other restaurants have — prep cooks and pastry chefs and the whole nine yards. It's just us. So I need someone reliable and hardworking. Creative. Also someone who, if the worst case scenario happens,' Charlie said, raising his arm now, showing her the cast, 'can completely run the show.'

Claire smiled. 'I'm your gal,' she said and she laughed lightly.

'You think so?' Charlie said, admiring her confidence.

'Yup,' said Claire.

'I haven't tasted the chicken yet,' said Charlie.

* * *

Holding a towel in her hand, Claire reached into the oven and removed the hot pan. She took the bird out of it and put it on a cutting board to rest. She removed the cubed potatoes and the julienned carrots. She dumped most of the liquid out of the pan and then added back some of the stock and a glass or so of white wine, and Charlie watched as it came to a rapid boil.

While the sauce was reducing, Claire returned

the bright green haricots verts to a frying pan and added a good pat of butter and some lemon juice and she shook the pan and then seasoned the beans with salt and pepper.

Next she carved the chicken. Her knife work was expert, and she frenched the thigh bone where it came off the breast and plated the pieces of meat in the center, using the roasted root vegetables as a bed, removing several thin slices of the breast on the bias and laying these against the thigh. She strained the sauce through a chinois, and while it was filtering through the fine mesh she placed a handful of the bright green beans on one side of the chicken. She spooned the sauce on the meat and in a circle moving away from it on the side of the plate opposite the beans. She quick-chopped some parsley sprigs and these with a quick flick of her wrists she tossed over everything. She pushed the plate across toward Charlie.

'Voilà!' she said.

Charlie looked at it, and shook his head as if in mock disapproval. 'I'm not sure it's up to the standards of Charlotte's,' he said.

'Oh, be quiet and just taste it,' said Claire.

And he did, he tasted it, and it was just what it should be, moist and satisfying, the flavor of the lemon and the rosemary at once bright and earthy. The green beans were crisp and perfect. All of it seasoned with a light touch even his father would have appreciated.

'When can you start?' he said.

'Are you serious?' she said, a wide smile lighting up her face, her eyes.

'You bet,' Charlie said, and as he said it he looked at her dark eyes and then he looked away, as if the looking was too much.

★ ★ ★

That night, back at the house on Signal Ridge, Charlie Bender cooked for himself. He grilled a salmon fillet and finished it simply with brown butter and capers and some wild rice. He ate in front of the woodstove and after, he sat and watched the snow that came with the dusk fall past the twelve-pane windows, the porch light just bright enough to allow him to see the large flakes floating to the ground. He slowly worked through a bottle of Burgundy, and the wine was good and the stove warm and despite the restaurant being closed Charlie was not restless. In his mind, he replayed the day over and over again, meeting Claire, showing her the restaurant, watching her cook. It all seemed somewhat unreal to him, as these things often do. Had she really been flirting with him, as he thought she had? Was the chicken as good as he thought it was? Was she wearing a ring, or had she mentioned a boyfriend? He could not remember seeing anything on her fingers, but he had not thought to look, either.

Charlie leaned back in the leather chair and he half closed his eyes. It was warm and the room had the comforting smell of wood smoke. His mouth was filled with the taste of red wine. In his mind he studied Claire as he had seen her that afternoon. Now that he was free from her presence, he could let his eyes linger on any part of her that he wanted. Her beautiful hair, dark eyes, the pale lovely skin, the shape of her breasts beneath her shirt. It would be two weeks before she would begin to cook for real inside the kitchen his father and some of his friends had built so many years ago. And when that time came, Charlie would need to be professional about it, pretend she was just another employee, no different from Joe Collins or Peg or Althea. Tonight, though, with the soft snow falling outside the windows and the woodstove ticking with a hot fire, he had no such need, and in his heart he knew he was indulging himself, but he did not care; it was a luxury he was willing to avail himself of, and when he finally fell asleep where he sat, the now-empty wine bottle propped against the arm of the chair, the image that endured was Claire Apple as she left the restaurant, the door closing behind her, her fingers reaching behind to let her hair down as she walked toward her car, the long dark curls tumbling for a second before coming to rest on her shoulders.

5

From the moment she drove her old Toyota across the border from New York State into Vermont, Claire Apple fell in love with what she saw. It had been a long day of driving, her second in a row, having started the day before from her childhood home on the outskirts of Cincinnati, Ohio. This was in late summer and the whole ride it had been threatening rain, dark gray skies, low heavy clouds, occasional drops that fell yet yielded nothing else.

Entering Vermont, the land suddenly changed, no longer flat and indistinct, forested hills looming up in front of her, lush fields of clover on the sides of the road, a ridge of blue mountains rising in the distance. As she crested a large hill in her car, the rain came, falling so hard she had to pull over. Then, just as quickly, it stopped, and the sun broke through the clouds, bright and hot on her windshield, and when she started driving again she saw the rainbow, its base obscured by dark clouds, bright colors against the clear blue of the sky, curved and massive over the forest. She wondered where it touched the earth.

She was on her way to culinary school in Montpelier. Twenty-two years old and she had never left home before, other than family vacations, which in her mind did not count. She was both nervous and excited; she was stepping into a new world, one of her choosing, and one her parents did not completely agree with.

Claire Apple's father was an executive at Procter & Gamble and her mother had never worked outside the home. She grew up an only child in a subdivision where all the houses looked essentially the same, a land of three-car garages and plush lawns with underground sprinkler systems. It was a normal and uneventful childhood, and Claire was expected to go to college like her parents had, and in her mother's eyes use those four years as a time to meet a husband as she had done. When she started to take an interest in cooking, her mother encouraged her, as she considered it a good skill, something that a daughter of hers who would go on to marry well and spend a lot of time as a hostess in her own home could certainly use. What she did not imagine was that Claire would begin to see it as a career. Her final years of high school, her mother kept pushing her to look into different colleges, but in time it became abundantly clear that she had no intention of doing so. After graduation she went to work in restaurants in the city, having no trouble finding jobs waiting tables and working the front end as a hostess, for her looks were an obvious advantage in these jobs.

Inside these high-end restaurants, Claire would linger in the kitchen, watching the chefs, all of them men, cook. She loved the pace of the kitchen, the way they had six things going at once, frenetic and yet somehow choreographed at the same time. She liked the giant stoves with their high butane flames, the pans bent and warped from use. Mostly she liked the creativity that went into the work, watching all those ingredients lined up in aluminum tins become transformed in minutes into something approaching art.

One afternoon, one of the assistant chefs, Jose, who had emigrated from Brazil and was ten years her senior, asked her why she spent so much time watching them cook.

She told him she was fascinated by the cooking and thought she wanted to become a chef. He did not laugh at her as she thought he might, but told her that the hours were long and the work hard and it was no life for anyone who wanted to have a family or vacations or the many things that other people liked to do.

'I don't care about any of that,' Claire said.

On some nights when it was slow in the kitchen Jose would tell Claire what he knew, show her what he was doing. In return, though she did not think of it this way, she began to follow him to his apartment and, before she drove back to her parents' house in the suburbs, she gave herself to him. Jose was her first and he was not handsome but he was kind and she liked the feel of his hands on her body, the feel of him when he was inside her. She liked the way he looked at her afterwards. The way his brown eyes smiled as he took in her nude body, the sharpness of his gaze as it moved over all of her. She liked how he spoke to her in Portuguese when they made love, words she did not mind not understanding for they were musical and she knew they were words of beauty and love and she was grateful for them. She liked how he smoked when they were finished, like an actor in a movie, the smoke rising in rings toward the ceiling of his small apartment while outside she could listen to the sounds of the city, the sounds of cars moving down wet highways. All of it combined to make her feel more mature than her years, even though she knew she was still a young girl from the suburbs, unwise when it came to the truth of the world. She chose not to give it words but she was smart enough to know that letting a man inside you was only that, letting a man inside you, and did not change things beyond it.

In time, though, as she knew she would, she grew tired of Jose, and she grew tired of life at home with her parents and their middle-class dreams, and she grew tired of life in the front end of restaurants and she knew she wanted more for herself. She wanted to be like Jose and the other men who cooked over fire; men who created while those around them simply carried out a vision built behind swinging doors hidden from the public.

To that end, during the mornings she had free, she began to research culinary schools at the downtown library. She wrote letters requesting brochures and opened a PO box to hide her intentions from the prying eyes of her mother. When the brochures came in the mail, she pored over them, the pictures of young men and women in white pants and tunics and with toques on their heads. She began to imagine herself as one of them, but oddly it was not the merits of the course, of the cooking, that swayed her decision one way or the other.

Rather, it was a picture from the school in Vermont that said to her that this was where she needed to go. It was not even a particularly impressive picture.

It showed a river, and across it ran iron trestle bridges, and lowhanging trees were on its shores, as were row houses with porches that leaned precariously out over the water. There was nothing especially beautiful about it; as the river looked black and still and the houses were not remarkable; but somehow it spoke to her, spoke to her of a life different from the one she had always known; a life where people lived on the banks of rivers, mingled with the world around them in a way they did not in her subdivision in Cincinnati. She began to imagine herself in an apartment overlooking the river, though as it turned out she would spend her life in Vermont and never discover where it was that this picture was taken; and in truth, it was not something she thought of much unless she was asked how she had ended up in Vermont, and then it was the first thing that came to her, came to her whole, unlike most memories, which seem to appear in fragments that the mind then reassembles.

So it was that Claire Apple applied to culinary school, and so it was that she broke it off with the first man to make love to her, and so it was that she told her parents, when she was accepted, that she intended to go. And it was almost as if everyone, Jose, her parents, the owners of the restaurant where she worked, saw no use in protesting her decision, for none decided to challenge her on it.

On the night before she left, a night filled with lazy summer heat, she lay in bed with Jose and they had made love and outside she could hear the sounds of cars on the main drag, and she could hear the voices of diners leaving restaurants, voices that wafted up the alley and up the fire escape to his small apartment.

Jose had his arm around her, and she rested her head on his chest, ran her fingers over the muscles of his stomach.

'I don't want to leave,' Claire said.

'Yes you do,' Jose said.

'How do you know?'

'You're a strong woman,' he said. 'I can see it in your eyes. This place is not for you. None of it.'

Claire sighed. 'I don't know what to say.'

'Don't say anything. Get dressed and walk out of here and don't come back. And I don't mean this to sound the way it does. But I'm kicking you out,' he said, and as he said it he began to laugh, a deep-bellied laugh that she had only heard from him a few times, and she began to laugh too, and she was thankful that he was the kind of man who was willing to let her disappear without a fight, for at this time it was what she needed.

Three days later she drove into Vermont, through a summer rainstorm, past a magnificent rainbow, and by the time she reached Montpelier she had been driving for nine hours, but she did not care, for as she reached the apex of the highest part of the highway before her exit, below her she saw the sun setting over the mountains, and she saw a web of river valleys running north, and she saw the lush green that was the hills of Vermont, and though she had never been here before, she knew she was home.

★ ★ ★

The two years of culinary school flew by. She had never worked so hard. Up at dawn and in the bakery, off to meat fabrication class at midmorning, lunch and dinner spent in the busy restaurant kitchens the school ran. At night many of her classmates went out to the bars, and at first she did as well, but later she stopped going altogether and she ignored the entreaties of all the boys at the school who wanted her. There will be plenty of time for boys later, she told herself. She was focused and determined, and it was almost as if she could not learn enough, that they could not teach her enough. She was a competent student, perhaps not as skillful with a knife as some of her male counterparts, but she was praised for her creativity, her ability to see dishes before they were prepared, her intuitive sense of food, that allowed her to know when things worked and when they did not.

As graduation approached, it was time to look for work. Most of her classmates were eager to get out of Vermont, to get jobs at prominent restaurants in big cities. Jobs that paid well. Others were determined to open their own places, and some already had financial backing to do so. For Claire, the thought of leaving Vermont depressed her; for in her two years she had grown fonder of this corner of the earth, with its harsh winters and hot summers, with its breathtaking foliage in the fall.

She scoured the Vermont papers looking for jobs. There were a few that seemed interesting, but they were at ski resorts and did not fit her idea of what she wanted to do. She wanted to be at a small café or a bistro; a place where rules could be broken, where she had some freedom to cook the way she had always wanted.

And then she saw it. It was a small ad in the classifieds of the local paper. On the bottom right of the page in a small box. It read: *Chef wanted to assist owner-chef at small rural restaurant. Seasonal cooking. Northeast Kingdom location. Send letter stating philosophy of food with résumé.*

Claire spent two whole days working on her letter. What was her philosophy of food? Her education had given her a foundation in the major cuisines of the world, with a particular focus on the Continental, but nowhere had anyone talked about philosophy. She had learned the detailed workings of the commercial kitchen. She had learned knife skills. She had learned how to break down meat and poultry and fish. How to make sauces simple and complex. She had studied Escoffier and the other greats. All the things that one did in culinary school. But had she graduated with a set of beliefs that could form the basis of a philosophy?

In the end, she wrote what she felt. She wrote that, when you got right down to it, all food was rooted in culture and tradition and could be not removed from either. In America, she wrote, we have greater freedom as chefs to draw from different cultures. She wrote that food needed to appeal to all the senses, with taste being the most important. And she wrote that she believed in doing things the right way. That there were no shortcuts to good cooking. It took time and patience and hard work. Finally, she said that she did not like the trend toward architecture on the plate, where food was arranged and stacked high like sandcastles. She preferred a simpler preparation, where you let the strength of the ingredients speak for themselves, as good home cooks had done for centuries.

When she finished the letter, she put it with her résumé, sealed the envelope and mailed it from the post office in Montpelier. Two weeks went by and she had put it out of her mind and kept looking for other cooking jobs in the state. And then Charlie called, and on a winter day she drove her old Toyota out along the country roads to Eden, crossing the frozen Dog River on a covered bridge as the light snow fell on to the hardened earth, the boughs of the spruce and ash on either side of her laden with a winter's worth of snow, threatening to fall as she passed.

★ ★ ★

Charlotte's took Claire's breath away. It was almost as if someone had taken all the things she felt and believed but had never been able to give words to and made them real. Even in the dead of winter, with gray skies and softly falling snow, she could see its beauty. She saw it in the long valley that led to Hunger Mountain, in the frozen river that she could see through the bare trees behind it. She saw it in the building itself, small and perfect, so in harmony with all that was around it, the smoke curling out of the chimney and rising into the air. She saw it in the dining room with its woodstove and its tangerine walls and its family pictures. Its large blackboard used for writing the daily menu. And she saw it in the kitchen that was like no commercial kitchen she had ever seen; oh, it had the basic equipment, the grill and the stove and the walk-in, but to her eyes it looked more like a farmhouse kitchen than that of a busy restaurant. She had never before heard of anyone cooking professionally in a place that had windows looking out to the world, where she could watch the snow as it fell and whitened the floodplain, where she could see a glimmer of black water where it flowed beneath a small frozen waterfall in the Dog River.

What surprised Claire even more than Charlotte's itself was her reaction to it, to the job interview. She felt completely at ease. Not even the slightest of flutters in her stomach. From the moment Charlie greeted her at the door, and she looked up at his icy blue eyes, his face craggy for a man of his age, and shook his strong hand, she knew this was where she was meant to be. And then, in the kitchen, all distractions receded, and she was only barely aware of his watching her and she did not mind it, for all she could see was the task in front of her, the roasting of the bird, the making of the sauce, the dicing of vegetables. It was as if she had never cooked anywhere else; was never meant to cook anywhere else, and later, when she drove away from the restaurant, the day's light fading, she could not help but smile, a wide smile that turned into a laugh, her hands leaving the steering wheel with excitement, returning again as she turned on to the covered bridge and crossed it, leaving Eden.

★ ★ ★

Claire Apple found an apartment on Main Street above the hardware store. It was not much, one bedroom, and the living room had shag carpeting. But it had a small porch on the back that looked out to the Dog River, wider and more open here than it was three miles to the south at the restaurant, ice floes on the banks, black water moving freely in the middle. It was also cheap and available and convenient for work. She told herself it was just a place to sleep.

She moved on a day when the sky was cloudless and the sun was bright enough that she wore sunglasses to reduce the glare off the snow. There was no wind but it was bone-jarringly cold. She rented a U-haul and two men from the class below her at the culinary school helped her move the simple furniture she had. They both wanted to sleep with her and she had grown used to this now, judging men's intentions with skill, and she was able to be artful about soliciting their help. She was able to use their desire to her advantage.

After all of her things were inside the apartment, the two men wanted to take her out for dinner and drinks.

Claire said, 'I just want to be alone in my new space, you know? I hope you understand.'

And so they left, and she thanked them each with a hug and a kiss on the cheek. She spent the next two days turning the small apartment into her own, moving the furniture around until she was satisfied with it, arranging what art she had on the walls, hanging the new stainless steel pots and pans her parents had given her for graduation from the rack above the small propane stove. She bought flowers from the florist in town and placed these in vases around the rooms. She laid out her jewelry, her earrings and necklaces and bracelets, on the top of her bureau. She hung her clothes in the closet. And when she was tired of working on the apartment, she poured herself a glass of wine and took long baths in the large clawfoot tub, next to a window where she could look out to the frozen river. She cooked simple dinners for herself. She had another week before she started at Charlotte's, before Charlie had his cast off and could work in the kitchen again. She enjoyed the winter days, short with light but full of freedom. She had a space of her own, and there are times in a woman's life when that is enough.

6

The end of that winter was a long one, even by Vermont standards. Nor'easters roared up the New England coast in late February and early March and they lingered for days over Eden, the snow piling up to the windowsills against the side of Charlotte's. The roads were snow-covered and slick, and the only saving grace was that the banks were so high there was no danger of going off. Tree branches in the forest strained and groaned from the oppressive weight, some of them eventually giving way, crashing silently to the covered floor.

Once a week, Charlie Bender climbed on top of the low roof of Charlotte's and shoveled as much snow off as he could. Although it had never happened in the history of the restaurant, this year there was a real danger of a collapse.

Meanwhile, in the kitchen of Charlotte's, Charlie and Claire were learning how to move around each other. In the mornings they made stocks and reductions; they marinated meat and fish; and they prepped vegetables for that evening's service. Charlie taught Claire the workings of Charlotte's, all the things that his father had taught him. How they prepared certain dishes, where everything was stored, how the inventory worked. What days the producers and growers made deliveries, who to call when they needed more meat or vegetables or other supplies.

They worked well together. Kitchens are intimate places, and even though Charlotte's was unusual in its space, oftentimes Charlie would feel Claire's thighs against the back of his legs as she moved to turn something on the grill; sometimes he would reach from behind her to shake a saucepan, and when he did so, he could smell the soap on her neck, the fragrance of the shampoo she had used that morning.

The simple fact was that with each passing day, Charlie Bender was growing more smitten with Claire Apple. He loved working with her; he loved being with her; and it was not just her physical beauty, her dark eyes and her hair and the loveliness of her skin. The fullness of her breasts. No, that was a large part of it, certainly. But there was more. The inexpressible part of desire, an ache that comes from somewhere deep within, the part you cannot control or give voice to. Where you stay up at night not wanting to sleep for she is in your thoughts and you are afraid that the sleep will take her away, only to discover that she is still with you when you wake, that even if you try to will her away, she is not going anywhere. It was like nothing he had ever experienced before and it scared him. It made him nervous. Like his father before him, he had grown used to being his own man, to governing his life by some internal compass that could not be adulterated by others. The very stuff of his independence, in other words, was built on a lack of interdependence, with the obvious exception of the relationship between his food and those who provided him with the raw ingredients, and those who then sat in the dining room in the glow of the woodstove and enjoyed the fruits of his labor.

There was also the undeniable truth that Charlie was Claire's boss. He had no sense that she was even aware of his feelings, let alone that she might return them. And so, at the minimum, he needed to treat her as he would any of the people who worked for him. As it turned out, he was incapable of doing so.

As time passed that winter, he grew afraid that he wore his affection openly on his face; that both Claire and the other workers saw it in his goofy smile when he joked with her; saw it in his body language; saw it in his eyes which at every opportunity drank in the entirety of her.

And so, in response, Charlie did the last thing he should have done. He began to relate to her differently than he did to the others, than he did to Joe Collins or Althea or Peg. And he related to her not in the way he wanted to, not in the way he did when he dreamed about it; in his dreams when they were lovers.

Instead, he treated her harshly.

He criticised her work; went out of his way to taste her sauces before they made it to the plate, suggesting they were missing something when he knew they were just what they should be. Once he even snapped at her when in the heat of service a pot containing pasta boiled over on her watch — the most natural and innocent of mistakes — and as the water cascaded down the sides and on to the large flame he told her to pay attention. And he saw her brace when he did so, and he wished he had not said it, wished he could tell her how he really felt; wished he could explain that everything he did now was an outgrowth of the fact that he was crazy for her; wished that he could explain that he could not help himself.

All men smitten live with a certain duality of self. Charlie Bender was no different. His only hope was that he was not building a wall between them, something from which they could not recover to reach the place where he thought they belonged.

★　★　★

One afternoon in the second week of March, on a day when the temperature soared into the fifties with a bright sun and from the kitchen they could hear the sound of the water melting off the roof, Charlie was in the walk-in, kneeling on the floor, sorting through potatoes, when he heard Claire behind him.

'Can I talk to you for a second?' she said.

'Sure,' Charlie said, turning around, standing up and wiping his hands on his apron. 'What's up?'

Claire looked at him and then looked away. 'This is hard,' she said, and when she said it, Charlie felt his heartbeat in his throat, for he was certain that she was about to tell him she was leaving.

'Okay,' he said.

'Is there something wrong with my performance?' she asked. 'Is there something wrong with my cooking?'

'No,' said Charlie. 'No, absolutely not.'

Claire nodded, a little vigorously, for she was angry. 'Then how come you're so critical? It wasn't like this when I was first here, but lately it doesn't seem like I can do anything right. I don't season well enough. The temp is wrong on meats. Salads are overdressed. My risotto is not 'soft waves'. I mean, Charlie, I love working here, don't get me wrong. I love this place. The restaurant. The people. The food. And I think you're a brilliant cook, I do. I know I'm not your equal, not yet anyway. I'm working on it.'

'Claire,' Charlie said.

Her eyes flashed. 'Let me finish,' she said.

'Okay.'

'I work my ass off,' said Claire. 'Maybe you haven't noticed, but I'm here an hour earlier than we agreed on. I stay as late as you do. I work my ass off. And I'm not complaining. I just want to be shown some appreciation for that. For what I do. There, that's it. That's what I got.'

Claire stood in front of him and her hands dropped from where they crossed her chest to her sides. Charlie wanted to tell her that he loved her; that was what this was all about, that it had nothing to do with how she cooked, but everything to do with how much she consumed him. But he knew he could not say this, that beyond the fact that it might scare the hell out of her — might send her running out faster than she had come in — it was a truth that had no place in this conversation.

He said, 'You're right. You are. You are right.'

'Thank you,' said Claire, still nodding her head at him.

'You're an excellent cook, Claire. I guess I haven't been used to sharing this kitchen with anyone else since my brother took off. I can be a little possessive.'

'A little?'

'Okay.' Charlie smiled. 'A lot. I can do better. And I will.'

'I love my job, Charlie.'

'I know.'

'Good,' said Claire. 'Thanks for hearing me out.'

'Sure,' said Charlie, and with that, Claire turned around and walked out of the cold storage room, into the kitchen, and the first warm sun of spring streamed through the windows, a golden light dappled across the hardwood floors.

★   ★   ★

At the end of March, the days grew consistently warm, sometimes touching the mid-seventies, and the winter's snowpack began to melt faster than it should. Mud season began in earnest, the roads impassable in places, and business at Charlotte's slowed as a result. Streambeds in the woods that had been dry for more than a decade now ran hard and fast with whitewater. The roads themselves often resembled small brooks, water moving over washboard grooves. The ice on Mirror Lake began its slow melt, moving away from the shorelines, turning from a hard white to a pigeon gray. The water ran consistently off the roof of the restaurant and at the old farmhouse on Signal Ridge the roof leaked steadily in the bedroom that had belonged to Charlie's parents. Every day when he returned home he emptied out the large bucket he had placed there and then returned it to collect for the next day. The first sounds of spring appeared in the air, birds in the morning that no one saw but that yet could be heard singing in the half-dark of dawn. And on the Dog River the ice upstream began to break up and started its seasonal crawl southward, stopping in place, the river forced to flow around it until it calved off and could move again as one.

The river flooded every year, though generally it took the form of water in the fields that bordered it; in new paths it carved through the forest.

Once in a man's lifetime, though, all of the elements came together in such a way that a larger flood was certain to happen. The last time it had happened in Eden was 1937. Charlie, like nearly everyone who grew up here, had seen the pictures. Men wearing suits and hats riding canoes down Main Street. Cattle swept up in the raging river water, found dead three miles from the farm where they lived. Iron trestle bridges broken away from their moorings, left in pieces at a bend in the turbulent river. Most of the buildings in the low-lying part of the town dated to that year as they replaced ones that had existed previously.

Charlie remembered that it was something his father was concerned about because of where the restaurant was situated. Charlotte's had fire insurance but it did not have flood insurance. No company would insure it because it was built on a floodplain. Normally, in the spring, the water came on to the floodplain, as it was meant to, but it was never closer than a hundred yards away. A bad year was when the basement filled partway with water and they needed to run two or three sump pumps to clear it.

Meanwhile, March turned into April. The warm weather continued and the snow left the lowlands, though it was still deep in the woods. The Dog River overflowed its banks, and behind Charlotte's you could see where it spread out into the woods, instant marshland, white birch trees sticking out of the water. And then the rain came.

It was a Tuesday. It started slowly, a light drizzle under cloudy skies, but by late afternoon as they were readying for the first diners at Charlotte's, it was falling hard. All that night the rain fell in torrents over the hills and valleys of Eden. On Wednesday it slowed for a bit but then picked up to where it had been the previous night. The soggy earth could not hold any more of it and pastures were filled with pockets of standing water. The river began to rise beyond its already precarious heights. It moved further into the woods, and from the bridges that crossed it you could look down and see it raging in angry currents.

From the back porch of the restaurant, Charlie watched the water, the river, the woods, and he knew it was rising, but nothing in his life prepared him to be concerned. It rose every year and sometimes it flooded. But he had never seen the building threatened and despite the heavy rain he did not expect it to be any different this time. Still, the river was moving out into the floodplain, increasing its reach with eddies of debris-strewn water moving out in concentric circles toward where he stood. Thursday brought more rain, and Friday, when it was still raining, Althea called to say her road had been washed out by the brook that gave it its name and she could not get past it. The radio carried news of a flash flood warning and late that afternoon Charlie took a call from the fire chief.

'Charlie,' he said.

'Hi, Len.' Charlie knew him from around town, though he was not a customer at the restaurant. He was a big man, with a handlebar mustache and a head of thick gray hair.

'How are things up your way?'

'It's rising pretty good but still out a good way in the fields. I think we'll be fine.'

There was silence on the other end of the line, as if Len was chewing this over. 'Yup,' he said. 'Listen, tomorrow morning, if it hasn't stopped raining, we're going to need to break up the last blockage of ice upstream at Fisher's Bend or we'll have a hell of a lot of water on Main Street. What that means for your place, I don't know.

91

But my guess is that there will be a whole lot more river there than there is now.'

Charlie took this in. 'What are you thinking, Len?'

'I'm worried about your business, Charlie. I would definitely close. That's a no-brainer at this point. With the way the roads are, I don't think too many folks are heading out anyway. But your building could be in danger. I hope not, but it could be. What I'm offering is our help. Tomorrow morning we can send some of the boys over to do some sandbagging. Hopefully it won't be necessary. But if it is, it sure could help.'

Charlie sighed, thought about this. His father would have said no way, that the Benders took care of their own place and did not need help from anyone else, no matter what the issue. But he weighed this against the possibility of losing Charlotte's, all he had ever known, a place that was in his blood, a place that meant more to him than anything. 'Thanks, Len,' he said. 'I hope we don't need it. But I appreciate it.'

When Charlie hung up, he called Claire and Joe Collins and Peg and Althea and told all of them they were closing. That they were expecting the river to continue to rise. He told them about the fire department. About the sandbagging. He told them to take the weekend off, and though both Joe and Claire offered to help, he told them not to worry about it. There was nothing they could do at this point.

Next he called the reservations they had and told them the score. That night he cooked for himself inside Charlotte's, and he drank a bottle of wine and sat on the porch and watched the rain fall in the black night. He could hear the river rushing through the woods. He could hear its edges sloshing on the floodplain a few hundred yards away. He watched it until the wine was gone and his eyes grew heavy. He slept fitfully on a makeshift bed on the dining room floor, and when he woke to a near lightless dawn, it appeared to be raining even harder than it had the day before, spilling off the roof so quickly that to look out the windows was like trying to see through the backside of a waterfall.

★ ★ ★

Charlie made a pot of coffee, and while it brewed he went out back to the porch. The floodplain had been transformed overnight, almost half of it now under water and you could no longer tell where the river began and where it ended. Where it normally flowed, grayish-black water swirled angrily around trees. The rain fell steadily.

Inside, he walked down the narrow, rickety basement stairs. It was a typical Vermont cellar, low-ceilinged and earthen-floored. There was standing water, about a half-foot of it, and he walked into it to the recess in the middle of the floor where the sump pump was and he reached down and turned it on. He found the hose and pushed it through the window and out. He waited until he heard it working and then he returned upstairs.

There was not much else he could do now, so he drank his coffee and made himself an omelet with Cheddar and mushrooms and ate it with yesterday's bread. He tried to ignore the rain but it was difficult for it was everywhere, the only sound beyond the clank of his dishes when he placed them in the sink.

By ten o'clock, the first of the volunteer firefighters began to arrive. Men in pickup trucks with sirens on their dashboards who stood in huddled groups oblivious to the rain and smoked cigarettes. Charlie went and greeted them, brought them mugs of coffee. They exchanged pleasantries, talked about the rain, and like the chief, Charlie knew some of them from around town, in the roundabout way that people in small towns know each other, but none of them he ever remembered seeing inside of Charlotte's.

'The Chief should be here shortly,' a large bearded man told him. 'And a truck with sand.'

Charlie nodded. 'I really appreciate you guys coming out,' he said.

The man shrugged. 'It's what we do.'

More arrived and Charlie stayed busy bringing them coffee, freshening up those who already had some. The men did not seem to mind the rain. They stood and talked and smoked and they seemed happy to be away from the house, to have the company of other men, and it occurred to Charlie that this was something he did not have in his own life. Not since Owen left. Other than Joe Collins, who was a strong and steady presence but would go entire days and not say much more than a few words, Charlie was now used to working only with women.

Soon the Chief arrived, the only full-time employee, and though the men were volunteers, Charlie could see they respected his authority. Shortly after the Chief's arrival a dump truck came, and right in the parking lot of Charlotte's, where cars would normally park on a night when dinner service was going on, it dropped a large pile of sand.

The men got to work. Charlie joined them and they worked on all sides of the massive pile, filling burlap bags with sand. Some of the men formed a bucket brigade that led from the parking lot out to the floodplain. When each bag was filled and tied it was passed down the line to the last men who began to build a levee. It was hard work and the rain was soaking through their clothes but no one appeared to mind.

They had been at this for about a half-hour when a car pulled into the driveway. Charlie looked up and he saw Claire Apple emerge out of her old Toyota and she gave him a smile as she did so. The men momentarily stopped and stared at her, and her hair was down and was already wet, plastered against the sides of her face, and she wore a long-sleeved T-shirt and jeans and boots, and Charlie knew the men would continue to stare at her until he did something. He went to her.

'Hey,' he said when he reached her.

'I thought I'd come help,' she said.

'You didn't have to do that,' Charlie said.

'What am I going to do? Stay shut up in my apartment all day?'

Charlie laughed. 'You're getting soaked.'

'Yeah, well, so is everyone else.'

'You could help me make some lunch for these guys.'

'Later,' said Claire. 'Looks like there's more to do right here.'

Charlie watched as she reached behind her and tied her hair up, and then she walked with him back to the sand pile, and several of the men nodded at her, and if they were surprised to see her pitch in and start filling bags, they did not say so.

While he worked, Charlie would now and again look up and see Claire, wet with rain, working as hard as any of the men. Her shirt and her face were smudged with mud and she looked more beautiful than he had ever seen her, strong and capable, and she did not have to be here and he loved her for it.

By early afternoon the pile was half gone, and out on the floodplain Charlie could see that they had the makings of a pretty good levee, bags stacked high and stretching longer than the length of the building. Charlie stopped what he was doing and went and found the Chief where he was supervising the brigade.

'Think these guys would like some lunch?' Charlie asked.

'You put it out,' the Chief said, 'I'm sure they'll eat it.'

'All right,' Charlie said and went to Claire. She stood and wiped her hand across her forehead, leaving a black mark from the wet sand as she did so.

'How about helping me with lunch now?' Charlie said.

Claire looked around. She smiled. 'I suppose they can survive without me for a minute,' she said.

'At least they'll try,' said Charlie.

* * *

In the kitchen, while the rain continued to fall, they could see the men continuing to build a high wall against the river that raged ever closer. Charlie and Claire cooked quickly, without speaking, and they were still both soaked through but they did not care. Charlie browned meat in a large stockpot and Claire diced onions and garlic for the chili. To the meat he added fresh chilies, the onions and garlic, beans from a can, and the first of the season's hothouse tomatoes. It was not anything they would have served in the dining room, but it would be hot and warm and filling, and they knew that for those who were working so hard to save something that they had no personal stake in this was all that mattered.

For an hour they let the chili cook down, the flavors all mingling together, while both Charlie and Claire returned to the building of the levee. For a while the rain slowed, which made the work easier, but as they grew closer to finishing the wall it started up again, and the first of the river water was lapping against the base of the bags.

'Do you think it will hold?' Charlie asked the Chief.

'Time will tell,' Len said. 'We've taken it as far as we can, I think.'

Charlie and Claire set up a makeshift mess line in the dining room and the men, all of them soaking wet and tired, filed through and filled large bowls with the chili. They ate at the tables in the dining room, and since Charlie did not allow them to take their boots off — partially a show of gratitude but also not wanting to seem too precious — water pooled around their feet while they ate. The chili could have used a few more hours, but it was spicy and good and most of the firefighters returned for seconds. Charlie managed to eat some as well, though his mind was on the river, and while he knew it was out of his hands, he also knew that it was going to be a long night.

After lunch, some of the men lingered out in the parking lot and smoked but most of them got in their trucks and drove down the wet roads to their homes, to their next call. Charlie talked with the Chief under the eaves of the front door while Claire cleaned up inside. They looked at the rain and Charlie thanked him profusely for the work.

'I hope it's enough,' said the Chief. 'You should go home, Charlie. There's nothing you can do by being here and if things really pick up you could be in trouble. It only looks like water, but if it gets moving it can be dangerous.'

Charlie nodded. 'I know it.'

'But you're not going anywhere, are you?' said Len.

'Probably not, Chief,' Charlie said.

'I figured as much,' he said. 'Well, hang in there.'

Charlie watched him go, stopping to admonish some of the men for their smoking, and they laughed with him and then turned back to each other, none of them appearing to be in a rush to go home, the rain falling on to their yellow coats and then to the ground. The Chief climbed into his bright red pickup and gave a big wave, drove off toward Eden center. Soon all the men had left and Charlie returned inside, to Claire, to a river that was swelling beyond his kitchen, moving in eddies closer and closer to the walls of Charlotte's.

7

They were in the restaurant with nothing to do. The wan gray light of day began to disappear. The dark began to gather. The rain continued its steady and incessant fall, sometimes coming in sheets that rippled in great waves across the whole of the floodplain, other times slowing to a near drizzle before picking up again. The river water rose, the bottom bags on the levee soaked through.

'You should go,' Charlie said to Claire. 'When it gets dark the road might wash out and you won't be able to see it.'

'Do you want me to go?' Claire said, looking at him.

'That's not the point.'

'Do you want me to go?' she asked again.

'Of course not.'

'Then I'll stay.'

'There's no work to do.'

'Do we always have to work, Charlie?'

Charlie looked wounded, like he had been scolded. 'No, it's just — '

'I could use a drink,' said Claire.

'Good idea,' said Charlie, anxious to have something to do. 'Let me get some wine.'

Charlie went into the dining room. Behind the bar he looked through the bottles lined in the cabinet. He picked a big Italian, an Amarone made from sun-ripened Sangiovese grapes. A good winter wine. A good wine for a day when the rain would not stop. He returned to the kitchen and pulled two large glasses off a rack above the fridge, opened the wine, and poured each of them a healthy glass.

'Cheers,' Charlie said.

'To the flood,' Claire said.

'To no customers,' said Charlie.

'To no customers,' said Claire.

They clinked glasses and they each took long sips on the wine. It needed to open and was big with fruit but the strong alcohol felt good and it was just what Charlie needed.

'I'm still soaked,' said Claire.

Charlie reached down, felt his own T-shirt. 'Me too.'

'We should light a fire. At least try to dry off.'

'Sure, I can do that.'

'And then we can make some dinner.'

Charlie looked over at her. Her hair was still wet and her big eyes suggested that she was kidding with him. 'What do you want to eat?'

Claire pursed her lips. She pushed her hair away from her ears. 'I haven't seen the menu yet, have I?'

'So you want me to cook for you, then,' Charlie said.

'Yes.'

'And light you a fire.'

'Yes.'

Charlie shook his head with mock incredulity. 'Is there anything else you would like, princess?'

Claire ran her hand along her cheek, as if

pondering this. 'Maybe a little more of this wine,' she said.

★ ★ ★

Claire sat down on a chair in the dining room in front of the woodstove. She pulled another chair up and on this she put her feet. It was not cold out but the fire was drawing well and she watched the orange flames in the firebox and the heat it gave off was warm and what she wanted. With no other noise in the dining room besides the crackling of the fire and the sound of the rain drumming on the roof, she could hear Charlie moving around in the kitchen, pans clanking, the creak of the walk-in.

'If I'm cooking,' Charlie had said to her after he lighted the fire, 'then I'm cooking. I don't want to be disturbed.'

'Fine,' said Claire. 'That goes both ways. Just leave the wine here.'

Now, watching the fire, she sipped her wine and asked herself what she was doing. There was something between them, she knew, and when there was something between people there were only two ways it could go. One was for both to walk away, or at least for one to walk away fast enough that the other had no choice but to give in. The other was to move inexorably toward one another in such a way that there was no turning back. Claire thought that by being here she was choosing the latter and she did not want to think about it too hard, for she knew that if she did, the practical side of her would take over and know that there was no good that could come of it. He was her boss; she worked for him; she needed the work, and nothing tended to screw things up as much as when co-workers slept together.

On the other hand, she found herself favoring the impractical side of herself, the side of herself that was drawn to Charlie. There were plenty of men who were better-looking, she thought. But he had those clear blue eyes, and he was tall and strong, and when he was not obsessive about the work in the kitchen, he showed her that he had a good heart. He showed her that he could be sensitive, and she respected his talent immensely. Every day, it seemed, she learned something new from him. Of course, that did not mean she needed to sleep with him. Have dinner, Claire, she said to herself, keep him company, but don't drink too much, and don't go to bed with him. It's a quick path to screwing things up.

Claire slowly sipped her wine, felt the stove warming her feet. She looked over to the kitchen. She could hear the sounds of cooking and she smiled. Her clothes were still wet but since she figured he would honor their agreement for her to stay in the dining room, and for him to stay in the kitchen, she stood and grabbed another chair from one of the tables and placed it inches away from the side of the hot stove. She glanced once more at the swinging doors, at the small plastic windows that looked into the kitchen. Then she took her T-shirt off, laid it over the back of the chair. She stepped out of her jeans and laid them on the other side. She chuckled to herself. She was in the dining room of Charlotte's wearing only her bra and panties. If it was not something she had chosen to do herself, it would have sounded awfully like a nightmare.

★ ★ ★

In the walk-in there were six Maine lobsters that despite the rain and the season had been delivered the day before. Charlie took two of them out of a box, one-and-a-half-pounders, still lively in light of the cold, their bound claws waving in the air as he held them up. He laid them side by side flat on the cutting board and with the sharp chef's knife he quickly killed them by cutting below the eyes through the thorax. Next he separated the tail from the body, the claws from the head, and he put these aside. He removed the roe from the body and the tail and scraped it into a bowl. He sliced the tails through the shell, into four pieces each. He smashed the claws with the flat of his knife. With flour and water and eggs he made a quick dough in the mixer and into this he folded the grayish-green lobster roe. He then forced it through the pasta attachment on the commercial mixer and the long threads became a dark green linguini that would turn red when he cooked it.

On the stove he boiled water and on another burner he placed a large sauté pan. In the pan he put a pat of butter and when the butter began to foam he added chopped shallots and cooked these until they were translucent. Then he added the pieces of tail and claw and knuckle, shaking the pan while he watched the lobster start to change color. He poured some Scotch whisky into the pan and then flambéed it, tilting the large pan so that the butane flame reached up and touched it and the alcohol caught on fire. He lifted it off the burner and shook it until the flames stopped. He let the whisky sauce continue to reduce and the lobster to cook and then he added some heavy cream that came from a farm on the other side of Eden. He chopped fresh tarragon and threw a healthy handful around the lobster. He turned the flame to low.

When the water came to a boil he tossed the fresh pasta in and he timed its finish by going to the fridge and pulling out a bottle of champagne, popping the cork. As soon as he did that, Charlie strained the fresh pasta, adding a quarter cup of the starchy water to the sauce pan, loosening the sauce where it had thickened. It was all of a sudden smooth and velvety and this was how he wanted it.

While he had a moment now, Charlie went to the door and looked in on Claire. She was next to the stove, and at the moment he looked through she was putting her jeans back on, jumping slightly as she pulled them up over her hips. She wore only a black bra and he got a good look at the shape of her breasts, and a touch of thigh before her jeans came over them. She had no idea he was seeing her, and he understood that she was drying her clothes next to the fire, and it was beautiful and natural, a completely rational thing for anyone to do given the circumstances, but it was sexy to him nonetheless, the sight of her pale skin, the curve of her breasts, the red of her mouth as it opened slightly from the exertion, from the heat.

★   ★   ★

Charlie tossed the now-red pasta with butter, salt and pepper and divided it between two stark-white oval plates. He took the tail meat out of the shells but he left the claws whole and these he put on top of the pasta, scattering the tail meat around it, on the edge of the plate. He finished the dish with the sweet sauce of reduced Scotch and tarragon and cream, pouring it over everything. He quickly checked the window to make sure Claire was dressed. She was back in her clothes and she sat facing the stove. He could hear the rain on the roof and if he looked toward the windows he could see it falling and he knew what it meant but it did not matter to him at all, not right now.

He moved through the swinging doors like a waiter, one plate in his right hand, the other balanced higher up on his arm, his left hand holding the champagne.

'Wow,' Claire said when Charlie placed one plate in front of her. He put his down on the table, and then the champagne, and then went to the bar and got two flutes. Claire rose and moved candles from other tables and lit them and they ate in the firelight and the candlelight and there was the ticking of the stove and the sound of the rain. They talked about the food, about the pasta, how the roe changed the

106

linguini from green to red, just as the lobster itself did. Claire was surprised that the Scotch worked; she thought it would be too much, too heavy, too sweet. But it lent a smokiness to the dish, a touch of sweetness and nuttiness that brought out the best in the seafood.

Charlie explained to her how he had come up with the recipe, during one of his father's blind baskets, how his father thought he should have used brandy instead of Scotch but was surprised, as well, that it stood up the way it did. 'Lobster Charles, he called it,' said Charlie.

'I wish I'd known your father,' said Claire.

Charlie played with the stem of his champagne flute. 'He was a complex man.'

'Aren't they all?'

'More than most. He was brilliant. Bullheaded. Difficult.'

'Sounds like someone else I know.'

'My father and I are very different.'

'How?'

'I don't know,' said Charlie. 'I don't like to talk about it.'

'I didn't mean to pry.'

Charlie looked across at her. 'It's okay. I'm sure you know what happened. There are no secrets in this town.'

Claire nodded, told him the truth. 'Yes, I heard about it. You don't need to explain.'

'I appreciate that. But let me say this. He was dying. That was clear. Would I have done the same thing in his shoes? I don't think so. And what confuses me about it is that I don't know if that makes me a coward or if it makes me brave.

Maybe I'll never know.'

'Maybe you're looking at it the wrong way,' Claire said. 'I mean, maybe it's not so clean-cut. Maybe it's not a question of cowardice or bravery. Maybe it just is what it is.'

Charlie finished his glass of champagne. 'This conversation is getting as grim as this rain.'

'I'm sorry,' said Claire. 'My fault.'

'No, no, it's not. But can we talk about something else.'

'Sure, of course. What?'

Charlie smiled. 'I don't know. The weather?'

★   ★   ★

Claire insisted on cleaning up, and while she did, Charlie went out the back door to the small porch that overlooked the flood-plain and the river; the porch on which his father used to sit at night and smoke. The dark was thick and it was difficult to see through the falling rain. Twenty yards away he could make out the gray-white sandbags that made up the levee. The sound of water was everywhere, all around him. Coming off the roof, falling on to the soggy earth, moving loudly in the dark closer and closer to him. There were gradations of sound. The loudest being the river water at its ambiguous center. It rushed like a train.

Charlie walked off the porch and the rain immediately soaked his hair and his clothes. He walked toward the levee, his boots making deep impressions into the soft earth. Thin light from the kitchen glowed behind him while in front it seemed to get darker and darker. There was no sky. Only rain and water and darkness.

Before he reached the levee, he stepped into pooled water up to his ankles. It was cold and wet and he thought: the levee's broken. But as he got closer he realised the levee was still there, the black river water lapping against its sides, about halfway to the top, and what he had stepped in had simply been what had risen up through the earth.

Charlie looked at the black water and he thought: I should be more worried about this than I am. I should be fixated on it. There must be more that I can do.

But he remembered the fire chief's words, that they had done all they could do. All he had now was hope, and the distraction of a woman who he was in love with, though he felt certain that she did not know that.

Charlie returned to the porch and he turned once again and faced the river. The air was alive with rain. The door behind him opened and Claire stepped out. She moved next to him.

'How is it?' she asked.

'Still rising.'

'It will stop.'

'We should do some thinking about what we do if it doesn't.'

'I'm not worried,' said Claire.

'How can you be so sure?'

Charlie saw her shrug in the dark. 'It's a feeling.'

'I just hope we're not fiddling while Rome burns,' he said.

'It's an end-of-the-world party,' Claire said. 'Those are the best kind.'

*   *   *

They set up chairs on the porch and they sat down next to one another and they watched the dark and listened to the sounds of the swollen river. They drank snifters of Armagnac and the liquor tasted of soil and of apples. Claire was getting drunk. It was not a bad drunk. She felt slightly euphoric and carefree and her thoughts were not on the river but on Charlie next to her, and when the rain began to slow to little more than a light drizzle, Claire put her hand on his shoulder as she said, 'Look.'

'It's done this before,' Charlie said.

'I think it's stopping,' said Claire.

'I hope you're right.'

Claire playfully reached out and punched him on the arm. 'You should be more optimistic,' she said.

'I'm trying,' he said.

'Maybe this will help,' she said, and she left her chair and half bent down to him, and before she had time to think about it and before he had time to react to it, she kissed him. She kissed him softly, and he kissed her back, and she felt his hands go to her face and she felt him holding her cheeks and she kissed him again. This time she tasted the liquor on his tongue and she stayed with it longer, reaching around the back of his head to move her fingers through his short hair. Charlie pulled back.

'Should we — ' he said.

Claire put her finger over his mouth. 'Don't,' she said.

'I'm just — '

'Shush. Don't,' Claire said. 'Don't think.'

Claire climbed into his lap and he held her with his strong arms, and she let him just hug her for a moment. Her hair was hanging in his face and she shook her head and with her hand she pushed the long bangs behind her ears. She moved in to kiss him again and this time they clanged teeth and Charlie said, 'Sorry.'

'It's okay. Slow, like this.'

Claire tilted her head, and now they kissed long and hard and she was aware of his breathing. And then she was aware of his shaking. He was shivering.

'Are you okay?'

'I'm cold,' he said.

'Let's go in.'

'Okay.'

Claire led him by the hand and they moved through the kitchen, under the suddenly harsh overhead lights, and then through the swinging doors and into the dining room. The candles they had used had been blown out and the only light was from the woodstove, a diffused orange glow that was enough to see by. In front of the stove she went to him, put her arms around him and he put his around her, and they kissed standing up.

'Wait,' Claire said, 'I have an idea.'

She left him and went back the way they had come, into the kitchen. When she returned, her arms were full of table linens. 'Help me,' she said. 'Let's make this floor bearable.'

They carefully laid tablecloth after tablecloth down on the wideplank hardwood. 'That should work,' Claire said when it was about twenty thick. 'Lie with me, Charlie.'

Charlie was scared and felt awkward but he also wanted her as he had never wanted anything. He watched as she sat down on the makeshift bed and started to take off her boots.

'Get down here, mister,' she said.

Charlie sat next to her, followed her lead, removed his heavy boots and pushed them across the floor away from them. They rolled into each other, and Claire rolled on top of him and she kissed him, with greater urgency now, and Charlie could feel her breasts against his chest and his hands moved under her shirt and down her back. Charlie rolled her over on to her side and he slid his hand under her shirt and he felt the soft skin of her belly and she leaned up and unhooked her bra and he ran his hand over the curve of first one breast and then the other, feeling her nipples stiffening under his fingers.

'Undress me,' Claire whispered.

Charlie knelt above her, and he helped her lift her shirt over her head and he unbuttoned her jeans and jerked them over her hips and then guided them down her legs and off until she sat naked before him, her pale body beautiful in the light from the stove, her full breasts and the slope of her belly and the dark triangle below.

'Come to me,' she said and when he lay down next to her and kissed her he felt her hand on the

112

buckle of his belt and she deftly unfastened it and he arched toward her as she undid his zipper and took him out and into her hand. He felt her hand moving up and down on him and he said through clenched teeth, 'I don't know how long I can handle that.'

Claire laughed. 'Okay,' she said and she took his hand in her own and she brought it down to her, held her own over his and showed him how to open her with his fingers, and she said, 'Gentle. Yes, like that.'

Claire let him do this until she could not take any more and then she climbed on top of him and she guided him inside her. She moved slowly, bringing him along, and while she did, she closed her eyes and felt the warmth of him; and when she opened her eyes, it was the shadows she saw, the reflections of the flames of the woodstove on the wall.

When she began to move faster, she looked down at him, her hair swinging in his face, and his expression was contorted with bliss, and she knew she would not finish herself and she could, should she want to, finish him now, but instead she decided to draw it out, slowing down, teasing him, before increasing again. Right when she knew he could not last any longer, she pulled off him and he came outside of her.

They collapsed into one another. They rolled on to their backs and their breathing came fast and ragged. Claire looked up at the ceiling. There was an exposed beam above that she had never noticed before. Then again, she had never had an occasion to lie on the floor of Charlotte's.

Charlie found an old blanket in the storage room and they pulled this over themselves and in minutes Claire was asleep with her head resting at the place where his arm met his chest. Charlie lay still and stared at the ceiling. He could no longer hear the rain and he guessed that it had stopped. He did not know that outside the flood had crested and that in a few hours it would recede beyond the levee.

The sandbags had held their ground. While she slept, he stared at the fire that he had stoked before they went to bed. He watched the ash logs burning and he sipped water to guard against the hangover to come. He thought of the river. He imagined it crossing the sandbags, rising up in a giant wave that rushed through the back door of the restaurant, picking up chairs and tables, picking up him and Claire and the tablecloths and sweeping them back up with it. He imagined moving quickly downstream in currents so fast that both of them were kept afloat. It should have been an unpleasant thought. Curiously, he found it strangely comforting. The cool water, the trees lining the shore, the two of them like loose branches, bobbing along, rising over small waterfalls and then slowing down in the still, wide parts of the river.

Sometime later, he drifted off to sleep. When he woke, Claire was turned away from him and he could hear her slow, steady breathing. He lifted himself up on his elbows and looked at her beautiful face. Her upraised cheek was flushed and her eyelids fluttered slightly but she did not wake. He could see where the blanket barely covered the swell of her breasts. Slowly, he rose. The rain had stopped and he walked out on to the back porch. He wore no clothes and his head ached. He saw the chairs they had sat in and he saw their snifters of Armagnac on the floor of the porch, one of them empty and the other with half a glass of the amber liquor. The day was gray but there was no rain. The river had receded but he could see it was still raging through the trees, whitewater swirling around the bone-white birch. The floodplain was full of debris and standing water. Above the clouds flew swiftly through a gray sky. A stiff, warm breeze blew. Wispy black clouds cut across the floodplain at eye level. Later the sun would emerge and the drying of Eden would begin. Twin sundogs would appear on either side of Hunger Mountain, like stained-glass windows in the sky. For now, though, the world around the restaurant had been altered, and inside it had as well, for in the dark of the flood Charlie and Claire had come together. And while the water would eventually return to where it always was, while the river would become the river it used to be, Charlie knew that he would never be the same man again. And though it made him happy, happier than he had ever been, he also was wise enough to know that what had happened last night would not recede like the water. It was here to stay.

8

It was just after ten in the morning when he led her into the woods. They left the restaurant and crossed the dirt road and then blended into the trees. The day was warm with bright sun but under the shadows of the tall spruces it was dark and the forest floor was covered with ferns, and these they walked through and their pant legs grew damp from the residual water on the broad leaf cover. They moved slowly as the growth was thick but soon he found the deer run and they began to move uphill, climbing the base of the steep escarpment.

'Where are you taking me?' Claire asked.

'It's a secret,' he said.

'You're so cryptic, Charlie Bender,' she said. 'What if I told you it was turning me on?'

Charlie turned and looked at her. 'Shush,' he said.

The deer run was narrow but the dirt was hardened and the hiking was not hard. The canopy was high here and in places shards of sunlight shot through to where they were and they could feel it warm on their arms. As they climbed, the tall spruces at the bottom of the hill gave way to poplars and reed-thin birches, their bark the color of sandstone, their leaves the palest of greens, almost silvery. The sun splashed through now, and its dappled light spread across the forest floor in waves. At one point they

116

startled a whitetail and Claire said, 'Look,' and Charlie turned in time to see it bounding up over a small hillock and out of view.

It had been two weeks since the flood and they were into it. In the kitchen of Charlotte's they had been doing their best to hide the truth between them but like all new lovers, they were no good at it. Theirs was a palpable love, as clear to those who looked for it as the slight hum that hung in the air following summer lightning. Their hands lingered for a moment too long when they accidentally came together; they made less effort to avoid one another while moving around the tight area that comprised the stove and the grill. When they thought no one could see them, they sneaked kisses and they held one another. In the mornings they arrived separately, and at night they spoke loudly and obviously about their respective plans for after work and for the weekends; and Claire always left first, in her car, Charlie meeting her at the house on Signal Ridge minutes later. Naturally, they both thought that their secrecy was working, that no one associated with the restaurant had any idea that they were together. And if Charlie had been only a little more perceptive, he might have recognised the laughter that stopped when he entered the kitchen for what it was. Althea had just bet Peg and Joe Collins ten bucks that, in her words, 'those two are doing it'. Now, moving up the steep hillside on the deer run, Claire looked back and saw the distance they had traveled and she saw through the trees to other hills and when she looked down she could see

Charlotte's as she had never seen it, from above, a little box, the sunlight catching a glint of river behind it.

'So are we going to walk all the way to Canada?' she asked.

'Work with me,' said Charlie. 'It's not much farther. Trust me, it's worth it.'

Soon the deer run began to level out, and Claire realised that they had crested the hill, and to her surprise it did not immediately head downhill again, but instead flattened out. Up ahead she saw bright sunlight and in a moment they reached a clearing large enough for thirty people to stand in. To the west it dropped steeply off and they could see over the trees to all of Eden, dimpled hills and trees and sky. The blue puddle of Mirror Lake amidst the green. All around them was the bright forest and when Charlie stopped, Claire stopped too, and he reached out with his hand in front of her as if to prevent her from walking another step.

'Look,' he said, pointing across the clearing. 'Do you see them?'

Claire stared ahead to the far tree-line and she did not know what she was looking for. She saw the remainder of the clearing and then the shadows of the trees, the play of the light across the deep green leaves.

She said, 'What? What should I be seeing?'

'Focus,' Charlie said. 'Look again.'

She did. Still nothing.

'There,' said Charlie, taking her hand in his own, using it to point. 'On the ground, near the trees, do you see them now?'

Claire suddenly saw them, amazed she had not before, for they were everywhere. She smiled. 'Wow,' she said, 'there are tons of them.'

'This is the time,' Charlie said. 'My father always said it was right after the full moon in May. The window is about a week long, and if you don't get up here, they're gone.'

They moved across the clearing then, and when they got near the woods, Charlie bent down and he plucked one of the mushrooms from the earth, held it up to Claire, and they were perfect chanterelles, yellowish brown stems, large floppy caps. From the pocket of his jeans he removed a folded-up trash bag and opened it. They got down on their knees on to the moist forest floor, and while a soft warm breeze blew through the clearing they picked mushroom after mushroom, working in silence, and the only sound that Claire could hear was the wind through the treetops, the rustling of the bag as they filled it, the gentle plop of each chanterelle as it left the earth for their hands.

★   ★   ★

Claire had never seen the ocean. One night lying in the bedroom of the house on Signal Ridge, moonlight streaming the windows on to the floor, she told Charlie this. They had just made love, and sex made the normally taciturn Charlie talkative, and it was something about him that Claire was growing used to. It was as if the love-making opened some valve within him, and out came words and stories and fears; all the things that he normally kept hidden. This night while she lay in the crook of his arm underneath blankets made warm by their exertions, he told her about the trips they had taken to Maine as kids, how their father never gave them any warning that they were going anywhere; he simply woke them when it was still dark and the next thing they knew they were crossing over the White Mountains and into the Maine woods, heading for the Atlantic.

'My mother hated the beach,' Charlie said. 'She'd usually stay at the motel and read. My father couldn't get enough of it. We were usually there off-season because it was cheaper. And the water was as cold as hell. But Dad didn't care. He'd throw us in there and then he'd come in himself and we'd bodysurf. And you'd be frozen after about ten minutes. But then you got to take that shower back at the motel and it was the best shower you've ever taken. All the sand washing off you. I remember how a shirt felt different after that. Felt different against your skin. Amazing. And in the mornings he'd get us up early and we'd go clamming. With our rakes and buckets. And we always rented a place with a kitchenette because, no, he wasn't going to pay to eat someone else's food. We ate tons of clams. Fried them. As chowder. Stuffed them. With linguini. In a stew with garden tomatoes. You name it.'

'It sounds nice,' said Claire.

'It was. Of course, Owen loved it even more than I did. Some people take to the sea and he was one of them.'

'You don't talk about him much.'

'I know,' said Charlie, his eyes staring up at the ceiling.

'Why is that?'

'It's hard. We were once very close and now we're — '

'You are what?' said Claire.

'We're,' Charlie said, pausing, as if looking for the words. 'We're nothing.'

They lay in silence for a few minutes then, as if digesting what was said, what was not said. Claire knew his brother was something he tried to keep from her. She thought that Charlie imagined that she could not understand their relationship, but she also knew that there were things between people that they kept to themselves, and that was part of it too.

Finally Claire said, 'I've never seen the ocean.'

'What do you mean?' said Charlie.

'Just that. I haven't seen it.'

'Are you kidding?'

'No,' said Claire. 'I mean, I've seen it in movies and stuff, of course. But I've never been there. I grew up in Ohio. We always went on vacations to the Great Lakes, places like that.'

Charlie sat up, pulling Claire up with him, so that now she was between his legs, her back resting on his chest. He said, 'We're going.'

'Going?'

'Yes, to the ocean.'

Claire laughed. 'When, right now?'

'If you want, yes, right now.'

Claire tilted her head back and looked at him. 'You're crazy.'

121

'Okay, tomorrow then.'

'What about the restaurant?'

'We'll close. Gone fishing.'

Claire leaned all the way back, and she kissed him as best she could this way, though the way their faces lined up she got more of his nose than his lips. 'Whatever you say,' she said. 'You're the boss.'

'And don't you forget it,' Charlie said, wrapping his arms around her tight, rolling her over so that she was beneath him, sliding his body over hers, running his hands underneath her, pulling her to him.

★   ★   ★

In the morning they rose and Charlie called the waitresses and he asked Peg to call the reservations and reschedule them for later in the week. Unlike when his father had done the same thing, Peg asked him what was going on, and for the first time, Charlie lied to her. He told her he was going to visit his mother; that she was moving to a new place in the city and needed his help. It was the only plausible story he could come up with, and if Peg was skeptical she did not say so.

She said, 'Tell Charlotte we all miss her.'

'I will,' said Charlie.

'You want me to call Claire and Joe?'

'You can call Joe. I'll tell Claire. I need to talk to her about something else anyway.'

'Okay, Charlie,' said Peg.

An hour later, Charlie picked up Claire at her

apartment where she had gone to pack a bag for the night. By ten o'clock they were driving east out of town on the dirt roads and the day was warm and they rode with the windows down. The sky above was cloudless except for some high cirrus, brushstrokes next to the sun. A light breeze blew through the cab of the truck and it moved Claire's hair off her forehead and from time to time Charlie sneaked a peek at her, at her arms which looked tan in the sun, at her hair blowing back in the wind, and sometimes she caught him looking and she returned his gaze and in her gaze he saw all that he wanted to see and he loved her. In the silence through which they drove, Charlie realised he was absolutely comfortable with her, more comfortable than he had been with anyone in his life except his brother, Owen, and he liked not having to talk. He liked the driving, watching the road disappear under the tires of the truck, the tree-lined path that they had all to themselves; he liked the warmth of the late-spring sun; the sense of journey that lay before him, full of promise and her wonder, the joy in knowing that he was about to give her something, the sight of the ocean, that she had never had before. And perhaps it was that he had never realised he was capable of giving someone from beyond Eden something they had never had before; and perhaps it was that he was crazy in love with her; perhaps it was that his love was no longer unrequited; but driving on those roads, leaving Eden behind, Charlie had never felt more whole in his entire life.

They crossed the Connecticut at noon, the river wide and blue in the sunshine. The land flattened here, and they moved through small towns on the rural highway, towns that looked like stage sets on Western movies, façades of buildings a few blocks long, and then a gas station and then back into the woods again. Soon they entered the National Forest and the foothills rose in front of them like great waves of green, Mount Washington, craggy and gray standing above it all, sending descending curtains of shadows down the hills below it.

The air grew cooler as they climbed in elevation and in front of them were tourists towing trailers and driving slowly on the winding roads but they did not care. The vistas stretched out in all directions at the high parts on the two-lane and they could see broad sweeps of green valley moving away from the mountains toward the north, toward Canada. Here and there they could see white church steeples pointing out of the earth, reminders that not all of this country was forest, that down below there were towns and people whose lives did not differ so much from theirs.

Claire played with her long hair, pushing it behind her ears against the breeze. 'It's nice not to be in a rush,' she said.

'I know it,' Charlie said. 'No deadlines, right?'

'No deadlines,' said Claire, and as she said it she turned and smiled widely at him, reached over and put her hand on his thigh and squeezed.

In time the mountains gave way to low-lying woods, whitewater brooks running along the side of the road, and then they saw the sign welcoming them to the state of Maine, and the roads were instantly bumpy and ill-kempt, and the truck bounced as it took the sharp turns through the birch forest that began right at the roadside. Claire unfastened her seatbelt and moved next to Charlie on the bench seat and he turned and looked at her.

'What are you doing?'

'Be quiet, will you?' Claire said, and she dipped her head then and he felt her fingers on his zipper.

He said, 'You're going to drive us into a tree.'

She looked at him with her big eyes. 'You just drive, okay? Let me handle this.'

And with that, he felt her mouth close around him and he felt her moving up and down him; he felt the coarseness of her tongue and it was warm and gentle and he knew he needed to focus on what was in front of him, on the turns to come, on the road and the other cars, but the sensations spun through him like light through a prism, and he gave in to it as much as he could, knowing that in that moment he was in two different worlds, each of them containing their own dangers.

They drove through old mill towns and by dammed, fat rivers and the air was rancid with the stink of rotting pulp. They drove on narrow roads past convenience stores where men loitered in the parking lots smoking cigarettes and wearing their despair like clothes. They drove past small highway diners with the spaces in front of them crammed with cars. They drove past small lakes packed with sickly-looking camps, paddle-boats cutting across their still surfaces. Mid-afternoon, they stopped at a roadside stand and they ate lobster rolls sitting on the hood of the truck. The lobster was fine and sweet and covered with mayonnaise and in a buttered hotdog roll and it was just what they wanted.

Then they were back in the car and it occurred to Claire that the road itself was no different from a river, moving down from the mountains and through the woods and eventually, to the sea. There was an inexorableness to it, as if it knew where they were going better than they did themselves. At one point, when they were past Augusta and its confluence of rivers, she tried to express this to Charlie.

She said, 'I can sense it.'

'Sense what?'

'The ocean.'

He laughed. 'Okay,' he said and his tone was sarcastic when he said it and he immediately felt bad for it.

Claire reached out and lightly pushed him. 'I'm serious,' she said. 'Does it ever strike you that the road is a river? That it moves toward the sea, only instead of emptying water there, it leaves us?'

Charlie looked at her with his pale blue eyes and he was going to make fun but he saw in her look that she was not messing around and so he smiled at her. 'I like that,' he said. 'Roads like rivers. I see it.'

★   ★   ★

They left the forests behind as they approached the coast. The character of the land and the towns changed as well, the gritty hard-scrabble life of western Maine giving way to small, gentrified postcard New England towns, towns built around churches and village greens. Towns with gourmet food shops and upscale restaurants.

'We're almost there,' Charlie said.

'Where is there?'

'Camden,' he said. 'It was always my father's favorite town.'

They came into Camden from the west, and Charlie chose this way because he did not want her to see the water until he was ready for her to, and soon they had reached Main Street and they drove past the stately old white homes and the large churches and Claire said, 'Where's the ocean?'

'Can you smell it?'

The air was redolent with salt and brine. 'Yes,' she said, smiling. 'I can.'

'Right here,' Charlie said, and he turned the

truck into the harbor park and it appeared between the façades of buildings, the small harbor, full of white-sailed boats, a few small fishing trawlers. Beyond they could see the islands and then the blue-green Atlantic, the horizon interrupted by large freighters like cities against the sky.

They parked the truck and climbed out. Claire was out first and she ran right to the seawall, stood on it and looked out at the boats bobbing on the soft chop, and the breeze was cool and smelled of salt and fish and the sun was warm on her arms.

'God, it's beautiful,' said Claire.

'I know it.'

'Let's walk out.'

They followed the narrow seawall out the right side of the harbor and men on boats looked up from where they were working at the two of them moving like children along the top of the seawall. They passed the busy yacht club, a hotel where people sat on a veranda and looked out to the water, and when they reached the place where the few private homes started, they sat down and dangled their legs over the water. Soft waves slapped against the concrete below them. It was late afternoon and they watched the boat traffic moving into the harbor, sailboats mostly. They waved to the men and women on the boats. They leaned into one another. A few puffy clouds moved overhead in an otherwise crystal-clear blue ocean sky. Seagulls swept down over the harbor, their stark cries somehow, for Claire, completing the tableau, all of it feeling like a gift made especially for her, put together by a man whose strength she had always known about, but whose generosity was starting to surprise her.

9

They rented a room at an old Victorian inn on High Street and the room took up the whole top floor of the house. Their four poster bed was directly under the interior cone of a turret and it had small windows at its top and the afternoon light made waves across its walls when they lay down and made love. After, Claire took a bath in the jacuzzi tub and Charlie stood and looked out a picture window at the harbor and beyond it to the ocean. The day was getting on and the sun had fallen lower in the sky. He watched the boat traffic move around the small islands and then in through the mouth of the harbor. Small fishing vessels dotted the ocean out past the islands. Against the horizon, as far as he could see, were the thick grayish masses that were freighters, commercial vessels. Seeing them, Charlie thought of his brother.

It had been six years now since he had seen Owen. The postcards still came with regularity, but there was something remarkably impersonal about a postcard. For one, everyone could read them and so they never said anything important. Second, there was no way for Charlie to respond — it was as if his brother, from whatever corner of the globe he was in, was holding his hand out, palm toward Charlie, and saying, you have your life, let me have mine. This card is simply my way of showing you I am still here. And that you can't find me.

Charlie knew that his own life had gone on as it should, with the exception of Claire. Not much had changed and he knew that Owen, who now lived on ships, would see it that way. But what would he think of Claire? Of the small changes in the restaurant? What would he make of the fifty-year flood that had almost taken everything away? Where was he? Was he out on the blue-green Atlantic, standing on the deck of some massive boat against the horizon, looking toward the room in which Charlie stood?

Standing in the window of the old inn, listening to Claire moving around in bathwater behind the thick wooden door, looking out at the great freighters at the edge of the world, Charlie suddenly longed for his brother. He longed to tell him what he knew, what he had learned. He longed to share his life with him again, to have someone who understood him in a way that no one ever could, not even Claire; someone to hear him out, to help him make sense of it all, in the way that only brothers are capable of doing.

★   ★   ★

After Claire had bathed and dressed, they left the inn and walked back toward the harbor. Other couples were on the streets, some of them clearly tourists as they themselves were. Claire and Charlie held hands as they walked. The sun was starting to fall behind the Camden Hills to the west, and the sea breeze was cool and Claire moved into Charlie, letting go of his hand and moving into him, hooking her arm into his, and she liked the way she imagined they looked to others, wearing the badge of new lovers for all to see, none of the secrecy they had taken on back at Charlotte's.

They ate at a small café that overlooked the harbor and the hostess seemed surprised that they wanted to eat on the deck since it was definitely growing cooler out.

'We're Vermonters,' Charlie said by way of explanation. 'We'll be fine.'

They drank a bottle of chardonnay and they watched the sailboats, and they watched the sunset, reds and purples over the hills spreading toward the ocean, the water in the harbor darkening as the sun set and as the night sky emerged, the outline of the pale moon rising over the town. They ate seared halibut fillets and the fish was fresh but cooked too long for their liking, and they both understood why it was cooked long as it was a tourist place and the chef would rather not have people send food back because it was 'undercooked'. They talked about how they should have recognised this and requested it medium rare, but they decided that nothing was going to spoil their night, not overcooked fish anyway, when they had cool wine and the cooling night and a fresh breeze that blew off the ocean and rustled their hair pleasantly.

Soon the lights on the sailboats came on as the darkness grew, illuminated masts rising out of the water, like Christmas trees in May. The wine was going to their heads. Everything suddenly effervescent and good. Claire, looking out over the water from the deck, at the boats and the harbor and the town beyond it, let her eyes linger on all of it before turning them back to Charlie. She ran her foot up his leg and he smiled at her. She smiled back, her joy in that instant not capable of restraint and he looked back at her as if he understood this, as if it was their secret, as if the truth of what was out there belonged only to them.

★ ★ ★

Back at the inn, they made love on the floor of their room and it was a thick carpet and in the morning they would both have rug burns on their knees but they did not care. After, they showered together and they were drunk and they knew it but they did not care about this either. Charlie stood behind Claire while the water ran over them and he wrapped his arms around her and under her breasts and the water spilled off both of them and then fell to the porcelain tub-bottom at their feet.

They climbed under the sheets and their hair was still wet and they were naked and cold and they rolled into each other for warmth. Charlie went to sleep first, and when he did he fell away from Claire, and though the alcohol had gone to her head she was curiously full of energy and could not sleep. She lay and listened to the comfort of his snores, loud and steady, falling the way they did when he had drunk too much, all of it coming up and through his nose. Then she rose and stood and walked to the window. In the glass she could make out her reflection, the heaviness of her breasts, her hair, though the reflection was partial enough that she could not see her face, not completely, and the effect when she looked suggested a lack of features, as if she were breasts and hair and arms but, ultimately, faceless. No eyes. No nose. No mouth. Or wrinkles. Characterless. A blank slate.

She looked through herself until she could make out the lighthouse at the point, its beam moving rhythmically across the small sound. She watched it bounce across the darkness, as predictable as a metronome. She watched it until she could not watch any more. Until she felt her eyes grow heavy. Then she climbed back under the now-warm sheets, slid her body next to Charlie's, and dreamt of ocean waves slapping against the large stones of a jetty.

★　★　★

In the morning they showered together and checked out of the inn and ate breakfast in town. Then they drove back to Eden and got there in time to open for that evening. For another month they kept their relationship secret, or at least thought they were keeping it secret, though it grew harder since the trip to Maine had drawn them closer together. They were inseparable now, Claire only making it back to her apartment every few days to pick up some things, and more and more she found herself simply leaving her stuff at the house on Signal Ridge. For both of them it was a lovely time, for they had the work in the restaurant and they had each other and they had the warm summer nights when in the lightless dark they explored each other's bodies, staying up way too late and making love, neither of them wanting to sleep for sleep signaled the death of another day, and when you are young and in love you want the days themselves to linger as long as possible, and there are moments when you are naïve enough to believe that if you want it, it will come true.

Inside the kitchen of Charlotte's they might not have fooled anyone about the truth of their relationship, but if anyone noticed how it affected what they did when they were working they did not point it out. And it was as if their lovemaking at the house on Signal Ridge somehow found its way into the cooking taking place in front of the stove overlooking the floodplain and the river. They fed off one another; they relaxed into each other's creativity; they pushed each other in new ways, experimenting with new ideas, some that worked, others that did not, all of them, though, helping to elevate Charlotte's to new levels of excellence it had never seen before. Charlie was motivated as he had not been since his father died. He wanted, through all his actions, to fill Claire with wonder, to show her what he could do. In doing so, he willingly stepped outside his comfort zone, beyond the recipes that his father had passed on, beyond those he had tested in his home kitchen, those that the regulars had come to rely on to define what it meant to eat at Charlotte's. He took risks. Like the Vietnamese carpaccio, local beef that he half froze and then sliced paper thin, marinated in lime juice, chilies and fish sauce and served raw. It was pungent and he liked it, but he knew that it was different from what people had come to expect from this restaurant. He did not care. All that mattered to him was Claire, what she thought, how she liberated him to do what he wanted. For the first time in his life he felt unshackled from the past, as if the ghost of his father, of his life before he met her, was receding into the shadows and no one could recall it but himself.

He wanted to show her everything. He wanted her to know all that he knew, and he thought that in the knowing she would take on more of him, and he of her, and the divisions between them would grow increasingly blurry. Charlie figured this was the natural evolution of things and it was his job to encourage it.

Once he took her to a place he had not been since he was a child, a place his father had taken him and Owen to show them what he considered the most magical thing in all of Eden. It was something they did for a number of years in a row when they were just boys and he did not know why they stopped going. Perhaps, he thought, it was because they outgrew it; though he knew when he took Claire there that it could not have been true. For when, he asked himself afterward, do we become too old for beauty? When do we lose the ability to see things with the eyes of a child? To see them as if for the first time?

It was the end of May, and a Friday, and though it was expected to be a busy night at the restaurant, Charlie said the prep could wait. They drove in the morning under azure skies through Eden, past Main Street, into the old village, and then up the sloping hill to where the glacial footprint of Mirror Lake sat between steep forest walls of spruce.

At the southern end of Mirror Lake, across from the old Fiske house, was a small stream that was unknown to those outside of Eden, a stream that ran through a cove and then out of the tooth-shaped lake and that was, in fact, the headwaters of the Dog River. They parked on the side of the road and they walked to the lake's edge. In the windless morning the lake was as still as glass. Charlie did not tell Claire where he was taking her, and she did not mind, for he had also not told her anything when he showed her where to forage for the chanterelles on the forest floor; and as a result she trusted him to lead her to something she could not discover on her own; something she would want to see.

They walked in silence. They followed the shore of the lake to the small peninsula that jutted out and was filled with scrub trees. The cold of the night was burning off and the day was suddenly warm as they went. At the mouth of the stream Charlie said, 'This way,' and they entered the woods to their right, moving gingerly along the banks of the small stream.

Though the stream was narrow, it was deep

and the water was muddy and filled with silt and they could not see the bottom. Near its first bend, they flushed a wild turkey from some heavy brush and it was visible for a moment, waddling in front of them, before it disappeared into the darkness of the deep green forest.

'That would have been some good eating,' Charlie said.

'Not the season, is it?'

'No, not until fall.'

The land began to climb here, a gradual sloping upward, and they walked again in silence. As they went up the hill, the trees grew closer together and the going was slower. The undergrowth was heavy and for a time they had to move away from the stream, for the banks of it were impassable. Soon though the growth gave way to a hard forest floor and they made better time. They caught up to the stream again, and it was on their right now, below them, a drop of about four feet to the dark water.

'Almost there,' said Charlie.

The stream in front of them meandered to the right through a grove of trees. They bee-lined to where it bent back, and when they reached it Charlie said, 'Look.'

Claire looked up. In front of her was a waterfall, falling perhaps seven feet into a deep pool. Above it, thin birches grew and their bark looked silvery in the sunlight filtering through the canopy above. The tumbling water frothed and foamed as it fell.

'It's beautiful,' said Claire.

Charlie smiled. 'You haven't seen the half of it. Come on.'

He took her hand then, and they jogged toward the pool, stepping over thick roots and small bushes on the ground below. When they reached the edge of the pool, Claire saw that it was lined with granite, and they stood only a few feet from the waterfall and when the cold spray reached them it dampened their shirts.

'I love it,' Claire said.

'Look,' said Charlie, pointing toward the water.

Claire looked and she saw the water churning and not just from the sharp current where the waterfall met the pool. Underneath the surface she could see them, large shadowy shapes.

'What are they?'

'Steelhead,' said Charlie. 'Rainbows. Or they will be. Later. Now, watch.'

Claire watched as first one and then another long, slender fish, slightly speckled, left the water in front of her eyes, giant graceful leaps toward the heart of the churning water above, their bodies flying straight like tiny planes. One after another they hit the out-cropping of rock where the water began its plunge, and one after another they fell back into the pool.

'They're not making it,' Claire cried.

'Don't worry,' Charlie said. 'They will.'

And as he said it, one large fish propelled itself out of the water, landed where the others had, only this time she saw its silver tail kick and it sat almost still for a instant, the water running over its sleek body, and then it was almost as if it were pulled forward, inexorably, as if chasing something beyond their comprehension, disappearing upstream as fast as smoke.

They stayed there for an hour and they did not talk. They sat on a mossy log and they listened to the sound of the falls and they watched the steelhead on their annual migration. They watched their flight through the air, the success of some, the failure of others, the persistence of all. Sunlight fought through the trees and made undulating waves of shadow on the water in front of them.

★ ★ ★

About a week later, Charlie rolled over one morning in bed to find Claire gone. Out the window he could see that the sun was already high in the sky. He had slept longer than he normally did. He shook the grogginess of sleep from his head and half sat up in the bed. It was then that he saw her through the open door of the bathroom. She had just showered, and she wore a towel around her waist like a man would, and her breasts were naked to him, and from the profile she presented to him he could see their slight upward curve, and her belly below, and he saw where the towel ended and her thigh tapered to her knee; and he could see how she looked at herself in the mirror as she combed the tangles out of her long hair, tilting her head first to the right and then to the left, running the brush through it. She was still wet from the shower and the bare skin of her shoulders glistened with

140

water. She had no idea he was watching her. Charlie thought: I could watch her for ever. Just like this. And as he thought it, she turned and saw him watching her, and she smiled at him, as if she could see the arc of his thoughts.

'Hey, sleepy,' she said.

Charlie climbed out of bed and she giggled as she watched him walk toward her, and he realised he was half-hard but he did not care. He entered the bathroom and Claire saw the way he was looking at her, his face full of intent, and she said, 'What?'

Charlie fell to his knees in front of her, and with this supplication he ran his hands up over her towel, up toward her breasts, and he looked up at her. He turned his head to the side for a moment and hugged her legs, the way a child would, and then he turned back and looked up at her.

'Marry me, Claire,' he said. 'Marry me.'

Claire laughed. She shook her hair and water spilled off it and landed on him. 'You're crazy.'

'I'm serious,' he said. 'Look at me.'

And as he said it, the corners of his icy blue eyes grew wet and she knew he was serious, that he was dead serious.

'Do you know what you're doing, Charlie Bender?'

'I want you to be my wife, Claire Apple.'

Claire shook her head again. Charlie saw her gulp hard. 'I don't believe this, it's been like six weeks.'

'I don't care, when you know, you know. And I know this. I don't ever want to spend a moment away from you if I can help it. Ah, shit. I'm no good at this, Claire, help me out. I don't know what to say. I'm dying here.'

'Okay,' she said.

'Okay?'

'Yes,' she said. 'Yes, Charlie. I will marry you.'

'Say it again.'

'I will marry you.'

'Shout it,' said Charlie.

'I will marry you,' Claire shouted, and now the tears ran freely over her high cheekbones, and Charlie rose to his feet and he picked her up in his arms and he leaned back and held her, and then he put her down and she kissed him hard on the mouth, and he kissed her back, and then he held her and he realised that she was shaking, and he wrapped his arms around her as much as he could, doing everything possible to keep her warm.

10

Some mornings that summer, she woke after the heat had already risen, and lying naked next to Charlie she could feel his warm skin next to hers and her thoughts, looking out the window to the fields and the trees and the green hills of Eden, almost always turned to the creeping shadow of doubt that the sobriety of this time of day gave her. There was something about the morning, with the long day in front of her, that made her anxious, allowed her to doubt what they intended to do, allowed her to doubt the coming marriage. She knew that these were ephemeral thoughts; that by the afternoon they would have all but disappeared and that by the evening she would find herself wondering how she had thought them at all. But they came to her, and the fact that they did alarmed her, and she told herself as she felt him against her that she needed to address them. If only for herself.

It was not that she didn't love Charlie, for she thought she did; and it was not that she did not want to marry him, for she thought this was true as well; it was more a feeling she could not place, a creeping dread, something that she suspected was particular to her, an insecurity perhaps, a flaw, but not something that could actually be true to them. She told herself that if she willed it away it would go. But still it persisted.

While he snored next to her, she thought of all

the reasons she loved this man. There were his eyes for one. Icy blue and translucent, she loved how they fixed on her, inscrutable and yet all-knowing at the same time. There was his height, his strength, the way he carried himself. He walked with humility and confidence at the same time: it was almost like he knew himself, knew what he was good at, but he was also wise enough to know that he should be without arrogance. And there was his cooking, his quiet grace in the kitchen, the best she had ever seen, born to it, with instinct and talent, creativity and a sharp understanding of all that had gone before him. He knew what should be done and then he executed it and he never questioned himself. He did not look back.

Most of all there was how he related to her; how he looked at her; how he seemed incapable of suppressing his desire for her. He made her feel wanted and sometimes she thought that that was all any woman wanted and when she found it she had an obligation to hang on to it.

Still, her own behavior mystified her. After he proposed to her in the bathroom that morning, Claire felt something come over her like a rush of heat, something ineluctable, and she could not describe it but it made her want to crawl under the comforter on the big bed and stay there and sleep. Charlie, by contrast, was ebullient, picking her up and whirling her around the room, and he wanted to immediately tell everyone that they were engaged. And he did not want to wait to get married, initially even talking about doing it right away, showing up at the town hall on

Monday with Joe Collins and Peg as witnesses, getting it done. But she succeeded, at least, in convincing him to hold off until the fall, until they could plan something, until her parents could make it out from Ohio. She had not even told them yet about Charlie, beyond telling them that he owned the restaurant that she worked in and that he was good to her.

She sat in bed on the morning he had proposed and she pulled her knees up to her chest and she listened to him on the phone, talking to his mother, a woman she had never met, and she wanted to be touched by the words he used as he told her how happy he was, how much he was in love, how beautiful and smart and talented Claire — his fiancée, a new word, as foreign as Greek to her ears — was. And when he was done, he wanted to know if she wanted to call her parents, and when she said she needed to wait, he looked puzzled, and she could not stop herself. She started to cry.

'What is it?' he said.

'It's nothing.'

Charlie sat down on the bed next to her. 'You're crying.'

'It's nothing. It's me.'

'Okay,' he said.

'I'll be okay,' she said. 'I will.' She managed a thin smile. 'I'm just a little scared, that's all.'

Charlie pushed her hair away from her face, and then he stood up, and he left, and when he returned he did not speak, though he handed her a cup of herbal tea, and she loved him for this, for he seemed to know when to leave her alone, and when to be present; and he seemed to know what it was that she needed without her having to say anything. And though she had only been with one man before in her life, she knew enough about men to know that his ability to read her was exceptional, and that she should be more grateful for it.

★　★　★

Summer in Eden is both glorious and short. The days themselves are long and languid, sometimes tropically hot, other times as cool as fall, so that at night when you sit on the porch you need a sweater. The muted golden green of spring gives way to lush rainforest-like growth everywhere. The rivers run fat and lazy. The sunsets over the mountains are brilliant on clear days, bright pink turning to red and then to purple as the moon rises through the color and the stars appear suddenly, millions of them, their light growing with each passing hour.

There are hazy days when the temperature soars into the high nineties and the humidity is oppressive, but you cannot complain, for in the quiet deep freeze of January, this is what you dream of. There are also days when the thunderheads move across the foothills and you'll hear the thunderclap and an instant later the rain falls torrentially, the black horizon fills with white flashes of lightning, and then just as quickly it passes, and the hot late afternoon sun emerges and burns the moisture off the leaves, off the dirt roads.

In the kitchen of Charlotte's, the heat was often unbearable. Some nights it would be in the eighties outside, but over a hundred in front of the stove and the grill, the water that always seemed to be boiling on the range filling the air with moisture it did not need. At the end of a busy night, Charlie and Claire would be soaked with sweat, and on some of these evenings, after everyone else had left, they went out back and in the dark they crossed the floodplain to the Dog River where, lit only by the moon, they would strip off their clothes and wade into the cool mountain water, sitting down on smooth rocks beneath the surface, the water deep enough so that every part of them except their heads was submerged, the soft current swirling around them, the black woods all around them, another day gone.

★　★　★

They were married in September of that year. Claire's parents had flown out for a weekend in August, and on a Sunday night when a soft summer rain fell, Charlie cooked them dinner in the farmhouse on Signal Ridge. He did not go out of his way to impress them, grilling veal chops over wood on the open grill on the porch, serving them with a sage jus and a salad of baby arugula, corn on the cob that he cut in half and rolled in truffle butter. He decided to be himself and it seemed to work, for Claire was nervous about it, and said so; there had been some tough conversations with her mother where Claire

147

thought that her mother felt that she was throwing her life away. Charlie remembered, in particular, something Claire had told him her mother had said after she told her parents that they were engaged.

She had said, 'Jesus, Claire, don't confuse sex with love.'

Though in truth they were nothing but charming to Charlie. They were nice people, not unlike the tourists who occasionally found their way to Charlotte's, people with a degree of money who found the restaurant picturesque and perfect for a vacation, but nothing they could ever imagine for themselves, not full-time anyway.

Still, he liked them, for he could not help it. They were Claire's parents and in each of them he saw her. Her mother had her dark eyes, her tumble of black hair. She was in her fifties and Charlie thought she was a beautiful woman, even if she seemed wary of him. Her father had the firm handshake and demeanor of the corporate executive he was, but he also had a soft smile, lines coming off his mouth at the corners, as they did on Claire when she laughed.

After her parents left, they were in the kitchen, cleaning up, when Claire suddenly leaned up and kissed him.

'I love you, Charlie Bender,' she said.

'I love you too,' he said.

Her face was aglow. 'I mean it, thank you.'

'What for? I didn't do anything.'

'For being you,' she said. 'For being nice to my parents.'

'Of course I was nice to your parents,' he said with a shrug.

'No of course about it,' said Claire. 'You were great. I mean that.'

'So the wedding is on?' he asked jokingly.

'Yes,' she said, leaning up and kissing him again, resting her hand on his broad chest. 'The wedding is on.'

★　★　★

A week before the wedding and still no word from Owen. Charlotte was coming from New York along with some of her friends from way back, Sam Marsh and the others who were there at the birth of the restaurant. Charlotte had not heard from Owen either, except for the postcards which came faithfully to her door too. She did not know what to tell Charlie and he did not expect her to tell him anything. But he was getting married and he wanted his brother to be there. One day in a life, he thought. That is all I ask.

He called the union offices for the Merchant Marines in Boston and in New York. In Boston no one knew the name, and while in New York the second guy he talked to did know Owen, he had not seen him for months.

'Last time I saw him he was waiting for a ship,' the man said.

'Waiting for a ship?'

'Yeah. I'm guessing he got it because I haven't seen him.'

And so Charlie gave up hope that his brother

would make it and got down to the business of making this wedding go.

Claire and Charlie decided, after much deliberation, to cater the event themselves. It was going to be a small wedding, around forty people, and they knew that they were the only ones in the area who could do precisely what they wanted.

Two days before the ceremony, they made their wedding cake. They worked all day and deep into the night, baking round after round of cake, renting a massive mixer for the different frostings, using more than a hundred eggs in the process. It was warm in the kitchen and by the time they had assembled the large tiered cake, constructing it with wooden dowels that held it all together, it was after midnight, and they were focused but drunk on sherry, covered with flour, and more than a little sweaty from the exertion of the work.

When they finished they stood back and looked at it, two and a half feet high, a thing of beauty, Charlie said, and they collapsed into each other with exhaustion.

They swam in the river that night, and then slept on the floor of the restaurant as they had during the flood, and when they moved together they did so wearily, still wet from the cool water, and afterward they dozed off in a half-hug, before Charlie fell away, on to his back, Claire slinging her arm across his chest.

The morning of the wedding they cooked a dinner they could serve at room temperature. They poached whole sockeye salmon in white wine and fresh herbs. They roasted a beef tenderloin and let it rest before slicing it thinly. They made a horseradish sauce to go with it. They made a large salad of fresh tomatoes, basil and goat cheese. They blanched green beans and tossed them with olive oil, tarragon, shallots and lemon juice. They made nori rolls filled with smoked tuna to pass before dinner.

When they finished cooking, Charlie kissed Claire goodbye, and stayed at the restaurant until Joe Collins arrived with a borrowed van to take all the food, and most delicately, the cake, up to the house on Signal Ridge. After Joe had gone, Charlie walked outside and he stopped for a moment before getting into his truck to drive to the house and change into his suit, prepare to get married. It was beautiful out, just what he wanted. A deep blue sky, lazy, fat clouds moving past the mountains. The forest was still all green; the first leaves had not started to change. He looked down the valley, toward Hunger Mountain. A red-tailed hawk made wide circles above the spruce trees. A light comfortable breeze rustled his shirt. He breathed in deep, closed his eyes and looked toward the sun, orange and yellow streaks on the back of his eyelids.

★　★　★

Charlie wore a crisp white shirt with a vest over it, no tie, black pants. He stood under the arbor next to the Reverend Smith. Reverend Smith, now eighty, and mostly blind, wore a baby blue jacket, a thin black tie, coke-bottle glasses more out of custom than for utility. He jokingly called himself the marrying man, for since he had retired after thirty years at the Methodist church in Eden village, he had done nothing but marry the youth of Eden and drink the brandy he made from his blueberry patch. He rocked slowly back and forth, clutching a worn and aged bible in his hands. In front of him, Charlie surveyed the guests, all seated in white rental chairs. In the front row was his mother, on her right old Sam Marsh, his father's best friend, who Charlie had not seen since he was a child, a shock of white hair falling over his forehead. To the left of her the seat was empty, as if deliberately, as if Owen might show up at the last minute and fill it.

Charlotte sat there and emanated strength; for Charlie knew this was difficult for her, being back in Eden, being back in the house she had shared with her husband, and he also knew that she would never admit to it. To his right, and a little behind him, a woman from town that Claire had found softly played classical guitar.

They were in a field behind the house, what had once been an apple orchard under previous owners, and a few of the gnarly small trees were still present, though they had long ago stopped yielding fruit. Below them was the house, and beyond it he could see the woods where he'd grown up hunting and where his father had ended his life. Beyond this, he could see other hills and then the mountains in the distance, blue peaks against a bluer sky.

Charlie held his hands behind his back and he looked at the house below him, and he watched

152

the cow-path that ran along its side and he thought: any moment now. Any moment now she will round that bend and this will become real. And no sooner had he thought it than he saw the dark brown of the horse, and then it emerged into the opening, and he saw her and her father on a wagon behind it. A murmur went up through the crowd and all eyes turned toward where his already rested. The old wagon they were in made its way up the path toward the ceremony, and from where he stood Charlie could see it swaying slightly as it negotiated the rutted old road. Soon they were close enough for him to see Claire, and she wore her mother's wedding dress, which she had told him she would do, though he had not seen it. Her thick curly hair was piled high on her head and she was wearing makeup, though she had never done so in front of him before, and when they reached the edge of where everyone sat, and her father pulled on the reins and brought the big chestnut horse to a stop, Charlie got his first good look at her and he felt something give within himself. I would die for her, he thought. If I had to, I would die for her.

Claire's father stepped out of the wide bench seat of the antique wagon and walked around it and held his hand out for his daughter. Claire took his hand and smiled wanly out toward the guests and she stepped down. Together they began to walk, toward the back rows, and in that instant everyone stood from where they sat and watched her as she went and the guitar player played with greater intensity now and Charlie took his eyes off his future wife for a moment to make sure that Reverend Smith knew what was happening.

At that moment, the Reverend's eyes opened behind his thick glasses and his head swiveled toward where Claire was now moving behind the last row of chairs, arms locked with her father, preparing to make her way down what passed for an aisle.

As they entered the aisle, Charlie turned and faced the audience, faced Claire, and for a moment they locked eyes and she seemed to smile at him, though he knew she was all nerves now; he could see it in her face, and he thought that he should be too, though he was curiously calm, everything slowing down for him with each step she took closer to where he stood.

Claire and her father marched slowly, conscious of the ritual, and the guitar played plaintively, and to Charlie it seemed to take for ever. Soon they made it, reached to where he stood, and Claire's father leaned down and gave her a kiss on the cheek, before letting go. Before he went to his seat, he stopped and shook Charlie's hand, and his smile as he did so was wide and warm and Charlie smiled back at him, thankful to him for all that smile imparted.

The Reverend began to speak. Slow, incantatory words, and in truth later neither Charlie nor Claire would remember anything he had said. He spoke of love and he spoke of marriage and he spoke of family and he spoke of the land. He closed his eyes when he spoke, and he rocked back on his heels and he raised his arms to the

154

sky and the words were good words but Charlie and Claire were both fixated on each other, on each other's eyes, his as light as ice, hers as black as the river in the dark. When he said to repeat after me, they did; when he said to exchange rings, they did, Charlie taking both of them out of the breast pocket of his shirt, handing his to Claire to put on his finger, while he slid the simple gold band on to hers. And when he said you can now kiss the bride, Charlie said, not fully realising until the moment had passed that it was out loud, 'It's about time.'

Behind him he heard the laughter, and some clapping, and he went to his bride and he took her into his arms, leaned her back away from him, and under the arbor he kissed her, harder than he probably should have, and when he pulled her back up, they turned and faced the crowd, bright faces with the woods behind them, the sound of guitar again, of the Reverend, of clapping, all of it rising quickly before fading into the mist of the moment.

★   ★   ★

In front of the house there was a large tent and under it were tables, and before dinner the guests huddled in groups and talked and drank champagne out of tall, stemless flutes. Peg and Althea, though they were guests, took the time to pass the nori rolls, refresh people's drinks. Joe Collins laid out the food on a buffet table, and a three-piece fiddle band set up a mock stage behind the wooden dance floor. The afternoon

155

was warm and many of the men took off their jackets.

Claire and Charlie walked from group to group, her arm locked in his, and they accepted the congratulations of all. Charlotte gave Claire a big hug, and when she looked up at Charlie her face showed the pride and happiness she had for him.

There was no best man, so before they ate, Charlie rose from his seat to speak. He raised his glass of champagne and everyone else did as well. He was not normally given to eloquence but today he found it within himself. He thanked everyone for coming. He talked about what it meant to him. He told them that he had found in Claire what he had always been looking for. Someone to share his life with, his vision, his love of food and this town with its lakes, streams and forests.

'Today,' he said, 'we are bride and groom, words unique because they are only used for one day. There are no other words that I can think of that are like that. And I think we use them because for one day we are perfect. We are just what we should be. Our love is perfect. And like all people, Claire and I are imperfect. Oh, we strive for perfection. We strive to be a good husband, a good wife, a good couple. Good neighbors. Good friends. And good cooks.'

'You got that one down,' someone shouted and everyone laughed.

Charlie smiled. 'There are two people missing today, and I hope that somewhere they know what is happening on this hillside. One of course is my father who I know we all miss tremendously. And the other is my brother, Owen, who will always be welcome in my life, wherever he is. I ask that you raise your glasses to Claire and me, but I also ask that you raise them to Owen, too. And while you're at it, spill a little on the ground for my father.'

'Hear, hear,' someone shouted, and everyone drank long and fast from the champagne, leaving a little in the glass which they dumped on to the grassy lawn at their feet.

'Let's eat,' said Charlie.

They lined up and brought their food back to the tables and they ate. The food was just what they needed for this weather, the tender beef, the rich poached salmon. They drank wine and after, they danced. Charlie and Claire took the first turn, and then Charlie danced with his mother while Claire danced with her father. The fiddle band picked it up, playing hard and fast and many of the guests took to the floor, bodies moving in the late afternoon sunlight.

Soon the afternoon bled into evening, and the guests gathered outside the tent to watch the September sunset. It fell behind the hills, and after it was gone a tapestry of red stayed in the sky, before fading to dark. Some people left but most stayed and the wine flowed. At nine o'clock, Joe Collins brought the horse and wagon around, and this time it was Charlie who would ride with Claire on it. The band stopped and the guests gathered to see them off. Claire threw her bouquet now, and it disappeared into the darkness for a moment before coming down into the waiting hands of Charlotte herself.

'Claire,' Charlotte shouted. 'What am I supposed to do with this?'

Claire smiled and shrugged, and Charlie gave a big wave and pulled on the reins, and the horse began its slow clop away from the tent. Above, in the sky, it had started on the far western horizon, moving toward Signal Ridge. At first it looked like bright starlight, but as it grew, there were different colors, greens and reds and shades of gold against the black firmament. Soon it covered the whole sky, the first time the Northern Lights had been visible in Eden for almost ten years. They were like great arms, pulsing with color, and now that Charlie and Claire had ridden away for a night at the inn, the guests who were left lay down on the dewy grass and stared up at the sky, watching the celestial event, wondering whether it was a blessing on this union today, or a harbinger of something different, something beyond their shared comprehension.

BOOK II

11

He came down the dirt road, his longish hair tucked under a baseball cap, a duffel bag, the kind that hockey players use, on his back. His boots sent little cyclones of dirt into the air with each step he took. He wore jeans and a leather jacket over a T-shirt. It was early October. Indian summer weather and the day was warm, too warm for his jacket but he did not stop to take it off. Peak foliage had passed, though the bright red of the maple leaves still leaned over the road and danced across it when the wind blew. Without the bag he would have fitted in, another hunter casing a road where he might look to get his deer. With the bag, his look tipped over to that of a vagabond, and you would not have stopped to pick him up had he had his thumb out. At one point he took a break from his walking at a bend in the Dog River and he sat down on a large granite rock that looked as if it were left here for this purpose and he lighted a cigarette.

He looked into the woods and he smoked. Buying the cigarettes had been a test. Stopping at the general store in town, he was not surprised to see Mrs Morse still working the counter. She filled his request for the Camel Straights and looked right through him, as if he had not come in here nearly every day when he was a boy, as if he had not bought penny candy here, not picked up milk and cream and bread for home.

Below him the river ran low, water swirling around the smooth stones that made up the bed. Beyond the river the dappled light in the forest cast strange shadows, a fallen-down beech tree, caught in the branches of an evergreen, for a moment looked like the roof of a small cabin before he was able to make out what it was. He stubbed his cigarette out on the ground and stood and began to walk again.

The dirt beneath his feet was the color of sand. The land felt solid to him and he walked with the slightly bow-legged gait of a man accustomed to life at sea. Seventeen years had passed as fast as a rainstorm and he was coming home.

★　★　★

Claire Apple was in the dining room at Charlotte's, replacing the flowers in the vases on the tables, when she suddenly realised she could no longer hear the steady bouncing of the tennis ball that her seven-year-old son Jonah had been throwing relentlessly against the side of the building. She stopped and listened for him. Nothing. Maybe he'd run around back, she thought.

Claire went to the front door of the restaurant and opened it. She looked out and she did not see her son. Then, stepping on to the granite block that led to the walkway, she saw him in the small parking lot and a man she had never seen before was down on one knee talking to Jonah.

Panic rose inside her. Charlie was out at one of the farms and would not be back for an hour at least and she did not like the look of this man. His hair was long and his face weathered and he had a bag next to him that suggested transience to her.

'Can I help you?' Claire shouted, moving quickly toward the two of them. Jonah turned and looked at her.

'Mommy,' he said, his voice calm, not displaying any distress.

The man rose up. He was tall and he looked at her. A broad smile came across his weathered face. She saw now that he was handsome, remarkably so, with bright green eyes and high cheekbones, a firm jaw, a straight nose.

He said, 'I heard you were looking for a chef.'

'No,' Claire said. 'I'm sorry, are you sure it was Charlotte's?'

Jonah came to her, her little curly-haired boy, and stood half behind her legs. Good, she thought, this is where you should be. She unconsciously ruffled his hair.

'Yes,' the man said, 'I'm pretty sure it was Charlotte's.' He looked away now, as if pondering this. 'That's what I was told.'

Claire shook her head. 'Again, I'm sorry. But we're not hiring.'

'The place looks good.'

'Thank you,' said Claire and she turned to go.

'Ma'am,' the man said. 'Just one more question, if you don't mind.'

Claire stopped. 'Sure.'

'Is my brother around?'

163

She brought him into the dining room. She had the curious feeling of displacement, the way one feels when suddenly the home they have always known is no longer theirs. She did not know whether to offer him something, or if she should wait for him to offer something to her. Outside she could hear Jonah once again playing his game with the tennis ball, the steady smack smack smack of ball against the old wood of the door. She had long ago given up asking him not to play it here, for this was a restaurant and there was nothing for a boy to do.

'Do you want some tea?' she finally asked.

'That would be great,' Owen said.

'I'll be right back,' said Claire and she was grateful to have something to do. She walked through the swinging doors into the kitchen and she filled the kettle and cranked up the burner underneath it. He is your husband's brother, she told herself. Your brother-in-law. She wished Charlie would come home, but she also wished there was some way she could warn him. She knew his affection for his brother: he often said the two of them were raised like twins, inseparable, with a bond that ran deeper than others could understand. At the same time, it had been years since he had mentioned Owen's name, and the postcards that once came with numbing regularity had stopped altogether. She knew that Charlie felt betrayed somehow by this, as if his brother blamed him for their father's death, for the decision that had left Charlie with Charlotte's.

Claire returned with the cup of tea, placed it in front of Owen.

'Thanks,' he said, and when he looked across at her, she found his gaze to be the most intense she had ever met, stronger than Charlie's, whose icy blue eyes always seemed benign, searching. Owen, by contrast, had deep green eyes, as bright as turquoise, and when he looked at her fully she needed to look away, for it was as if in the looking he could see into her, though she knew that was not possible. He made her feel small, powerless, and she did not trust him. Everything about him unnerved her.

In just a few minutes, though, she heard Charlie's voice outside, talking to Jonah, and she said, 'Here he is.'

Owen stood up. 'Let's surprise him,' he said.

'You don't think he's going to be surprised already?'

'I know, but let's really surprise him.'

Owen moved toward the door, and leaned against the wall, so that when it opened he would be behind it. He was only there for a second when the door swung open and Charlie stood on the threshold, looking at Claire where she sat at the table, a cup of tea at the place across from her.

'Hey,' he said.

'Hey,' said Claire, trying to signal him with her eyes, looking over toward the now-open door. Charlie looked puzzled.

He said, 'What?' And in that moment the door

behind him moved back toward closed, and he turned, and for an instant Claire saw his body coil, as if preparing to fight, and then she saw the recognition run through him, his arms going slack, and he said, 'Holy shit.'

'Hello, brother,' said Owen.

'I don't fucking believe it.'

'Believe it, I'm here.'

'You look like shit.'

'Thanks, is that any way to treat your kid brother after, what, seventeen, eighteen years?'

'You need a haircut for starters.'

'Give me a hug,' said Owen, and Charlie did, and as Claire watched the two tall men wrap their arms around each other, as she saw their obvious affection, their sense of loss regained was palpable, and in that moment Claire thought, it's going to be okay. It's going to be okay after all.

★　★　★

Owen had always known he would return. He knew it the way you know when it is about to snow, intuitively, a feeling somewhere in your bones. The truth was that Eden and Charlotte's were imprinted in him, in the same manner that certain spawning grounds were imprinted in the steelhead trout that Claire and Charlie had watched swim the falls on that spring day many years ago.

He had done things, seen things his brother never would. He had watched a giant orange sun fall into the South Pacific from the deck of a

166

boat. He had made love to strange women and, sometimes, prostitutes, in port cities. He had smoked hashish in Turkish cafés. He had slept on benches; had been in fights in foreign bars where he was lucky to escape with his life. He had stolen. Once, while out on a Portuguese fishing trawler, he woke from a deep sleep to hear a commotion on the deck, where he found a circle of grown men having sex with a large fish that they held down with their boots.

Owen had dealt with the boredom, the hard work that was life at sea. He had spent countless hours applying heavy white and dull gray paint to all parts of ships under an unforgiving sun. He had cooked for men who had no appreciation for food beyond the bare sustenance it provided. He had grown used to the unyielding horizon, the sameness of the broad ocean, water all around him, but all of it useless except as a means of travel, and for the fish they sometimes caught with the lines they used to troll off the back of the large container ships.

Like his father, he took up smoking and he grew to love it. He smoked, like all the men he knew on freighters, to mark time. He drank more than he should and when he could find drugs, no matter what they were, he used these too. At least until their hold on him began to scare him or when a captain got a sense of what he was up to. Getting caught sniffing heroin was enough to blackball a man from the service for a long time. Not to mention the dangers posed by a small kitchen. You did not want to be too high in a kitchen at sea. Fire was the enemy of all boats.

He had slept with many women but he had loved none of them. Oh, he loved them at the time, when they lay in his arms in the tropical heat; he loved their smell, the differences in each of them; he loved when they first undressed and he saw them, their breasts and their nipples, the darkness or paleness of their skin. He loved their shyness and their boldness and he loved that they gave themselves up to him even though they knew he had little to give them in return. Even though they knew that in a few days he would leave without ceremony, moving on to wherever the ocean — and the company — took him next. He loved the sounds of their voices, speaking to him in Vietnamese or Spanish or French. He did not care what they said, as long as they said it, as long as when they moved together they talked, they cried and they spoke to him. In the mornings he loved sitting in a chair and smoking and watching them sleep. Times when he could take in all of them and revel in the fact that they meant nothing to him beyond the warmth of their bodies in the dark of night.

Sometimes, though, as his brother had, he became aware of his heart. There was one woman in the Canary Islands, ten years, or more, older than him, with dark skin and long black hair and cocoa-colored eyes. He spent two weeks with her without learning her name, and back at sea he ached for her in a way he had not for the others. Smoking under the ocean stars, he thought about her. And he thought, so this is what it is all about. But he knew that like the others he would never see her again. And in that lay a certain comfort. If you did not get too close, Owen figured, they could not hurt you.

★　★　★

That night, back in Eden, Owen lingered around the kitchen at Charlotte's and watched Charlie cook and tried to stay out of the way. He would never admit it but he was exhilarated by watching his brother cook, how accomplished he had become, better than their father, while Owen's skills had eroded from years of cooking simple food for men at sea. Claire was home with the boy, as she was now on all but the weekends when she joined her husband in the kitchen and a sitter watched Jonah. It was busy enough that Owen did not have much chance to talk to Charlie and spent much of his night out on the back porch smoking cigarettes, looking at the black river running through the trees in the dark.

After Charlie closed down, they returned to the house on Signal Ridge, and Jonah was in bed now, and Claire cooked for the two of them, a simple dinner of pan-fried steaks, roasted potatoes and a green salad. They drank a big-bodied cabernet and Owen told them about life at sea.

He told them about the sunsets over the Pacific, the islands he had seen, the general monotony of the endless ocean, broken up by occasional storms, sometimes a fire that they all rushed to put out. He told them about the exotic cities he had visited, the foods he had eaten in

169

places like Brazil and Vietnam and the Philippines. He told them about pirates, how they still existed, and sensing their acute interest he leaned forward and told them a story that had happened on another boat, to other men.

'Once,' he said, 'we were coming into the port of Guayaquil, in Ecuador, and it was late at night, and the large stick ship I was on moved slowly down this wide river. I was on watch, with two other men this night, since this was an area known for pirating. As the ship moved through the narrows, pulled by a tug, they came from all sides. Four or five speedboats pulled up alongside. It was dark. Quiet. Then the sound of the grappling hooks they used landing across the rails of the deck. One of the men I was with ran inside, while the other two of us, without thinking, rushed the rail. Below we could see them. They were on rope ladders, climbing quickly toward us. I had a flare gun and I fired it quickly. The flares shot across the river and lit up everything. The trees on the shore, their boats, the men below. They stopped for a moment, looked up at us, and then they just kept coming. I fired another one and this time they didn't hesitate. By the time I turned to head inside, it was too late. The other man with me had already left. Three men scrambled over the railing, and when I went to swing at one of them, I was hit from behind. And that's all I remember.'

'My God,' said Claire. 'What happened?'

'They knocked me out,' Owen said, fingering his wine glass. 'Hit me with some makeshift weapon. No one came out to help me.

Apparently I lay there while they cut the locks off the containers and began throwing cartons of stuff down to the boats below.'

'What were you carrying?'

'Watches. That's what they got. Boxes and boxes of Rolexes.'

'They must have known,' said Charlie.

'Oh, yeah,' said Owen. 'Someone would find out what was coming in. We got hit at most of the major ports at least once.'

'So were you okay?' asked Claire.

'Yeah. I mean, I had a hell of a headache for about a week. And any time after that, if the ship got hit, I locked myself in my room. Let them have whatever they want. I'm not getting hurt protecting another man's stuff.'

Owen looked across the table at his brother and then at his pretty wife. He locked eyes with her, and he sensed her discomfort, but also her wonder. He did not know anything about her. But her look as she caught his eyes and then looked away was familiar. He had seen it before, on other women. Women from other parts of the world, women who looked on him as if he held answers to things they wanted to know about but did not have anyone to ask. Generally, like Claire, they were questions that went unspoken, but the look was enough for him. It showed that they were capable of thinking of such things. More important, it suggested to him that they thought he might be the one to solve a problem that they were just beginning to frame within themselves.

After dinner, Owen helped clear the dishes but since Claire insisted on finishing the cleaning, he retired outside and Charlie joined him. They stood on the porch and Owen smoked and the air was cool with fall and smelled of wet leaves.

'When did you pick those up?' Charlie asked, motioning to the cigarette his brother drew on.

'Occupational hazard,' Owen said.

'They'll kill you.'

'One can hope, right?' said Owen.

'I was never tempted. Thank God. After Dad.'

'You have any grass?'

'Grass?'

'Yeah, you know, pot. Like we used to.'

Charlie laughed. 'Not in a long time. Not since you were around, really.'

Owen looked at his taller brother, at his serious face, his receding hairline. 'I bet there's still roaches in the barn. Remember how we used to just leave them out there? For a rainy day?'

'Yeah,' said Charlie, 'I do. But they wouldn't be any good now.'

'Fuck it,' said Owen. 'Let's find out.'

And with that, he stepped off the porch on to the grass and began to move toward the barn. He suspected his brother would follow him, and he was right. They walked across the lawn and the light from Charlie and Claire's room upstairs shot across the grass and illuminated their walk. Above, the sky was clear and the moon was sliver-thin and the stars were muted, Venus bright this time of year, a small, yellowish light above the hills in the distance.

When they reached the barn, Owen opened the old doors and stepped into the darkness. He sensed Charlie at his back, and he stopped for a

172

moment and let his eyes adjust to the lack of light. When they had, he said, 'This place hasn't changed.'

'I almost never come out here,' said Charlie.

'No?' said Owen. 'This used to be your favorite place.'

'Things change,' Charlie said.

'You better go first,' said Owen.

Charlie stepped in front of him and in the thin light that came through the large doors, Owen watched his brother move across the earthen floor to the ladder against the south-facing wall and he followed him. Charlie hit the ladder and began to climb and Owen followed on his heels. When he emerged into the loft, it was even darker, and he waited a minute until he could make out his brother's shape, and hear his footfalls, moving across the beams toward where he knew from memory the large hay doors were.

'It's like stepping back in time,' Owen said.

'Just watch your step,' said Charlie. 'Some of these floorboards are like paper.'

Owen moved forward gingerly, one foot in front of the other, and he was following the beams and the wood was solid underneath his feet. He could not see his brother in front of him, though in a moment he no longer heard his steps, and then the hay doors opened and the wan light from outside suddenly streamed into the loft and he could make out the shadowy shape of his brother next to the opening. He had about fifteen feet to go and he made it easily now, and when he reached the edge, he sat down next to his brother, and he let his legs hang over the edge. Venus was at eye level now, the curved slice of moon above it, and the night was clear. A cold breeze came in from the east but it did not bother him.

Owen reached out and put his arm around Charlie's neck. 'How about this?' he said. 'Now all we need is a joint.'

'Check behind the door,' said Charlie.

Owen reached to his right, and felt along the wall, toward where seventeen years ago they had put their unfinished roaches. His fingers hit grainy wood and he moved them up till he found the small shelf that was there, and then he felt the small nubs of old joints, mixed in with the cobwebs. He grabbed whatever was there and brought it back, held the small pile in his hands and in the dim light he saw that there were a number of old dried ends of marijuana cigarettes.

'Look at this,' he said. 'Just as I thought. Get stoned with me, Charlie.'

'I can't,' Charlie said. 'But help yourself.'

'Why not?'

'Not my thing any more, that's all.'

'Suit yourself,' said Owen, and he began to unroll the old joints, the mixture of ash and dried pot crumbling into his hands. 'Most likely sucks anyway.'

From the pack of cigarettes in his pocket he took one out, removed the filter and then carefully took the paper away from the tobacco, letting it spill into the air below him. He took the mixture in his other palm and pressed it into the paper, rolling it slowly so that it would not rip. He licked it together and then shook it. 'There,' he said.

He put the jury-rigged joint to his lips and he lighted it, the flame like a candle in the night for a moment, his face and then his brother's caught in its brightness before it extinguished and the joint was cherry-red and he sucked on it. He inhaled deeply and then he coughed, for the old pot was harsh and hurt his lungs. But he felt its bite instantly, for though it was old, it still had what it took and it went to his head. He held it out for Charlie.

'You sure?' he said.

'Yeah,' said Charlie, 'I'm sure.'

Owen took two more long drags on the joint and then it was so low it was at his fingers and he tossed it into the yard, watching its red tip spin in the air before landing on the grass below them. The wind picked up then, and they could hear the weathervane on the roof above them as it spun on its rusty axis. To their left was the old house, and the kitchen light had gone off since they had gotten up here, and the only light came from the upstairs bedroom, around the corner from the barn, so that Owen could not see into it. They sat in silence for a while, as they had as youths, and they looked at the moon and the stars and the dark hills. They listened to the wind. They looked down at the earth below, their boots moving slightly above it.

Charlie broke the silence. He said, 'Don't take this the wrong way. But can I ask you your plan?'

'Let me see,' said Owen. 'I don't really have one.'

'You can stay as long as you want, you know that.'

'Thanks,' Owen said. 'Don't worry about it. I won't mess up your perfect life here.'

'I'm not worried about that, I was just wondering if you were going back. Back to the Merchant Marines.'

Owen sighed. 'I don't think so.'

Charlie did not ask. 'Okay,' he said.

'Can I get back to you?'

'Of course, I was just curious. You can have the downstairs room tonight and for as long as you need it.'

Owen nodded. 'I appreciate that.'

Charlie went to speak and then paused. 'You could — '

'What?'

'Nothing. I was just going to say you could come work at Charlotte's again while you figure out your next move.'

'Let me think about that one.'

'All right,' said Charlie. 'And now I need to get to bed. Tomorrow morning is going to come fast enough as it is.'

'I hear you,' Owen said.

They stood then, and walked back the way they had come. When they reached the porch, Owen stopped. 'I'm going to stay out for one more smoke.'

They said goodnight, and Owen watched as his brother opened the old screen door and disappeared into the house. Owen took his cigarettes out of his breast pocket and he took one out and he lighted it. He left the porch for the yard and he looked up into the black sky, the stars brighter now than they were earlier, the thin moon fully risen, almost directly above. He looked across the field, past the barn, to the black woods where a lifetime ago his father had taken his own life. Many times out on the ocean he thought about that day. He had thought about the two of them running through the woods in the heavy rain, knowing what was in front of them, but having no choice but to continue on. Sometimes he wondered if he could ever go in those woods again, if he could ever move through the forest with the innocence of childhood, and he decided that he could not. Their deep beauty, the groves of birch that caught the fall sunlight, had been, for him, for ever tainted.

Owen turned back to the house. There was a nightlight lit in the kitchen and up above the light in his brother's bedroom was still on. He saw his shirtless brother move past the window, and a moment later he saw Claire as well, and she stopped for a moment in front of it, as if looking out to him. She wore what appeared to be a white nightgown, and her arms were bare. He stared up at her. He drew on his cigarette, knowing that it would attract attention to his face. Claire moved away from the window. Owen smiled to himself. The lights in their room went out, and he was left alone, standing on the hard earth in the dark, the wind picking up again. He tossed his cigarette out into the field, watched it tumble through the air until it vanished into the high grass.

12

Shortly after they were married, Claire felt that she suddenly knew what it was all about. Rolling over in the mornings and seeing Charlie there, and then working together as husband and wife, all of it hers now too, she felt a comfort and a warmth from the certainty of it all. She loved their mornings together, making love while the sun spilled through the old dusty windows. She loved the coffee they shared with the paper, and she loved the daily drive to Charlotte's, cutting through those old dirt roads, the windows rolled up in the winter, days when she would move close to her husband on the bench seat of the pickup truck and watch the snowy woods that they passed through. Summer mornings when they drove with the windows down, the warm breeze entering the cab, the whole world bright and full of possibility. Mostly, though, she loved the restaurant itself, the bustle and noise of it, more than a job now, more than work to mark time, but a life, a life that belonged to both of them.

And then, their first spring as a married couple, a spring when the melt came early and steadily and the days grew gradually warmer and longer, her favorite time of year, she discovered that she was pregnant. Oddly, it was not something they had spoken of much. Oh, there were drunken talks about the idea of children, what they would look like. Would they have his height, her eyes? Would they be artists, poets, cooks, athletes? How would it work, bringing them into the life of a restaurant, a job that never ended?

But, unlike most married couples, they did not plan for it. It was not something they talked about in a concrete way, as other young married women Claire had known discussed it. In the third year, we will have our first, and then one each year after until we hit the magic number of three. No, there was none of that. It remained an abstraction, something that happened to other people, though deep within both of them they probably understood that this was denial, that by their resolute decision to not use birth control, relying instead on Charlie's ability to end things when he chose, they were relinquishing some authority over the choice of it all.

Claire knew her period was late. For a brief time she thought perhaps it was only that and she did not say anything to Charlie. Since she had been in Eden, her cycle had been in perfect alignment with the full moon, as regular as a clock. When one week passed she began to think about it, and when two weeks passed she began to worry about it. One morning she left the restaurant on the pretense of going to the bank and she drove out of town and found a drugstore where the clerks did not know her and she bought one of the instant pregnancy tests they had for sale next to the cigarettes and the condoms. She waited until that night and while Charlie slept soundlessly in the dark of their

179

bedroom, she took the test.

The results were not unexpected. She was with child. Still, she did not tell Charlie right away. Somehow she hoped that if she did not give it words it would not come to pass. And she knew this was the wrong way to think but she could not help it. A child threatened the life she had grown to love so much: just the two of them, the restaurant, the work, the freedom.

She waited until Sunday morning, until the one day they did not have to rise early and head to Charlotte's. She woke before him that day, and outside the late April sun was already bright. She had played this conversation over in her mind, what she would tell him, but when he finally stirred next to her, raised his arms above his head and smiled at her, rolling half over and slinging his arm across her belly, all she could say was, 'I'm pregnant.'

Charlie quickly sat up. 'My God. Really?'

Claire nodded. 'I'm pretty sure.'

'Ah, Claire,' he said. 'That's wonderful.'

Claire smiled thinly. She looked out the window to the green woods, to the high clouds in the sky. 'Yeah,' she said, her voice betraying her lack of enthusiasm.

'What, baby?' said Charlie. 'This is great news. I mean, it's not something we planned for. But still. It's amazing.'

Claire saw how his eyes lit up, and she thought to herself, how do I explain it? How do I tell him why this makes me so uneasy? How do I tell him how afraid I am? And as she thought this, he moved into her, put his strong arms around her

180

body and pulled her to him. She felt his lips on her neck and the stubble of his beard scraped the side of her cheek.

He said, 'I love you, Claire.'

'I love you too,' she said.

'This will be amazing, honest. It will.'

Claire nodded her head, and she wanted to tell him what she thought, that she was not cut out to be a mother; that some girls were, it was what they wanted from the time they were old enough to think about such things. She was not one of them, she knew that. She figured she was too selfish. Cared too much about her own life to throw everything she had into nurturing the life of another. And she hated herself for this, for what kind of woman did not welcome the coming of a child to a man she was married to? A man she loved? What kind of woman did not put a child above a job? Though she knew that was not fair either. Charlotte's was not simply a job, cooking was not simply a job. It was a life. But she could not tell him this. She could never tell Charlie this. So she simply returned his hug. She dug her hands into his back. She looked out the window to the broad valley below. To the hills and the mountains and the sun in the sky. To all that lay beyond her.

★ ★ ★

And then with the full acknowledgement of it, the uncertainty gave way to love, love for what grew within her. In the soft nights of spring the two of them lay together in bed and they talked about names, boy names and girl names, names steeped in personal histories, and they imagined the child they would have; and they speculated about him or her; and they talked about things that they had not realised were of import to either of them but that the prospect of a child suddenly made real. They talked about religion, and the truth was that neither of them was religious, Charlie being raised in a secular house and Claire as a Lutheran but not practicing since high school. They talked about school, about the possibility of home schooling, which had never occurred to Claire until she began to think about it, picturing in her mind her son or daughter coming home from some Vermont public school unhappy and unsatisfied, remembering her own unhappiness years ago in junior high outside of Cincinnati, the relentless teasing of a girl whose breasts were prematurely large and whose beauty had not yet become objectively apparent. They talked about all these things, and in the talking she found herself reaching a level of comfort that mirrored the physical changes within her, the growing baby, the new heft to her tummy, the sense of motherhood that seemed to cover all of her, the general warmth of it, the feeling of strength it gave her. And for this, she loved Charlie more and more, for in all the changes to her, she saw him, his power and humility: all that he so easily gave her. And in this, in the shared sense of future that only a child can provide, she saw the two of them growing closer together, as if they were old vines climbing the clapboards of a house. It made her happy.

Early in the pregnancy, she was sick, not in the mornings as she expected, but mostly in the middle of the night, waking and moving quickly to the bathroom where she retched into the toilet. If Charlie heard her, he rose too and came to her, held her head up, soothed her with his words. Sometimes she grew unfathomably emotional, stealing downstairs in the dead of night to be away from him to a place where she could sob in peace. But mostly, she learned to adjust to the change, and by the time she was six months along, her body full of the baby to come, her cheeks flushed with it, she knew she was ready. Ready for the birth, desiring it, and ready for the life to follow. For how their lives would change, for she knew enough to know that a baby could not help but change people, could not help but take them toward something more profound.

Those last months she worked whenever she felt up to it, and they never talked about it but Claire knew that Charlie would prefer that she did not but he was wise enough not to suggest such a thing. She went to Charlotte's in the mornings and she prepped for the night's dinner, sitting on a stool rather than standing up. In the afternoons she returned home and napped and came back for the rush of dinner, though she did not work the line as she once had. She admired how good Charlie was in the kitchen on these days, for he was doing the work of two and made it seem effortless. She watched him move from stove to grill and back again, as many as twelve entrées going at any given time, and all of it coming out just as it should. She watched how he never grew flustered, how he took the time in the chaos of things to turn and smile at her, to mouth the words 'I love you'. And sometimes when he did this, she felt herself overcome by it, and she knew it was the pregnancy, how it made you aware of the simplest of gestures, how it made you understand their greater human import, and she smiled at him and then walked out to the porch to let it wash over her like rain.

Winter came late that year. By December there was still no snow on the ground, though the earth had hardened and on the roads the grooves left over from the previous spring were now frozen ridges that jolted the truck as it went and made Claire uncomfortable. Her official due date was 13 December and she knew the baby could come any day now. Both she and Charlie were uneasy about it. If they were to talk about it, perhaps they would recognise that the life of the restaurant was one of rigid control: you did everything you could to manage the future. And they both knew, of course, that babies come when babies when come, and that there was not much use in expecting otherwise. Still, lying in bed as midnight passed and the thirteenth came, Claire turned to Charlie and said, 'It's not going to happen today.'

He rubbed his eyes and rolled toward her. He had just started to doze off. 'How do you know?'

'I don't know. I just do. It's going to be a Christmas baby.'

Charlie laughed. 'Okay,' he said. 'There are

worse things to get in your stocking than a new baby.'

'Christmas it is then,' said Claire.

'Christmas it is,' Charlie said.

★　★　★

As it turned out, the baby came on 23 December. They had had plenty of opportunities to discern the sex and did not, one of the things they both agreed on, deciding to be old-fashioned about it. And if they had a preference, they did not express it to each other. Claire secretly hoped for a boy, and she thought she knew it was a boy, not that she had any way to know, but something about the weight within her, the way the baby moved in those weeks before birth suggested to her a little boy. And then, that morning, she woke and knew it was happening. She felt it and she did not have to have experienced it before to know that this was no fire drill, the pain was hot and white and in her abdomen, and when she calmed her breathing the contractions came fast and regular.

Charlie was in the bathroom shaving. In a few moments, as he did every morning now that she did not join him at Charlotte's, he would kiss her goodbye and get in the truck and drive the snowy roads to the old schoolhouse at the banks of the Dog River. Claire felt the pain and as she did she looked out the window where big snowflakes floated lazily past, the sky a dull winter gray.

'Charlie?' she called. No answer. Again.

Louder. 'Charlie?' And then even louder, practically screaming it. 'Charlie!'

The door to the bathroom opened quickly and he was there, shaving cream on his face, a towel around his waist, her tall, muscular husband. She almost did not have to speak for she saw in his face that he knew. But she said it anyway. She said, 'It's happening.'

Without the slightest hint of modesty, he removed his towel, wiped the shaving cream off his face and at the same time said repeatedly, 'Okay, okay.'

Claire tried to rise from the bed but the pain was intense and she lay back down. The pain was so strong she felt the first tears of the day come to her eyes. The room around her grew blurry. She had a sense of Charlie's frenetic movements, his sliding into jeans, his buttoning of his shirt, his rummaging through his closet for his boots. Then, somehow, she was in the truck and her hands were on the turbulence that was her belly, and they were driving, trees and snow and sky moving in front of her, Charlie's words sounding distant but soothing, nothing more than his incessant 'okays' but they helped nonetheless.

Soon they were leaving Eden, and she saw the sign that announced its presence and she remembered little after that. She knew he was driving fast, could feel the road vanishing beneath the tires of the truck. She watched the snowflakes sweeping past the windshield, big, cartoon flakes. The kind that held their shape for a moment when you caught them in your hand. And then they were at Copley Hospital, bright lights, people taking care of her, Charlie fading into the background except for his strong hand which refused to let go of her own.

'It'll be okay, baby,' he said to her.

Later she would remember the midwife, a round-faced woman with curly hair and a broad smile. And she would remember the doctor who came in to oversee things, gray-bearded and blue-eyed. And she would remember Charlie, more nervous than she had ever seen him before, his face the color of flour, his eyes furtive and darting. What she would not remember was the pain, though she knew it was there, all around her, and somehow she managed to block it out. What she would not remember was what she wanted to remember most, the moment they handed her the new baby, a baby boy, red-faced and screaming, eyes closed, his throaty yelling coming to a halt as she brought him to her cheek.

★ ★ ★

They named him Jonah. It had started as a joke, when they first realised Claire was with child and she had worried that the life of the restaurant would swallow a baby up. Charlie, with his secular upbringing, did not know the biblical reference but when Claire told him he immediately loved the name. 'My father loved the sea,' he said. 'And of course, my brother. I think if they were here they would appreciate the irony.'

After a few days she was able to take him

home to the house on Signal Ridge, and as she lay in the upstairs bedroom on a clear winter day when the sun sent sparkles of light off the snow she was overcome with the truth of it all. She breast-fed little Jonah and he nursed with pursed lips, his tiny eyelids closed and as soft as blankets. She watched the hills and the sunlight and was grateful for the heat from the woodstove that flowed easily up the grate to the bedroom. Charlie was downstairs and she could hear him making her tea, the whistle of the kettle before he turned it off. And she wanted to cry because of it, not out of sadness but because of the beauty of what it all meant, the two of them, and the baby who in only a few days had already become more a part of her than he had been when he rested within her.

By the time Charlie brought her the mug of warm herbal tea, little Jonah was done feeding and slept soundlessly on the lip of her chest, his little rib cage rising and falling with each tiny breath.

Claire said, 'Look, Charlie. Look at this boy we made.'

Charlie smiled wide, leaned down and kissed her forehead. 'I know it,' he said.

'I can't believe it,' Claire whispered.

'Believe it, Claire,' Charlie said. 'It's just the beginning.' And with that, he kissed her forehead again, reached down and held his big hand over the head of his baby boy, as if he was going to cup the bowl of his skull, instead holding it there for an instant before taking her free hand in his own and squeezing tight. He smiled at her and she smiled back and outside the short day moved on toward dark.

★ ★ ★

Jonah was a healthy boy and he grew like a tree. That is the way it is with babies. You want them to grow up and then they do and you long for those moments when they were so new and uncomplicated and so completely you and nothing else. The time before they began to take on any residue of the world.

New motherhood was a heady time for Claire. Each day brought new joys and new challenges and she surprised herself by how easily she moved into it. When she expressed this to Charlie one night with the baby upstairs asleep, the steady tick of the baby monitor on the table next to where they sat, he said, 'See? You're a natural.'

Claire looked at him. 'I really didn't think I had it in me,' she said. 'It's not something I wanted and I know that sounds terrible, but it's true. I really didn't. I don't think I even played with dolls when I was a girl. I was such a tomboy.'

'And now look at you,' said Charlie.

'If only we lived in the suburbs and you wore a suit to work. I'd be my fucking mother.'

'I like your mother,' said Charlie, feigning indignation.

'Me too,' Claire said. 'That doesn't mean I want to be her.'

And it was on nights like these that Claire

Apple, in the old farmhouse on Signal Ridge with her husband and her child, reached an accommodation with herself, something approaching peace. Nights when the cold outdoors did not matter for inside there was the steady pulsing of the woodstove with its orange glow of heat. Nights when the world had shrunk to include only the three of them and they were a family and on nights like this she did not know what else you could ask for. You had each other and the wood heat and the old house and that was enough.

But there were times later, as Jonah moved from infant to toddler to child, that she watched Charlie leave in the morning, watched him start the truck in the driveway from the kitchen window, and she felt something close to loss, and worst of all she knew it was not something she could speak about.

The truth was that she was jealous of her husband, of the restaurant, of the life he now led outside the home and that she did not.

Secretly she longed for the days when she had cooked with absolute abandon, when the food was what mattered and everything else came second. Claire missed the hot stove, all the burners fired up, the pans warped from the heat, waiting for a fillet of fish or pigeon thighs to be seared. She missed the tedium of the prep work, the endless making of stocks and mother sauces. She missed dicing onions and garlic, breaking down birds. She missed the ritual repeating of orders as they were called to her from the wait staff. She missed all of it, but most of all she missed the freedom, the sense of personal identity she associated with cooking at Charlotte's. In short, she missed being herself.

Sometimes Claire wanted to confess all of this to Charlie and she thought she should. But she seemed to stop herself. What kind of lousy mother wants to cook more than she wants to spend time with her beautiful boy, a beautiful boy who thinks that she defines the world, creates it for him anew every day?

In the mornings she watched Charlie leave and in the evenings she welcomed him home. In between she took care of Jonah and sometimes she visited Charlotte's, which only made it harder for her. And the seasons came and went, the falls with their color, the winters with the snow and ice, the springs with the melt and rising rivers and the first gold on the trees, the warm summers with the hot sun and the deep, lush green of everything. The years slid by like low-flying clouds. And Claire Apple never said to her husband what it was she felt, what it was she truly wanted. She never told him about the emptiness that grew somewhere within her, perhaps where the baby once was. She never told him how it spread until it was how she thought of herself. She never told him that sometimes in the middle of the day she dreamed of her life going in different directions, she dreamed of her own place, her own restaurant, of a life without a husband and a family. She dreamed of other men: imagined them when she took long baths, saw them running their strong hands over her body. Other men who made love to her with the abandonment of youth, not the careful, calibrated movements of marriage. Claire hated herself for thinking these things; for dreaming these dreams. She hated herself for wanting to stand alone. For wanting her life back. For wanting herself back. In her heart, she knew it was too much to ask. And so she only asked it to herself, and only during those moments when she was alone and it could eat at her in peace.

13

After a week at the old farmhouse on Signal Ridge, Owen sank his meager savings into the purchase of an old Silver Stream trailer on three acres of hilly woods on the Hunger Mountain Road. The land was not beautiful, thick and dense with high spruce and rocky forest floor, but it was high enough to have a sliver of view to the mountains to the west, and the sun fought through this gap and threw streams of afternoon light on to the small trailer. Inside there was a jury-rigged, pot-bellied woodstove, a small kitchenette with a two-burner cook stove and a tiny refrigerator, a narrow living room with a built-in sofa, one rocking chair, and a place for a television. A curtain divided the small platform bed from the rest of the living area.

It was a class-four road, and he had enough money left over to buy himself an old Toyota truck, one of those classic Vermont vehicles where the bed had been replaced by a wooden one. But he could lock the tires and have four-wheel drive and this was essential to climb the road in winter and in mud season.

His last night at the house on Signal Ridge was a Sunday and the restaurant was closed, and Owen cooked for Claire and Charlie as a thank you for putting him up in the house he had grown up in but that now belonged only to them. It had been a long time since he had done anything ambitious but somehow from the depths of his memory he summoned his father's coq au vin, and he broke down a chicken and browned the pieces in butter and oil and then slowly braised them in mushrooms, pearl onions, stock and red wine. It was a complex series of reductions, and as he cooked, he found it all coming back to him, the red wine turning syrupy and coating the back of a spoon. He served it, as his father had done, over buttered egg noodles and with lightly fried asparagus bundles.

Outside the night was dark and cool and they ate in the dining room and from the living room they could hear the woodstove as it ticked with the heat of new wood. Jonah had been put to bed and it was just the three of them. As they ate, they talked in general terms about the weather, about Charlotte's, about Owen's new place in the woods. Claire and Charlie were careful not to be condescending about his trailer, though both of them wondered how he could live there, in space that small, on land that dark and unforgiving. But what they did not know was that to Owen it offered, if less light, then greater space than he had grown used to on the tight quarters of a boat. And, for the first time in his life, something besides the clothes on his back would be his and his alone.

When dinner was finished, Charlie brought up the idea of Owen working at Charlotte's. Owen knew it was a pro forma gesture, that in truth neither Charlie nor, especially, Claire wanted him there but that they had to offer. And for a moment, the possibility of accepting intrigued him, if only for this reason, and as he looked across the table at Claire, at her big, beautiful eyes, he wanted to say yes, if only to see her discomfort increase.

Owen said, 'That's nice of you, Charlie, it really is. But you know it's not my bag. I've been making bad food for twenty years, why stop now?'

Charlie crossed his hands on the table in front of him. 'I think it would be nice. And I can use the help. Claire can only be there a few nights a week now.'

Owen nodded at Claire. 'What do you think, Claire? A few too many Benders in the kitchen?'

Claire smiled shyly and looked away. Owen knew she had trouble making eye contact with him and this did not surprise him, for he knew that a lot of women did. For the same reasons women were drawn to him they were also frightened of him, of the strength of his gaze. It was as if they worried that if they looked too long at his sea-green eyes, they might fall in, fall into him, and not be able to get out when they wanted to. Oftentimes they mistook it for worldliness in addition to his almost feminine beauty. What they did not know was that he was born this way, and no amount of experience would change it.

Claire said, 'We could use the help. That's true. Charlie's been doing the work of two, maybe three, really, for a long time now. Maybe he would even get a night off and we could do something as a family.'

Owen watched as she reached out and placed

her hand over her husband's own. It was a subtle and natural movement, one that wives the world over do. But in its subtlety he saw something else too. A reminder of how different things were, that seventeen years had passed and there was no going back.

Owen slowly stood from the table, making his way outside for a cigarette. He stopped and put a hand on his brother's shoulder, shot a long look at Claire. 'I appreciate it, I do,' he said. 'But I'll be all right. I will.'

★　★　★

Owen took a job cooking at Camel's, a dive bar on the outside of town. It was a low-ceilinged place with a wooden bar warped from age and scratched up from generations of patrons carving their initials and other things into it. It had a pool table and the light was dim and sometimes on Friday and Saturday nights there was live music and people danced. The food was nothing special, burgers and fries and the occasional salad, but it was work he was used to, not much different from cooking for men at sea, with the obvious and important difference that it was a bar that employed young barmaids and there was something, Owen thought, to be said for this.

On nights when the kitchen grew quiet, Owen sat at the old bar and nursed bourbons and smoked his cigarettes.

Sometimes he chatted with the women who worked there, local girls mostly, girls who wore blue eyeshadow and were killing time until they married someone they had known since elementary school. Girls who wanted dreams but could not dream beyond the confines of this town, the life they had always known. Girls who thought they wanted to escape but did not know what that meant.

He knew they were all curious about him. Where he had been, what he had done, what his story was. He knew they liked his longish blond hair, his weathered, handsome face, his green eyes, his tall, lean body, the way he carried himself, which spoke of stories from other places even though he, like them, had spent his childhood among these gentle hills. He knew they whispered about him, imagined fucking him, talked about it the way women always had in the lee of his presence, and sometimes, generally more out of boredom than desire, he allowed their want to be realised.

Occasionally one of them came home with him to the trailer at the base of Hunger Mountain and in the half-dark he would undress her, lay her down on his narrow bed and move his hands over her. Bring her, slowly and deliberately, to places boys her own age could not. Knowing where she liked to be touched, how to be slow and patient, refusing to give in to his own need to slide inside her until he knew that to not do so would border on cruelty.

He made love to them in ways he knew they wanted to be made love to and he did so not out of some great sense of selflessness or passion for the particular woman, but rather because he understood what it was they ached for and he knew that there were few things in this life that came easily to him and this was one of them. He also liked their gratitude, often unspoken but as palpable as the play of the moonlight on the trailer walls when they were finished and lay together, sweaty and intertwined, falling apart naturally, like objects caught in a vacuum after it lifts.

In the mornings Owen would wake and for a brief moment forget they were there, rolling over to find some woman half his age sprawled out on the other side of his bed, her makeup wanting to run off her face, her nakedness not nearly as interesting to him as it had been in the drunken dark of the night before. He would take in the whole of her: the pertness of her young breasts, the place where her thighs came together; how her body moved with the collective hum of sleep. And in this moment, watching her while he himself remained unwatched, he wanted somehow to give in to them, to know what love was, to feel it the way he had heard it described to him. He wanted to be the man he imagined himself capable of being, humbled by the beauty of a nude woman who had been kind enough to open herself for him. He wanted to pick them up, to wake them suddenly; to mutter lovely things into their half-woken ears. Owen wanted them to know that he might go away but that he would try to be right back. Be right back to feed them, make love to them, roll into them in the blue of the morning and stay with his hip pressed against theirs until the fragile sun rose over the hills and shone its golden light through the windows to where they lay. He wanted to be the man he imagined his father had been, the man he suspected his brother had become.

But Owen was none of these things. Instead he left before they woke, getting into his truck on mornings when he could see his breath, letting them find their own way to whatever corner of Eden they happened to call home. No promises, no commitments, nothing more than a warm body to mute the chill of the season, as if that were enough, as if anything were enough.

★   ★   ★

Right before Thanksgiving it snowed for ten days in a row, a heavy, wet snow that clung to the spruce trees and piled high against the sides of the buildings in Eden. It was snow that fell with the intensity of rain. Snow that made the roads tricky; that felled trees with its weight and knocked out the electric grid for entire days, sparing businesses like Charlotte's that knew enough to have generators for back-up. Snow that built small bridges of white across the still-flowing Dog River. Snow that blighted the light on these the shortest days of the year. Snow that was beautiful and white and cast a crystalline blanket over all of Eden, over the entirety of the small stamp of world that Owen and Claire and Charlie now shared.

By Thanksgiving Day it had stopped and the sunlight was almost blinding as it reflected off the snow that covered the meadows that Owen

199

drove by on his way to the house on Hunger Mountain. Charlie had come by Owen's trailer the day before, on a morning when the wind blew the heavy snow into drifts. Owen did not have a phone so Charlie had driven out to invite him over. They had stood together in the snow, Owen in only a flannel shirt, and the falling snow had clung to their hair.

'Turkey and all the fixings,' Owen said. 'How American of you.'

'It's just dinner,' Charlie said. 'Get you out of the bar for a day.'

Owen smiled. 'What makes you think I want out of the bar?'

'You know what I mean.'

'All right,' he said, 'you got me. What time?'

'There's one other thing,' said Charlie. 'Mom is going to be there.'

'I think I'll just hang here,' said Owen.

'Come on, Owen, it's not that big a deal.'

Owen brushed snow off his eyebrows. 'I thought she was never coming back here.'

'She doesn't. She came for my wedding. And now she's coming to see you.'

'That's too much for me, man. I'm just getting used to being back here. Getting my legs still.'

'She wants to see you.'

'Yeah, well.'

'Listen,' said Charlie. 'One day. That's all. Is that too much to ask? That for one day we try to be a family?'

Owen looked across at his big brother. At the earnestness coming from his blue eyes. He shook his head and laughed. 'Fuck,' he said. 'Fucking holidays. That was a good thing about being at sea, you know? We'd defrost the best steaks and get drunk and call it Christmas. Out in the middle of nowhere, somewhere near the equator. No bullshit. No drama.'

'There won't be any drama,' said Charlie.

'Sounds like I don't have a choice.'

'You don't.'

Now, driving through the bright blue-skied morning, Owen smoked cigarettes and thought about Charlotte, about his father, about Charlie, about how everything turned out. About how a moment in time could alter your life for ever.

★　★　★

His mother had aged well. She was the first one he saw when he came through the door and she smiled at him, crow's feet emanating out from her beautiful green eyes, the eyes he'd inherited. She wore a long black skirt, a red shirt, a black cardigan. She looked very hip for her age, very New York. She was the timeless beauty she had always been. Charlotte.

She held her arms out wide and he thought, if she does not cry then I will. But as his mother came to him, as he took her into his arms, doing what he did not want to do but what came naturally, he felt her hands running through his long hair.

'Owen,' she said and in her voice he heard the tears before he saw them.

'Don't, Mom,' he said.

'You smell like cigarettes.'

Owen held his mother away from him. 'That's funny,' he said. 'I just smoked a cigarette.'

'I'm still your mother,' she said.

'I know.'

'I can say things.'

'Say anything you want.'

Owen looked at her, her blonde hair now elegantly streaked with gray, his mother. He looked at her for signs of strain, to see if being back in this house redolent with memories was having any effect on her. But he knew her legendary strength, the sense of propriety she had instilled in all of them: the stoic Yankee widow, never showing the world her pain.

'I need a drink,' Owen said.

'There is stuff in the dining room,' his mother said.

'I'll find it,' said Owen and he left her in the foyer of the old house.

In the dining room the table was set for the four adults and for young Jonah who was nowhere to be seen. From here Owen could see through to the kitchen, and he caught a glimpse of Claire kneeling in front of the oven, her hair tied back, and she did not see him and for a moment he watched her. Watched her look in on what he figured was the obligatory bird. She stared into the open oven, brushed a lone bang of hair away from her face. Then she closed the oven and stood and suddenly, as if aware of his gaze, she turned to see him there, in the dining room and she smiled at him. Her black eyes flashed.

'Hey, Owen,' she said. 'Happy Thanksgiving.'

Owen lifted the bottle of bourbon off the table as a return greeting. He smiled. She moved out of his sight, into the kitchen. He poured a stiff three fingers of the bourbon into a tumbler and drank it right down. Filled it again and drank this in two swallows. Filled it a third time and moved into the kitchen. Toward the one day of family he had promised his brother.

★ ★ ★

They ate a meal their father would have been proud of. Fat Prince Edward Island oysters on the half-shell with a simple mignonette sauce. A roast wild turkey stuffed with chestnuts, black truffles, walnuts and rice. An au jus gravy. Leeks braised in white wine and cream. Sweet potatoes whipped with maple syrup, vanilla bean and butter. An apple pie made from local Macintosh apples and served with a coffee ice cream Charlie had made that morning.

They ate in the dining room and outside the sun was setting early, the sky a mottle of reds and blues, high wispy clouds, a portent of the bright star-night to come. They all sat around the table, even little dark-haired Jonah, who reminded Owen of himself and Charlie at that age, polite and quiet, used to formal dinners, a child of the restaurant. The alcohol was helping Owen. The bourbons before dinner and now the parade of wines with it allowed him to forget his misgivings, to look with kindness at his mother across from him, to share stories and smiles with his brother, glances with his sister-in-law, and most of all, allowed him to block out the history that this house, this life, this life that had once belonged to his father but had since been swallowed by his brother and by the comely Claire, did not normally let him bury the way he thought he must if he was to survive. For was that not what it was all about? Survival? Learning to let things behind you, be behind you? Embrace the present, live in the moment and all that other bullshit. That was what Owen said to himself when he was sober. For now, it was less relevant. He was drunk.

Still, he managed not to give in to it. Not to tell his mother what he thought about her running away to the city, to her friends from an earlier time, away from these hills and their secrets. Not to tell Charlie what he thought of his becoming their father, of the sickening domestic bliss in which he seemed to wallow: the beautiful wife, the successful restaurant, the handsome, well-behaved child. Instead he told stories of life at sea, drunken stories, stories he told in a rising singsong voice, not caring whether or not he embarrassed himself or insulted his mother. Grateful, instead, for the comfort of his voice, rising from within him with a power he had not anticipated. They were ribald stories, stories of women and of faraway ports, stories more suited for late night at the bar, stories more suited to the company of men. But with the telling his words grew more incantatory and unmeasured until he was standing to make a point, raising his glass above him, looking down at his elegantly dressed mother, his reserved brother, Claire with her downcast big eyes, his nephew who had now left the table and was imitating an airplane in the kitchen, moving in circles in front of the dishwasher, his arms stretched out on either side of his tiny body. Fuck it, Owen thought. Fuck all of it. This is me. This is who I am. This is how you made me.

★ ★ ★

After dinner, Owen moved to the porch to smoke. It was dusk now and in front of him was the snow-covered field and beyond it the spruce trees at the start of the forest rose like sentinels. The stars were emerging in the darkening sky and in the distance he could see the bluish-black mountains. There was little moon. There was the noise from the kitchen where the dinner dishes were being washed and there was the sound of his lighter as he lit his cigarette and there was nothing else, only the steady sound of his breathing as he smoked and the early-winter wind that twisted and turned the creaky, rusty weathervane on the roof of the barn to his right. Despite all the snow it was not cold. Or maybe it was the booze. He was immune to the cold when he was drunk.

He finished one cigarette and lit another. Above him a light went on upstairs and sent light out onto the snow and he knew from his brief time living here that this was Claire putting Jonah to bed.

Behind him the door opened and he half turned, expecting to see Charlie, but instead it was his mother. She gave an exaggerated shiver and pulled her small sweater closer around her. She moved and stood next to him.

'I don't know how you stand the cold,' she said.

'I don't think about it.'

'You remind me of Charles right now.'

'It's the smoking.'

'Yes,' said Charlotte. 'There's that. Standing on the porch, smoking in the cold. That was your father all right. But it's more the way you look. The way you are staring into the woods. Searching.'

Owen smiled at her. Dragged on his cigarette. 'I wouldn't read that much into it,' he said. 'I'm just not that deep.'

'Oh, I think you are,' said Charlotte. 'Deeper than you even know. You were always more soulful than your brother. And I don't mean that as an insult to Charlie. You just were. Love and life come easier for him, that's all. He isn't as verbal as you so I think that is sometimes mistaken for introspection. But you wonder and think about things. You have a harder time forgiving. Forgetting. We all do, of course. But sometimes, too, we need to let go.'

Owen field-stripped his cigarette, sending the cherry tip out into the yard, putting the spent filter back into the pack he kept in his breast pocket. 'Sounds like the wine talking, Charlotte,' he said. 'Trust me, I'm fine.'

'All I'm saying,' said Charlotte, 'is that you can't fool your mother.'

Owen turned to his mother. 'Give me a hug,'

he said. 'I'm going home.'

Charlotte moved toward him and he took her in his arms and hugged her briefly, and when they separated he saw that her eyes were wet and he wanted to say something but there was nothing. Only silence, only the sound of the wind.

★   ★   ★

That night, after Owen returned home, he sat for a while on the front steps of the trailer and he looked out to the gap in the trees where he could see the stars, bright and close in the near-winter night. Though his head was swimming from the gluttony of food and drink, he nursed a final bourbon and smoked his cigarettes and watched the night sky and the black spruce loom over him and he listened to the sounds of the forest on the mountain behind him. The groan and creak of the trees, the spooky cry of unknown animals that was the deep Vermont woods at night. It was cold but the density of the trees kept out the wind that rustled the branches high above. He drank and he smoked and he studied the blinking stars, almost as tangible as they were on the open sea, yet still ineffable to the point where he thought he should not stare at them too long. When he looked away he remembered his father's words: 'Don't think too much on what you can never understand. Focus instead on the small mysteries. What we can know. What we can hold in our hands. This is all that counts.'

And as he thought this, he turned his attention

207

to the day now past, to his mother, and to Charlie, to the old house on Signal Ridge that they collectively pretended held no significance. A house that did not hide the truth of the past, as if it were any other house on any other hill in Eden, his brother's residence and nothing more. Not the place of his childhood. Not the place where in the woods on a rainy afternoon his father had blown his head off with a single shot from a deer rifle.

He took a long pull of his bourbon and he saw in his mind his brother's wife, Claire. Saw her in front of the oven as he had seen her earlier that day, kneeling down to check on the progress of the roast. Saw her brush the hair out of her eyes, saw the shape of her through her clothes, and for the first time it occurred to him that they had more in common than he had previously imagined. They were both a part of this family yet somehow outside it. Claire because she was not born to it, had moved into it through Charlie, steady, capable Charlie, Charlie who acted as if everything happened the way it did because that was how it was meant to be. And he, Owen, because he refused to acknowledge that any of it mattered any more. He had seen too much, been too many places. He had tasted too many things, lived longer and harder than a man of his years should. He had stopped believing. And the truth was that while he could return to Eden, on some vital level Eden could never return to him.

14

That was the winter when the two brothers reached an unspoken accord around how they would share the small town of their birth. It should not have been difficult. Charlie was perfectly willing to let the years wash away, to return to how, in his mind, things should have evolved all along. He had no concerns about sharing the restaurant, as long as the years he had spent shaping Charlotte's into his own image were taken into account. He had no concerns about sharing his life with Owen, about bringing him closer to his family, to his work. In fact, when Owen first returned, Charlie thought that this was how it would happen. He thought Owen would become the friend he had never had all these years he'd been married both to his wife and to the business. He saw the two of them getting right back into it, as they had as children, playing and hunting and fishing and, yes, cooking, together. It never occurred to him that there was another way, and the only thing he worried about was how Claire would adapt to having his younger brother around. There were two of them and then there were three, and now he was asking her to allow room for a fourth. And a fourth who was also a chef, like her.

Still, even after it became clear that Owen intended to strike out on his own and build his own life amongst these hills, Charlie found himself trying hard to reach out, to understand his brother, to fulfill the promise of the lifetime friendship they had seemed destined for until it was all blown up so many years ago.

On Sundays, nights when none of them had to work, Charlie insisted that Owen come to dinner, and mostly he did. Some nights he simply did not show and since he did not have a phone, Charlie had no way of knowing until he arrived whether or not he would be there. But more often than not he showed and the three of them ate a late dinner after Jonah was in bed and they drank wine and they talked.

Sometimes Owen would stay late and they would sit in front of the woodstove and nurse Scotches, and on these nights whatever tension existed between them went away and they would wander back to earlier times, to silly stories about school as kids, about growing up in the restaurant, about their parents and their parents' friends, the drunken parties that in the early days of Eden filled the lawn behind the house they sat in. They were archetypal family stories, the kind every family has, and in the telling of them the two brothers grew closer together and this pleased Charlie. If Claire felt excluded from this bonding she did not show it. Instead she asked questions to keep a story going and she'd laugh when they did, the three of them shaking their heads with the knowledge of it all.

One beautiful January morning, Owen appeared in the kitchen window while Claire and Charlie were having coffee and he held up a pair of snowshoes at his brother. Charlie smiled and looked at his wife.

'What are you waiting for?' she said. 'Go ahead.'

Charlie suited up and joined his brother out on the snowy pasture. The sky was cloudless, the sun bright and high. Though it was cold the air was invigorating and their breath showed when they spoke. The snow in front of them sparkled like a field of crystals.

They set out toward the forest, not downhill toward where they had found their father, but uphill, behind the house, heading across what was once the apple orchard toward the high woods. The snowshoes moved effortlessly across the deep snow, and they used cross-country ski poles for balance.

Owen led and Charlie followed and they did not speak and the only sound was the steady crunch of the snow under the large aluminum snowshoes. Soon they had reached the woods' edge and the house was below them now, and they stopped for a moment before they hiked into the trees and watched the smoke spilling out of the chimney of the old farmhouse, the bright sky and the frosty mountains beyond it.

'Ready?' said Owen.

'You're the one with the pack-a-day habit,' Charlie said.

Owen laughed. 'Just for that, we're going all the way to Blue Pond.'

They entered the forest now, and it was mostly white birch and beech here, trees that dated from the turn of the century, trees that were

211

surprisingly tall and slender given their age. But they were trees that grew from fire and in the light that filtered down their bare branches and on to the unfettered snow covering the forest floor they were beautiful. In front of them was the closest thing to a path, not a deer run exactly but a place where the trees formed a natural canopy. The snow below them was white and unmarked by animals. It was a steady pitch upward and they went quickly, Charlie marveling at his brother's strength, strength that did not make sense given how Owen spent his nights, how he treated his body.

They climbed steadily and soon they were among groves of dense spruce, darker in here, and they picked up a deer run, the path worn with tracks, pebbly pockets of shit here and there on either side, bark missing from the trees from the spring rut. The land flattened and the run was wide enough that they were able to walk side by side.

'When's the last time you were up here?' Owen said.

'For ever,' said Charlie.

'Me too. I used to come here with Jill Cormier. Do you remember her?'

'Yeah. She's still around. Married with kids, I think. Lives in Walden.'

'We used to hike up to Blue Pond and smoke pot and skinny-dip off those rocks, those great rocks. On the western side. Then we'd lay out a blanket and screw in the hot sun. Talk about not caring about anything. Nothing mattered then.'

'I know it,' said Charlie, laughing. 'Especially

for you. You were the one who got all the girls. I remember how I was always Owen's brother. 'Aren't you Owen's brother?' Didn't seem fair.'

'Well it comes around,' Owen said, leaning back for a moment as the trail began to climb again. 'Now I'm Charlie's brother.'

'I don't know about that,' Charlie said.

'Charlie's no-good brother,' Owen said.

'No one thinks that,' Charlie said quickly.

'Except for your wife.'

Charlie stopped, breathing hard from the exertion. He leaned on one of his poles, looked at his brother, his brother with the long hair, the scraggly beard, the jawline he envied. 'What do you mean by that?'

Owen started to walk again, lifting each leg high, placing the large shoe down on the deep snow beneath. 'She doesn't like me,' he said.

'That's not true,' said Charlie, catching up. 'What makes you think that?'

'I can tell. I know women.'

'Well, I know Claire and she's never said anything like that to me.'

'It's not always what they say. It's what they do. What they show you with their eyes, their body language. She doesn't like me. I can tell.'

'I think she's probably just not used to having my brother around. That's all.'

'Blue Pond?' said Owen, changing the subject. 'I'm not sure you're up to it.'

'Catch me,' Owen said.

★ ★ ★

213

They made good time over the top of Signal Ridge. The winter light fought through the heavy evergreens and in front of them the woods were as they should be, snow-covered, and in places where there were small clearings the sun reflected brightly off the white of the pack. The forest was quiet, except for the insistent pressing of their snowshoes and the sound of their breathing. Once, before the ridgeline, they startled a hare, and they watched as it ran from them, a jagged bounding run through the high snow before it disappeared from their view.

Soon they had crested the large hill and they stopped. In front of them were more woods and the land swooped down away from them and though they could not see it, they knew that it rose again to the next ridge, and beyond that, another ridge. This land was a series of high ridges, mountain foothills leading to the west. Behind them, when they turned around, they could see where they had come from and they could see beyond to where the valley that was Eden proper resided, though they could not see the valley itself. Above it all rose the curved horn of Camel's Hump Mountain, white with snow against the deep blue of the sky.

From the pocket of his coat Owen took out a metal flask and unscrewed the top. He put it to his lips and sipped from it.

'What kind of rotgut are you drinking now?' said Charlie.

'Bourbon,' Owen said and handed the flask to his brother.

'What the hell,' Charlie said and drank from it.

It was sharp and sweet and warm but it tasted good. He took another pull and handed it back.

Owen drank from it and then he lighted a cigarette. The smoke spilled out of his mouth and nose and into the thin air.

'When you going to give them up?' said Charlie.

'As soon as you stop asking me,' Owen said.

'Well, if you're going to smoke, then I'm going to beat you to the pond,' Charlie said and he began to walk again. He did not look back to see if his brother was following him and he did not have to for he would hear the sound of his footfalls.

The escarpment was steep and he felt it in his legs, muscles he did not use every day. The tree cover was heavier as he went down and the air was suddenly cold and there was less light. In places the going was tricky, snow mixed with ice underfoot, and Charlie had to fix the claw of each shoe before moving forward.

When he reached the bottom, he turned and looked behind him. No sign of Owen. Charlie smiled to himself and he began the ascent over the next ridge, the one that led to Blue Pond.

By the time he reached the top, he was out of breath and he stopped for a moment and stuck his poles into the snow and rested his gloved hands on his knees. When the wind came back to him, he looked down and he could see the pond now, not blue at all but white and ice-covered. It was beautiful nonetheless, the forest walls moving up and away from it, a small hidden mountain lake. It had been a long time since he had been to it and he could never hike here without thinking of his father, who had taken them to the pond one summer morning when they were still young boys, forcing them along on the difficult walk. When they reached the shore, he told them that the lake contained a giant prehistoric fish, capable of eating children. Charlie remembered staring at the black water, wondering if it was lurking there, staring back at up them, waiting to rise from the depths. It was not until he was in his teens that he realised the story was nonsense, a story fathers told children to scare them away from swimming here on their own.

The memory of this energised Charlie, and he grabbed his poles and began to hike down the hill. The trees thinned out here and the sun was bright and he made good time. He looked back to see if he could see his brother but he could not. About halfway down the ridge, he was below the lake and he lost sight of it. He went quickly, one shoe in front of the other, using the poles to propel him along. He had a second wind and soon he was at the bottom and all that lay between him and Blue Pond was a small hillock dense with evergreens.

He charged up it, the path narrowing considerably through the trees, and as he hiked he listened again for Owen but his was the only sound in the woods. So much for beating me here, Charlie thought.

Finally he rounded the bend that led to the lake and there it was, the flat expanse of snow-covered water, a lake of resounding beauty in the summer months, stark and bare in the winter, the bottom of a bowl.

When he reached where the trees ended and the broad rocky shoreline began, he was so fixated on what was in front of him, the lake and the forest walls rising up on the opposite shore, that he heard his brother before he saw him. He turned to his left and in front of him was Owen, sitting on a rock as if he had been there for a while, smoking a cigarette, the flask of whiskey propped on his thigh, leaning against his jacket. It was his laughter Charlie had heard, a low, throaty chuckle.

'You made it,' Owen said.

Charlie just stood there looking at him. He shook his head. 'What, did you fly here?'

'I went around,' said Owen. 'It's a lot steeper but if you move it it can be faster.'

Charlie went to his brother, sat next to him. He pointed at the whiskey. 'Give me that.'

Owen handed him the flask and Charlie sipped long and hard from it. He looked at Owen and smiled. 'I got to hand it to you,' he said. 'I thought I'd left you in the dust.'

'And not for the first time,' said Owen.

★ ★ ★

That night at Charlotte's, Charlie could already feel the soreness that the morning would bring. But he felt awake and alive from the vigorous exercise. It was a slow night for Charlotte's, and he turned out a basic menu for the restaurant. A rack of lamb with a

217

marjoram wine sauce was the big seller.

Back at the house, Claire had made a polenta with pancetta and parmesan and it was hearty and warm and they ate in front of the woodstove with a rich red wine and watched the fire as it glowed behind the glass. Charlie normally stayed up after she went to bed, trying to wind down from the night of cooking, but tonight he followed her to bed and for the first time in a long time he rolled into her and lit only by the full winter moon, he made love to her.

Charlie did not know why their lovemaking had become occasional at best. They did not talk about it. Sometimes he chalked it up to their schedules, to having a child, but he knew it was more than that. They had grown stale with one another and he did not know how to breathe life into their sex. He still found her beautiful, remarkably so. Some mornings he'd watch her walking around the bedroom in her nightgown and the sight of her stirred him, her breasts loose under the thin cotton, the light framing her body for him. And then there was her great tumble of hair, how she combed it after she showered, letting it hang in her face, bent over, all of her beautiful and wet and ageless.

The times they did make love it was perfunctory, all business, Charlie sliding into her while she lay on her side, moving together without patience until they both finished.

Tonight, though, it was as if they were who they were many years ago, many years ago when she first came to the restaurant and he wanted nothing more than to linger over her, to let his hands play over her, to make love to her. Oh, how she seemed to want it, slow sometimes, fast others, but always engaged, their eyes locked together, their loving words echoing back and forth until their bodies went slack in each other's arms. Tonight, though, he climbed on top of her and she said, I love the weight of you and Charlie looked down at her dark eyes, the slight roundness of her mouth as it opened when he pushed into her, and with his hands he reached underneath her and pulled her as far on to him as he could. Claire stretched her arms above her head and with one hand Charlie held both hers together and in this way he loved her until he had nothing left and spent himself inside her.

They came apart. Lay together looking at the ceiling. Charlie caught his breath and then said, 'That was something.'

'Yes.'

'I love you,' he said.

'I love you too,' said Claire.

For a while they did not speak. Outside the window Charlie could see the smoke from the chimney caught in the moonlight as it drifted up and out over the valley. He could see the bright full moon, all alone in the black sky. He could hear Claire's steady breathing next to him. And he could hear the sound of the wind as it came against the old house, not like it was in a storm but still there, the slight creak of old wood and old walls. An old house moving and shifting in the world.

After a time, Charlie turned and looked at his wife. She was awake, clearly so, and as he turned she turned too and caught his eyes with her own. She looked at him in such a way that he wanted to tell her everything, tell her all that he knew and all that he thought she should know. He wanted to tell her what he had learned, though when he stopped to try to put words to it, all he knew was that there was not much there. Not much that she did not know already. On some level this bothered him. He wanted to share secrets, to tell her how things worked, but he understood, as all men come to understand, that no one ever sees completely how things work and that all there is to do is pretend. Play the game as if everything is dripping in significance. Proceed in the only manner we know how, for to do different is to acknowledge that our lives do not matter, that there are no choices, there are only endings and they happen as they do without any interference from us.

Instead what Charlie told her was what Owen had told him earlier, standing on a snow-filled ridgeline looking at the sun. He said, 'Owen thinks you don't like him.'

'He said that?'

From her tone Charlie sensed that he had made a mistake. He plugged on anyway. 'Pretty much. I don't want to put words in his mouth. But he worries about it.'

Claire sighed and as she did her breasts rose beneath the comforter. 'That's bullshit,' she said.

'I know.'

'You do?'

'Yeah.'

Claire looked toward the window, toward the

night. 'I like your brother, Charlie, I do. Maybe 'like' is the wrong word. He's your brother. I mean, that gives him a place in our lives that I cannot control. He's never done anything to offend me. He's never given me a hard time.'

'Hardly a ringing endorsement,' said Charlie. 'I'll talk to him.'

'No, don't. Really. I shouldn't have brought it up. I shouldn't have. I really shouldn't have. It was a mistake.'

Claire stared at him and then her eyes looked away, towards the foot of the bed. 'I will. I'll talk to him. Don't worry, I'll be nice. You know how I am. I don't believe in tiptoeing around things. I say what I think. But I'll do it at a time when it's right. He's my brother-in-law. That means something.'

Through the darkness Charlie nodded. 'I wish you wouldn't.'

'That isn't good enough,' said Claire.

'Let's go to sleep,' he said.

And after he said it, he slid down next to her and he hugged her, his face nuzzling against her neck. Claire put her arms around his neck and they stayed this way until he rolled away. His snoring came quick and heavy, through his nose. Outside the full moon cast its deep white glow across the snowy fields, woods and valleys of Eden. Soon it would be morning, the sun would rise in place of the moon and there would be the shocking white of winter and the bluest of skies. For now, though, it was dark. Dark and quiet. The world around them slept.

15

In the morning, Claire stood in the cold, clear air at the end of the long driveway and waited for the yellow school bus to makes its way down the hill and pick up Jonah. It was a ritual they shared together every morning when it was not summer. They stood and looked up the hill and held hands and they could see their breath in the air. Then the bus would round the corner and she'd pick her son up in her arms, give him a kiss, knowing that soon the time would come when she would embarrass him, as her parents had embarrassed her, but that for now he was young enough to take her affection, to genuinely miss her when he walked up those steps, turning around for a moment before disappearing into the depths of the bus.

When the bus had pulled away she waited until she could not see it any more, and then she began the slow, long walk up the driveway to the house. Inside, she warmed herself in front of the stove before she set to making Charlie his breakfast. It was some of the only cooking she did now during the week and the simplicity of it pleased her. Of seeing eggs sunny-side up in the pan, of listening to the toast click with the sound of bread that was done. Of smelling the local bacon as it snapped in the pan. The whole kitchen full of smells and sounds while her husband still slept upstairs.

When everything was done, she climbed the staircase and wandered into their bedroom and woke Charlie. He was a good sleeper and he always came to slowly, and when he rubbed his eyes and looked at the winter sun streaming through the window, she told him breakfast was ready. That it was time to go.

By the time he came downstairs, freshly showered, Claire was ready with his mug of strong black coffee, and she sat him down and fed him, and they ate with the silence of morning and it was the life of a housewife, a life she had never wanted, but one that on weekdays she resigned herself to. Soon he would put on his coat and she would watch his truck leave the driveway, the exhaust gray in the cold and spilling into the air as he went. She would wait until he was gone. She would let him go where she wanted to be, to Charlotte's, to a kitchen full of promise, to a day spent preparing to create, a day that no longer belonged to her.

★　★　★

Once he was gone, Claire took a shower. The water was hot and she stayed under it for a time, washed her hair, and for a minute she considered touching herself but then decided against it. Afterward, she dressed, putting on a black turtleneck and jeans, and downstairs she put on her winter boots and her coat.

Outside the sun was now high in the sky and there were no clouds. She climbed into her car and began to drive, down Signal Ridge, and then picked up the Old County Road. She passed cars and trucks as she drove on the dirt roads and the drivers all waved, the way people did in Eden, and she waved back.

She was on her way to Owen's, and though she had never been there, she knew where it was. The Hunger Mountain Road was a road that she used to drive on with Charlie, long ago, long ago on summer nights when the air was warm and they rode in his truck with the windows down and followed the curve of the earth up and over the eastern side of the mountain. It was a drive she loved back then, back then when they were young and first together, back when they wanted nothing more than to just be together and a truck on an empty mountain road in the quiet summer dark was the perfect way to do that.

By the time she pulled into Owen's driveway — seeing for the first time the small Silver stream trailer, looking small and buried in high snow — it was almost eleven. She had no idea what his schedule was, though his truck was here, next to several cords of stacked wood protected by a large blue tarpaulin. She pulled in behind it. Got out of the car. She suddenly got a sense of altitude, of space beyond the trees and when she looked she realised she could see halfway across Eden, to other mountains in the distance. Somewhere below her was Charlotte's, she thought to her west but she did not have her bearings. Claire took a deep breath and went to the door.

She knocked lightly and listened. Nothing. She knocked again, a little more assertively this time, and was about to knock again when it opened. In front of her stood Owen, wearing only a pair of jeans, shirtless and without shoes. He moved his shaggy hair out of his face. Claire looked away.

'I woke you,' she said.

'Don't be silly. I needed to get up anyway. Come in.'

Owen stepped away from the door and Claire climbed up into the trailer, and it was dark and it took a moment for her eyes to adjust. On her left was the woodstove and on the right a small kitchenette. Beyond it was a living room and then his bed. It smelled of wood smoke and cigarettes, the ripeness of old beer.

'You can put your coat on the chair,' Owen said.

'Thanks,' said Claire. She took off her coat and slung it over one of the chairs that surrounded a card table.

'You want some coffee? Tea?'

'Are you having any?'

'Coffee,' he said.

'Sure.'

'Have a seat,' he said.

Claire pulled out one of the chairs and sat down. Owen still had not put a shirt on, and while he made coffee Claire could not help but watch him. He was tall and lean and his long torso was wiry and heavily muscled. Unlike Charlie, he did not have a hairy chest, and the only hair was a small ribbon from his navel heading into his jeans. He was beautiful, like a man in a magazine, and this had never attracted her and she felt she could be objective about his beauty. She knew it was important that she did not see him how she understood women easily came to see him, as someone whose slightest gesture suggested sex.

Owen ground coffee beans and the sound filled the small trailer. Claire watched as he boiled water, and poured from the kettle through a sieve into a stainless-steel container. He filled two mugs and brought them over to the table.

'I hope black is okay,' he said. 'I don't keep any milk or cream in the house.'

'Black is fine,' said Claire.

Owen sat down across from her. He sat with his legs slightly open and he still wore no shirt and for the first time she noticed his tattoo: it was on his chest above his right nipple, a small black umbrella.

'I like your tattoo,' she said.

Owen looked down. 'Oh, yeah. You know, in case it rains.'

Claire laughed in spite of herself. A nervous laugh. He made her nervous. Uncomfortable. As if she were not a woman of her age, as if she were not fully in control. 'How long have you had it?'

Owen shrugged. 'I don't know. Ten, fifteen years? I got it in the Philippines.'

Claire nodded and sipped her coffee. She did not know where to put her gaze. She wanted to take it off his body, but looking at his green eyes was almost worse. They were narrow and intense and shocking in their brightness, brighter than a man's eyes should be. The eyes of a cat.

'So,' Owen said. 'Not that you need a reason, but why the visit? What's on your mind?'

Claire looked across at him. 'I just — I just wanted you to know that whatever you might think about how I feel about you, I don't dislike you. I know you've probably gotten that impression, but we're family now and I for one am happy that you came home.'

Owen did not say anything for a moment and then he began to laugh. A big hearty laugh. He shook his head.

'What?' said Claire.

'No, it's sweet, it really is.'

'Listen, I came over here to be nice. To clear up any misunderstanding.'

'There's no misunderstanding.'

'Good,' Claire said.

'Terrific,' said Owen, his tone cocky and condescending, and Claire thought, maybe I spoke too soon. He was being an asshole.

'I didn't come here to get laughed at,' she said.

'I'm not laughing at you, Claire.'

'Well, it sure feels that way.'

'No,' Owen said. 'I'm not. Listen, I appreciate you coming out here, I do. It's the family thing. That's all. It's not about you. The idea that I have a family still strikes me as, well, not possible. Charlie's my brother and I love him. And I love my mother. But a family is a whole other thing. Something that we stopped being a long time ago.'

Claire thought about this. 'I'm not sure any family is anything more than a collection of people that happen to be related to each other.'

'Anyway,' Owen said, as if that was all, that nothing else needed to be said.

Claire stood. 'Thanks for the coffee,' she said.

'Stay,' Owen said, and his voice was softer now, soft enough that she almost sat back down.

'I should go,' she said, and she put on her coat.

'I'm serious,' he said. 'Stay. I'll be nice. I promise. Plus, I don't get many visitors.'

'That's not what I hear,' Claire said.

'Ouch,' said Owen.

'I'm sorry, I didn't mean anything by that.'

'Please stay. Sit.'

Claire did as he said. She removed her coat and sat back down.

'You need more light in here,' she said.

'Yeah. I guess I'm used to it. Not many windows on a boat.'

'I don't think I could handle that.'

'You can get used to anything, I think. With enough time.'

'You like living by yourself?'

'I do. I wouldn't be much good at living with someone else. I like my freedom too much.'

'So you'll never get married?'

Owen smiled. 'Oh, no,' he said. 'That I won't.'

'Never say never, right?'

He leaned his elbows on the table and moved across toward her, tipped his head. 'I can say never on that one. Some things you just know.'

Claire laughed. 'And what about all the hearts you're breaking in Eden?'

'What hearts?'

'All these waitresses and local girls I hear about.'

'Ah, those,' said Owen, rubbing his chin as if

considering this. 'You shouldn't listen to town gossip, you know. I'm celibate up here. I'm like a monk.'

'Right,' said Claire.

Owen leaned back and took a cigarette out of a pack Claire hadn't noticed sitting on the table. He lighted it and inhaled. The smoke filled the air above her and normally she hated cigarette smoke but for some reason now it did not bother her. 'It's true,' he said, taking his empty hand and laying it over his heart. 'I swear.'

'Okay, I believe you.'

'What about you? You got something on the side?'

'Excuse me?'

'The grocery boy or something.'

'Oh, please,' Claire said and feigned astonishment but in truth she found herself oddly flattered by this. As if she was the kind of woman who would have affairs. 'I'm happily married, thank you.'

Owen shrugged. 'Married, I knew, happy, I wouldn't have guessed.'

'I like being married.'

Owen looked at her intently. 'Do you though?'

'What do you mean?'

'I look at you and I see,' said Owen, pausing for a moment and looking away, taking a drag of his cigarette. 'A woman bored. Maybe it's more than that, but bored, yes. See, I look at you and sometimes I see myself. The wanderlust. The need to be free, unattached. To be able to do what you want. Am I right?'

Claire was stunned. She glared at him and

wanted to say 'Where do you get off?' but she knew inside herself that he spoke the truth, that what she thought she kept hidden, in the place she allowed nobody to see, was as accessible to his view as her hair or her eyes. And this was where, she thought, any brotherly similarities ended. Charlie loved her, she knew that, but he was unaware of what this life was like for her, how she envied him. And for this reason, for his ability to suddenly see her she really was, Claire found herself telling Owen the truth.

She said, 'Yes, you're right.'

Owen smiled. He stubbed his cigarette out in the ashtray and leaned forward. His voice was almost a whisper as he said to her, 'What is it you want? What is missing?'

'I don't know.'

'You don't know, or you don't want to say you know.'

Claire looked at his hands on the table in front of her. Strong hands, prominent veins. She looked at his beautiful face, his eyes. Part of her wanted to rise out of her seat then, go to him, have him take her into his strong arms, have him make love to her the way she knew without having experienced it that he was capable of. She knew he would hold nothing back, would let loose all of himself on to her, and this was all she wanted. He was that kind of man and it thrilled her at the same time it scared her.

'I don't want anything,' said Claire.

'You mean, you won't say,' Owen said.

Claire looked away and was silent.

'It's okay,' said Owen. 'You don't have to say anything to me.'

'Jesus, you're my husband's brother.'

'Don't think of it that way. Really. You can talk to me. I mean that.'

Claire began to speak and then stopped. 'You're right. I am bored. I keep thinking there must be more and it drives me crazy that there isn't. And I'm a shitty mother, I really am. I work at it, I do. But I hate that Charlie gets to go to work every day, do what he loves and I stay home. It sounds so selfish, I know.'

'Not to me it doesn't.'

'No?'

'No, it sounds natural. I couldn't live without control over my own life,' said Owen.

Claire thought about this. 'Freedom is what it is.'

'Freedom to make up your own mind.'

'Yeah, I guess that's it,' Claire said and she reached for her coffee cup now and realised it was empty.

'More coffee?' Owen asked.

'I should go now,' said Claire, and she stood and put on her coat.

Owen rose as well and for a moment Claire looked up at his face, and she saw something different then, not the cockiness or the almost feminine beauty. Something different. A vulnerability, perhaps. But before she could put a finger on it, it was gone and he was the same man he was when she arrived.

'Let's do this again,' Owen said and he smiled.

Claire smiled back. She nodded. 'Okay,' she said.

'I'd walk you out but I don't have a shirt on.'

'I think I can make it,' said Claire.

'Bye then,' Owen said.

Claire opened the door and walked out into the bright sunshine. She heard the door close behind her and she stood for a moment and looked through the gap in the trees to the leafless hills in the distance. Bright, bright winter sunshine. She climbed into her car. She did not look back. She did not want to see Owen in the window watching her go.

★ ★ ★

On her way home, Claire stopped by the restaurant. The snow was high up the walls on the outside and beyond it the river was obscured by banks of snow that rose above it. She found Charlie and when he saw her come through the swinging doors he smiled wide and she was happy to see him.

'Hey,' he said.

Claire went to where he stood at the stove, wrapped her arms around him from behind.

'What are you doing?' he said.

'Hugging my husband, is that okay?'

'Of course,' he said. 'Though I'm making risotto.'

Claire let him go and moved next to him and then they said it in unison, words that came across the years from Charlie's father, a mantra almost. 'There are no shortcuts. Risotto waits for

232

no one. It is done when it decides to be, not when you wish it to be.'

They laughed. Claire looked down into the large Dutch oven at the rice taking on the stock, Charlie's spoon moving aggressively around the bottom of the pan, stirring it up. It was a bright red color and seeing this Claire said, 'Seafood?'

'Yeah. Scallops and shrimp and mussels. Lobster stock, big splash of cognac.'

Claire stuck a finger into the pot then, into the stock, granules of underdone rice clinging to the sides of her finger. She brought it to her mouth. 'Oh, that's good,' she said.

'Rich.'

'Very.'

'So what are you up to?'

'I was just up at your brother's.'

Charlie turned to his side, looked at her, still stirring vigorously. 'Claire,' he said.

'I know. I had to. It was fine, really.'

'What did he say?'

'Nothing, really. We had coffee. Talked. It was nice. He showed me his tattoo.'

Charlie shook his head. 'Owen has a tattoo?'

'Yup. A better question would be where is it.'

'Oh, no, you're kidding me.'

'Yes, I am. It's on his chest.'

'Well, he was a sailor.'

Claire said, 'It's an umbrella.'

'That's interesting.'

'I thought so.'

'The day my father, you know. It was pouring out. Raining almost as hard as it was during the flood.'

'I see,' said Claire. 'Well, he was nice.'

'I'm glad about that. Will you hand me the mussels?'

Claire turned and found a big bowl of cleaned and bearded mussels on the wooden table. She handed them to Charlie and he dumped them into the Dutch oven and let them sit on top of the rice, and in a few minutes Claire knew they would open and spill their liquor, flavoring the risotto with the musky essence of the sea. 'I have to get Jonah,' she said.

'Give me a kiss,' said Charlie.

Claire leaned up and kissed her tall husband, then she patted him softly on the shoulder and left him to his risotto. Outside she drove the snowy roads of Eden and as she did, in her mind she kept seeing the small black umbrella on Owen's chest. And though she had always known what had happened that day long ago, she suddenly felt its weight. She could see it in her mind with a vividness that filled her with sadness. Two brothers in the rain, carrying what was left of their father out of the woods. Water all around them. Water whose purpose in the world was to cleanse and purify, to renew. Water that might have washed away the blood from the base of an old tree, but on that day took little else with it, left everything else behind for time to sort out. Claire wondered if it ever could.

16

There are times in life when the world decides to reveal itself to you. Moments of utter transparent awareness when you see things as they always have been, as they always will be, and you try to find comfort by finding your place in the vastness of it all. And surely, you realise there can be no comfort, for when you look deep into the nature of it all you see only yourself and you see the smallness that is you, the insignificance, and any search you have for something larger, something greater, something that will make that which can never be understood as clear as water, will end in frustration, and if you are not careful, despair or worse.

On his small patch of earth on the side of Hunger Mountain, Owen Bender sat in a lawn chair and watched winter slowly become spring. He watched the first of the snow begin to melt under the heat of a sun that grew palpably stronger with each passing day. Streams forming in the woods around him where there had never been streams before. Water rushing everywhere. Great arteries of water that in time would feed the lakes and the rivers and eventually flow to the sea, the sea that he once called his home.

In his chair those afternoons before he had to be at the bar, Owen sat and drank cold beer and smoked cigarettes and he saw the geese return in the sky above. He heard the songbirds return to the trees and he listened to the trickling of water off the roof of the trailer. He listened to the snowmelt move through the forest. He heard cars and trucks sloshing through the mud on the road below. And he thought about things. Again and again he returned in his mind to the Charlotte's of his youth. To the image of his father in front of the large wooden table dicing vegetables, boning fish. His father whom he wanted nothing more than to please, his father whose approval he craved. The image of his mother in the front, his mother with the sun-kissed hair and the eyes he'd inherited from her. And he saw himself and Charlie, insepa-rable, working, always working, helping out, brothers and best friends, united by both blood and obligation. Of course he had known that nothing lasted for ever, that this life of theirs, this family, would inevitably change, as they all do. Still, when he thought back on it what he remembered was wholeness, and certainty, and a period in his life when the future seemed as distant as the stars. He did not see his father leaving them the way he had, and he did not see what would happen after, when it was as if the center could no longer hold and he was sent spinning out into the world to find his place.

Only he never did. He went to the farthest corners of the earth on giant ships, and he saw that on the most fundamental level it was all the same. People struggling with the minutiae of everyday living, of eating and drinking and shitting and sleeping. People who spoke different languages but slept under the same sky. Sure,

236

things were different, different in ways one would imagine, but no matter where he went, he discovered that he was always alone. Even when he was with others, even when he found some strange woman to take to his bed. Especially then. For though he lay with these women, for though they let him inside them, Owen never felt love, or connection, or anything deeper than the mutual pleasure the sex provided. Yes, he loved their bodies, and the sound of their voices, and the warmth of their skin against his own. But when they left, when they kissed him softly on the lips and spoke to him in words he often could not understand, he felt relieved, glad to see them go, so he could return to all he truly knew: himself.

Sometimes he blamed Charlotte's for this. When you grow up in a restaurant like they had, it becomes the entirety of your life. You do not have friends like others do. You have the work and those who share the work with you and as long as these things stay around, you are fine. For all of them, Charlotte's was their moorings. This was where he figured he and Charlie diverged, for Charlie was still tethered to it, still finding the beauty in the place and the food and a woman who felt the same way about it all as he did. The structure and meaning it gave to each day. It was Owen and his mother who were thrown out.

Owen did not blame Charlie for any of this. It was true that sometimes he grew angry, especially on days he did not work when he sat in the trailer or out on the chair and drank the time away until a bitterness came over him that he could not shake. But no, he did not blame Charlie. Charlie was doing precisely what he was supposed to do, what had been handed to him as the chosen one. Owen blamed his father, his father whom he had tried so hard to emulate, only to have him in death take away the one thing that made sense in life. He did not expect to get any of it back. And he did not expect to exact revenge of any kind. Life was not that tidy. But he wanted something. And that spring, while all around him winter gave itself up to the inevitability of its own demise, he listened to water flow like rain and he tried to understand what would make him whole, what he wanted, what he needed.

★ ★ ★

And so winter begat spring and spring became summer. These were the longest days of the year and the time of year when Eden met the promise of its name, its hills full of deep, lush green, new growth everywhere, the woods alive with sound, a rainforest with homes. Owen's days had a rhythm to them, waking late, coffee and breakfast, a light lunch, beer and cigarettes in front of the trailer, work. Some nights he slept alone, other nights he did not and on Sundays he made his way over to Charlie's for dinner.

He had grown to like these dinners more than he cared to admit. Perhaps it was because it was the season of optimism, the bright northern sun staying in the sky for what seemed like for ever, finally setting behind the mountains, filling the blue with color before it faded to black. And there was the food, always exceptional, and lots of drink and long nights after the boy was in bed of sitting on the old porch and looking at the stars and the moon and talking. Telling stories and talking. Trading stories with his brother and more important, with Claire, whom, Owen, if he had decided to be honest with himself, would have realised was the reason that he spent all week looking forward to Sunday.

She was different from other women he had known. She was beautiful, though that alone did not make her exceptional. Owen had known lots of beautiful women, had known them intimately, though he had not allowed more than a few to stay around long enough to have any effect on him. No, she was different, and it was not just her beauty, her dark eyes, her pale skin, her full breasts, the heavy curl of her long hair. It was something intangible about her; it was the fact that when she smiled at him he felt that the smile was for him and for him alone, as if she possessed about her a sincerity that he had never been around before. He thought that maybe this was what love felt like: a truth between people, a purity of expression and thought so honest that all artifice could not help but be peeled away, leaving only the sheer essence of a relationship behind it.

Of course, Owen never lost sight of the fact that Claire was his brother's wife. He could not. On those nights when they had dinner he saw them communicate with each other with the shorthand of husbands and wives; he saw their gentle touch to one another; he saw all of it and it served to remind him that he must give her distance regardless of what he felt, that she was off limits to him no matter how he felt about her.

Sometimes he wondered if he could have her: what it would be like to see her underneath him, to feel her body against his, to see her mouth open as he moved above her. He pictured this in his mind. He imagined her without clothes, what she looked like, all of her. He wondered if she was a good lover: if she would challenge him, push back at him as only the strong ones did. Or if she would disappear in his embrace, fall away from him and stay there until he released her. He thought about all these things and he knew on some level he should not but he could not help it. Claire had slowly taken a hold of him.

And then one evening Owen was at work in the kitchen at the bar, pressing burgers together for a rush that would not come, when Sue, one of the waitresses, stuck her head into the small place that he called his own six nights a week. She was a small dark-haired girl with bangs, no more than twenty-two, and she was one of the few who had not ever made it back to Hunger Mountain with him.

Sue said, 'Owen?'

'Yeah.'

'Phone.'

'Who is it?' Owen said, knowing that no one had ever called him at work.

'Some lady,' she said.

Owen wiped his hands on a towel and sighed.

240

What was this about? He went through the swinging doors and into the low-ceilinged bar area. A few regulars at the bar, men drinking Budweiser, some younger kids he did not recognise shooting pool. The Red Sox on the television. This was a Monday in late June and it was slow.

Owen went to the bar and Karen, an older woman who bartended early in the week, handed him the cordless phone. Owen nodded at her and took it, put it to his ear.

'Yes?' he said.

'Owen?'

'Claire,' he said softly, recognising her voice. He knew instantly that something was wrong, it was in the muffled way she said his name, as if she had been crying.

'I need your help,' she said. 'It's Charlie.'

His heart leapt in his chest. 'Charlie? What, Claire? What about Charlie?'

'He's okay, he is. He's going to be okay. He burned himself.'

'What kind of burn?'

'Oil. I don't know all the details. It's all over his left arm. Althea called me. Knocked over a pan full of oil he had used for deep-frying. It's pretty bad, Owen. They airlifted him down to Dartmouth.'

'Airlifted?'

'It's the closest burn unit. He's going to be fine. That's what they told me. But I need your help, Owen. I need to go down there. And someone needs to be here for Jonah. He's asleep and I'd ask Althea to do it but she drove to

241

Dartmouth already. I just need someone to be here in case he wakes up. Can you come?'

'Of course, of course. Shit, Claire, I'm sorry. Give me five minutes.'

Owen hung up the phone and told Karen at the bar that he was closing the kitchen. He told her the details quickly but in truth he did not want to talk about it, did not want to think about it. Once in his truck, he drove quickly down the dirt roads, the night warm and clear, the windows down, and he smoked as he went and he thought about his brother lying in a hospital bed. Owen knew the kitchen could be a dangerous place, just as boats were, and while both he and his brother and their father before them had always displayed nicks from knives on their hands and small burns from picking something up quickly, bar burns from cookie sheets on their forearms, none of them had ever been seriously hurt. Until now. And Charlie had ended up in the one place their father never would have gone. The hospital. Hospitals with their bright lights and cold floors, the ubiquitous sadness. Their father had ended his life not to be in such a place, and now Charlie was there because he had to be, because it was the only thing that could help him. All that had passed between them now fell away for Owen, and all he knew was that his brother needed him, his brother's wife needed him, and Owen could not remember the last time he had been needed by anyone.

Pulling into the long driveway on Signal Ridge, the headlights in front of him rose and fell with the bouncing of the rippled earth beneath. The trees tightly on either side of his truck. He pulled in front of the house. Owen got out of the truck, dropping his cigarette to the ground, crushing it with the heel of his boot. By the time he reached the porch, Claire was there, and she seemed so relieved to see him, he thought for a moment about hugging her, which was some-thing he had never done, and as soon as he thought it, she did it, wrapped her arms around him, and he held her for a brief moment and then they separated. Owen looked at his sister-in-law.

'Is he okay?' said Owen.

'Yes,' Claire said. 'He's hurt. They are going to do surgery. Skin grafts. It's a real bad burn. His whole arm. But it's not life-threatening and that's what counts.'

'He needs you.'

'Yes.'

'What do I need to know?'

'I put the number of the hospital on the fridge. Althea said she could come back. Jonah is asleep and he will sleep through the night.'

'Does he know anything about this?'

'Not yet. I didn't want to wake him.'

'All right.'

'I'll call. Just stay. Make yourself comfortable. And I can get Althea to come and take your place later if you — '

'No,' said Owen. 'I'll be fine. I can stay. Just go. Let me know how he is, okay?'

'Thank you,' said Claire and she hugged him again, quickly, and then she was gone into the night. Owen heard her car starting and he stood there until he saw her headlights moving out through the trees and down the drive, disappearing into the hills.

★ ★ ★

After she was gone, Owen walked through the doors and into the kitchen. It was dead quiet. There was the hum of the clock on the wall and other than that silence. He had not been in the house when it had been quiet like this since he was a child, and even then it was rare that he was alone. Upstairs Jonah slept without the knowledge of what had happened to his father and Owen wondered what he would tell him if he were to wake. Owen was not someone who related easily to children. They were a mystery to him, an annoyance that other adults had to deal with at certain times, and he tended to overlook them, the way he did when people had pets. It was not that he did not like children. If he were to think about it, he supposed he would think they were fine, cute and all that, but not his trouble, not his problem. Suddenly, his nephew was both. He needed a drink.

In the buffet in the dining room he found a half-empty bottle of Scotch and poured himself a generous tumblerful. He took a long pull of it and then began to walk. He moved through the living room and to the stairs. He stopped at the base of them and drank again from his Scotch and then he began to walk up the stairs, slowly, not wanting to wake the boy with the creak of the boards under his feet.

At the top of the stairs it was dark and it suddenly occurred to Owen that he had not been upstairs in this house since he was seventeen years old. He had spent his first time back in Eden here but he always slept in the small downstairs bedroom. Beyond that, there was never any reason for him to be anywhere but the kitchen or the dining room or the living room or the porch. He knew that Charlie and Claire slept in his parents' room, straight ahead from him, which meant that Jonah must be in the room Charlie and Owen had shared as boys. He moved toward it, quietly, one foot in front of the other.

When he reached the door, he put his hand on the knob and listened. Silence. He turned the handle and slowly opened the door, remembering that it creaked, and it did, slightly, but then it opened and he stood looking into the room he had slept in as a child. The moonlight streamed through the window that looked out over the pasture to the woods and on a single bed against the wall he could make out his nephew, curled into a fetal position, sleeping. Owen stood and watched the rise and fall of his soft snores. His eyes adjusted to the light but he could not make out Jonah's features and he might have been looking in on himself many years ago, lying in bed oblivious to things beyond his own life as a child. He wondered if the boy dreamed and what it was he dreamed of. Owen tried to remember dreams he had as a child and he could not. He wondered if he had dreamed at all and he thought he must have, for everyone dreams, but he did not remember any. He stood and watched the boy sleep. At one point Jonah coughed slightly and he rolled over and Owen thought he was awake, but he saw his arm go up behind his head, surrounding the pillow, and then he heard him snoring again. He stepped back and slowly closed the door.

Out on the porch, Owen finished one Scotch and had another. He smoked and watched the moon. It was at three-quarters and huge in a deep blue sky. It blotted out most of the stars though he could see the yellowish glow of Venus above the far hills. A light breeze rustled through the trees and the air was warm. It was a lovely night.

Owen stayed out there until his next Scotch was gone and then he headed inside. He looked at his watch. It was midnight. No sooner had he come in the door then the phone rang and he looked around for it, realised the sound was coming from the kitchen and he managed to catch it right before the answering machine picked up.

It was Claire. 'How is he?' Owen asked.

'Asleep.'

'How bad is it?'

'It's pretty bad but I was able to talk to him briefly. They're going to operate in the morning. Is everything okay with Jonah?'

'He's sleeping too.'

'Are you okay there if I stay the night?'

'Sure. What should I tell the boy?'

Claire paused. 'Just tell him what happened.

That I will call. But that his father will be fine. That we'll be home soon.'

After he hung up, Owen looked down at his now empty glass and he thought, I should go to sleep. Morning comes quickly with a child. But he decided to have one more drink, one more smoke, and he retired to the porch. He sat down again on the bench and again he watched the moon and the woods and the paleness of the night sky. He was drunk and he was tired but he did not want to go inside. In time his eyes grew heavy and the night seemed to gather around him. He knew he should go in but for some reason he could not. Perhaps it was the alcohol or perhaps it was the house, the quiet house steeped in unquiet memories. The next day he would not remember precisely when he fell asleep. But sleep he did, on a hard bench, slumped against the wall of the old farmhouse, the moon starting its slow descent behind the distant hills, the first glow of morning no more than the faintest rim of light at the farthest edge of the eastern horizon.

17

The boy woke him. A light touch on his bare arm and he jerked awake, aware suddenly of bright sun and warm air and the presence of a child to his right. Owen turned and saw him, a little boy with sleep-mussed hair and his mother's dewy black eyes. Long lashes. He wore pajama bottoms and a T-shirt and his feet were bare.

'Jonah,' he said.

'Where are my parents?'

'Jonah,' Owen said again, sitting up straight, rubbing his eyes, trying to find the right words. 'They'll be home soon. Your father had a small accident at the restaurant but he's fine. They took him to the hospital but there is nothing wrong. Your mother is with him. She'll be home soon. She asked me to cook you breakfast, would you like that?'

'Is he hurt?'

'He's fine. Really. Nothing to worry about. Trust me, he's fine. Your mother should be home by lunch. In the meantime, how about some breakfast? I bet you're hungry.'

The boy followed Owen into the kitchen. He was a dutiful and quiet boy and he did not say anything else. He followed Owen into the kitchen and then he sat at the table, the chair too high for him, his feet dangling, and he looked at Owen expectantly, and Owen was aware of his

248

looking and it unnerved him a little, for he was unused to anyone looking at him that way.

He put the water on for coffee, first things first, then he opened the fridge and looked inside. He saw a carton of eggs and he turned to Jonah and said, 'How about eggs?'

The boy nodded.

'How do you like them?'

'Scrambled.'

Owen cooked the eggs as his father had taught him to, not as he had done while in the Merchant Marines. He cooked them slow and long, running a spatula through the eggs in the pan, gently stirring them, bringing the curds to the surface. He cooked them until they were light and fluffy and then he and the boy ate wordlessly across from one another, with eggs and toast, Owen drinking coffee, Jonah with a tall glass of orange juice. Eventually their silence was interrupted by the ringing of the phone. Owen looked to Jonah and the boy did not react so Owen went to it. It was Claire.

She told him the surgery was over, that Charlie was sleeping, and that she was on her way home. Could he stay until she got there? Of course, he assured her, and then he asked Claire when Charlie would return.

'Well, that's the thing,' she said. 'It'll be at least two weeks. And then he won't be able to work for a while. He wants to talk to you about this. I think I'll let him do that.'

'What is it?' Owen said.

'He wants your help, Owen. With Charlotte's. The truth is we can't afford to stay closed that long. You know how that is. The places makes money but doesn't have the turnover or the tables to make a lot. He didn't want me to say anything. But there it is.'

Owen shook his head. 'I'll have to think about that one,' he said.

'Don't say anything to him, okay?' Claire asked.

'I won't,' said Owen, and then he brought the phone to Jonah. He could hear Claire's muffled voice and Jonah did not say anything as he listened to his mother. Owen watched him as he nodded his head, still chewing on a piece of toast, his feet moving where they dangled, his long-lashed eyes staring across the kitchen to the large window and the bright sun outside.

★　★　★

The next morning, while a light, warm summer rain fell, Owen drove his pickup the forty miles to the hospital where his brother lay recovering from skin grafts to his left arm. He did not want to visit Charlie in the hospital. He had not been in a hospital since he was born and he shared his father's revulsion for them and for doctors of all kinds. He did not know much about them, other than what he had seen on television and in movies, but he knew they were depressing places, places where people went to die. But he had promised Claire he would go, that he would go and talk to his brother, and he knew that at the minimum he owed Charlie this.

At the front desk he asked about Charlie and

the nurse asked if he was related.

'I'm his brother,' he said.

He took the elevator to the third floor and when he found the room he was looking for, number 314, he stopped and paused for a moment. Then he opened the door and there was his brother, propped up in bed, the television tuned to a talk show. His eyes met Owen's and he smiled. The entirety of his left arm was bandaged and an IV ran into his right arm but otherwise he looked the same.

'Come in,' he said.

'How are you feeling?' said Owen.

'Like shit. The drugs are strong,' he said, motioning to the IV. 'They keep them coming.'

Owen nodded.

'Sit,' said Charlie. 'Please. I can use the company.'

Owen pulled up a chair. 'Where are all the hot nurses?'

'I think that only happens in movies.'

'The least they could do is give you a bath.'

'No kidding. I think you have to break your legs for that. Oh, man. I fucked up.'

'It happens to all of us.'

'Not like this,' Charlie said. 'I'm not even sure how it happened. So fast. I was bending down into the oven and when I came up the whole pot of oil was coming toward me. I jumped back but too late.'

'You're lucky it was just your arm,' said Owen.

'I know it. You know both times I've been unable to work at Charlotte's it was because I hurt my arm.'

'I didn't know that.'

'I didn't tell you that story? That's why I hired Claire. Stepped out of the house on to black ice one morning. Broke my arm. Just like that. Couldn't cook.'

'Maybe it's a sign,' Owen said wryly.

Charlie shrugged. 'I'm glad you came, I am. Appreciate it. I know it's a long ride. Copley doesn't have a burn unit and these guys are the best around.'

'And they give you your own room.'

'Yeah, they do that for everybody. Place is like a hotel. Except for the food. The food is awful.'

'Can't be worse than Camel's.'

'The burger I had last night was a hockey puck.'

'Is there anything you need?' Owen said, wanting to get to the heart of the conversation, wanting to say his goodbyes and be back in Eden, back at his trailer with his beer and his view of the mountains.

Charlie sighed. 'I think I know what you're going to say to this, but I'm going to ask anyway.'

'Shoot,' said Owen.

'I need your help, Owen. With Charlotte's. It's going to be a month at least before I can cook. Being closed that long will kill us. If it was a week or something, I wouldn't ask. But a month is a long time. You are the only one I can ask. I mean that. The only one who could pull it off.'

'What about Claire?'

'She can't do it by herself. She's a great cook but that place gets ripping. The doctor doesn't want me near the place. And I know myself. I

252

couldn't go there without getting in the middle of it. Too much of a control freak.'

Owen looked away from his brother, across the bed, to the window. He could see a slice of building and the gray sky and beyond it the wide Connecticut flowing under the highway. 'I don't know, man,' he said. 'I've been making chicken wings and pot pies for twenty years now.'

'You're better than that,' Charlie said.

'I like what I do.'

'I wouldn't ask if I had another choice. You can do this.'

Owen ran his hand through his long hair. He looked at his brother, his brother jacked up in a hospital bed, good-hearted Charlie, good-hearted Charlie who knew so little of the world, his older brother, his older brother who knew only his father's legacy and for whom everything else was a mystery, the great other. If he even bothered to try to see, which Owen suspected he did not. 'All right,' Owen said.

'You'll do it?'

'Yeah. But I don't know any of the dishes, what you're trying to do.'

'That's no problem,' said Charlie, smiling. 'I'll write them out for you.'

'Dad would kill you for that, you know.'

'Dad's not here,' Charlie said.

★ ★ ★

Later the same day, the soft rain that had fallen all day stopped, and the sun emerged from dark clouds, and from the doorway of his trailer on

253

Hunger Mountain Owen watched the fullness of the dramatic sky above. To the east the clouds were still black, while to the west the bright sun shone and directly in front of him, through the parting in the trees, looking toward Charlotte's, he could see the thick end of the rainbow that had formed over the hills. He could not see where it touched the ground, and he could not see where it dissipated into the cloud bank, but he could see the meat of it, the full spectrum of colors, and it was beautiful.

He whittled away the afternoon drinking beer in the lawn chair in front of the trailer and he smoked cigarettes and watched the woods and he watched the rainbow fade into the blueness of the sky. He had not eaten anything since the eggs with Jonah in the morning and he thought he should eat but he was not hungry. At one point he switched from beer to bourbon and he knew he was getting drunk but he did not care. The day moved on. By sunset, he was in his chair and starting to doze off, the day suddenly long and the drink suddenly coming upon him, when he woke quickly because he heard the distinct sound of car tires on the dirt drive leading to his house.

He tried to shake off the drink and the tiredness and then he saw the car, its nose coming between the trees, the Subaru wagon that belonged to his brother's wife, to Claire. Owen stood and she waved from behind the glass as she pulled in front of the trailer, brought the car to a halt in front of the woodpile, turned off the engine. She got out and she wore a tight-fitting T-shirt and jeans, and with the sun setting behind her, the sky golden with its dying light, she was remarkable. Owen became aware of his feet, of his knees, of his thighs, of all that held him erect. He smiled at her. She smiled back.

Claire said, 'I brought you something.'

'Oh yeah?'

She had a sheaf of paper in her hand and she held it toward him now, moving across the dirt to where he stood. 'After you left,' she said, 'he spent all afternoon writing these down. It was good for him. Gave him something to do.'

Claire reached Owen and handed him the loose-leaf unlined paper, all of it scribbled on in his brother's familiar and nearly illegible handwriting. On the first sheet he saw the words 'Lobster Charles' underlined.

'The recipes,' he said.

'He was so happy, Owen. He'd probably kill me for telling you that. But he was. Knowing that you would help. It means a lot.'

'Didn't have much of a choice, did I?'

Claire stood in front of him and she put her hands on her hips and the small wrinkles gathered around her eyes as they did when she questioned things. He did not know her well but he knew her well enough to recognise this about her. He had seen it before and he was not a man who forgot such things. She said, 'Are you drunk?'

Owen laughed. A big, deep-bellied laugh. 'Ah, shit,' he said. 'You got me.'

Claire laughed back. 'Well, it is summer.'

'That it is,' said Owen.

'Have you eaten?'

Owen shook his head. 'Not since the eggs with Jonah.'

'I don't suppose you have any food in this place?'

'I'm sure I could cobble something together.'

'Let me,' Claire said. 'I owe you one.'

★ ★ ★

Inside the trailer, the last of the day's light streamed through the narrow windows and it was just enough for it was growing dark in here. Claire rummaged through his small pantry, looking for something she could put together, while Owen sat at his small kitchen table and smoked and sipped bourbon from a tumbler. In truth, she did not know what she was doing here, only that she wanted to be here. Back at the house, Althea had called and offered to come over and help with Jonah, and she was about to say, 'Don't be silly,' but then without thinking about it she found herself accepting and before she could consider it further she found herself driving on the dirt roads on the now-beautiful evening, the air sweet with the earlier rain, and there was nowhere for her to go, for they had no friends outside of the restaurant and Charlie did not want her at the hospital. He thought it made no sense for her to sit and watch over him when all he wanted to do was sleep anyway, sleep with the benefit of the painkillers that came from a bottle and into his arm. And so she'd ended up here, in her husband's brother's trailer on the flank of a mountain, trying to find something to cook.

She settled on pasta and she put water on the stove to boil. She chopped garlic and opened a can of anchovies and diced these on his cutting board. The only fresh food in the house was a bunch of tomatoes on the windowsill and she diced these as well. In the fridge she found salt-packed capers, the only giveaway that he was a chef, everything else, the beer, the carton of eggs, the loaf of commercial rye bread, suggesting typical bachelorhood. She rinsed the salt off the capers and chopped these into a rough dice. She sensed Owen watching her but she did not mind. At one point she turned to him and said, 'You have anything to drink besides beer and whiskey?'

'Only if you promise to get drunk with me,' Owen said.

'No promises,' said Claire.

'There's wine under the sink.'

Claire opened the small cabinet and next to some bleach and dish soap there were several bottles of red wine and she grabbed one, an Italian cabernet blend, and she said, 'Quite a place to keep your wine.'

'Space is at a premium,' Owen said, 'you have to make do.'

Claire opened the bottle, poured herself a glass and then she began to cook. In a large frying pan she heated olive oil and then sautéed the garlic and the anchovies, breaking up the anchovies with a wooden spoon so that they melted into the oil. Next she added the tomatoes and their juice that had collected on the cutting board and she turned down the heat and softly simmered the tomatoes with the oil and the garlic and the anchovies. The small kitchen filled with the smell of the garlic and while it cooked Claire sipped her wine, and when the water came to a boil she dropped a pound of linguini in and salted the water. She added the diced capers to the sauce and finished it with a smattering of red pepper flakes for heat. She drained the pasta and saved some of the water, and tossed the pasta in the pan with the sauce, adding a little of the water to thin it out.

She brought the whole pan to the table and they ate right out of it, with forks and spoons to twirl the pasta on, and outside the night had arrived and Owen lit candles and the intimacy should have been awkward but it was not. The pasta was lightly sauced in the Italian way and the anchovies and capers gave it a salty bite that was nice. Owen drank wine with dinner and the food seemed to sober him and while they ate they spoke of the restaurant, and it was the first time she had ever talked about the restaurant with Owen, and she liked the way he spoke. He told her how hard Charlie always worked when they were kids, how he loved all of it, while Owen spent all his time conniving to get out of doing the dishes or chopping vegetables. He told her how men used to come to the restaurant just to get a smile out of Charlotte and how their father knew this but did not mind, for he had never felt threatened by another man his entire life and because he knew it was good for business. He told her stories of the regulars, men like Rene from Montreal who came in three nights a week, ate at the small bar by himself and only wanted steak frites, which was not on the menu but which Charles cooked for him anyway, taking a big strip and cooking it 'bleu' as requested, barely touching each side to the grill so that the meat was as raw as when it was butchered.

'And I think that's why my father cooked him the steak whether it was on the menu or not. He loved that he wanted it bleu. Nothing pissed him off more than someone who wanted steak well done. He hated that. Then you get this French guy who wants to eat it raw. There was a purity to that he loved.'

'I wish I'd known your father,' Claire said.

'Ah, he was a bastard. But he could cook. Straight out. Guy could bone a whole chicken in ten minutes. No lie. Ten minutes. He'd turn the thing inside out and you wouldn't even see the knife move. Slice, slice, slice done. Never seen anything like it.'

Claire fingered her wine glass. 'I think he would be proud of you. Of both of you.'

'But he's not around is he?' said Owen, lighting a cigarette.

'Part of the reason is what's in your hand,' Claire said, and then was sorry she'd said it. 'I'm sorry,' she said. 'I shouldn't have said that.'

'No, it's all right,' said Owen. 'It is the cowardly man's suicide.'

And Owen smiled at her then and for a brief

moment, as she had once before in this trailer, she saw behind his façade. She saw the boy he had once been. She saw beneath the surface beauty of the man he was, a man who grew his hair long and kept a scraggly beard so as not to be so pretty. She saw that there was pain and sorrow in him and she saw for the first time that he longed for things he had never known and she did not know what they were and she knew she could not give them to him but she somehow wanted to help him, to bring him to her, to help him cross whatever divide stood between him and the promise of what he should become. And this was why, when he looked at her with those piercing green eyes and said for the second time, this time with greater force, 'Get drunk with me, Claire,' she did not go home as she knew she should. She did not stand and leave, walk out the door of the trailer into her waiting car and drive back the way she had come, back to the old house on Signal Ridge, back to her sleeping child.

Instead, she smiled and said, 'I can't,' knowing she was not convincing anyone, least of all herself.

At one point, they moved outside and they sat in the lawn chairs under the night sky, clear and full of bright stars, curving off and away from them, looking close enough to touch. The night was warm and they drank directly from a bottle of wine, passing it between them, and Claire felt it going to her head. It was not often that she drank and she felt now the exuberance and the high that alcohol could bring and she had so much she wanted to say, so much she wanted to tell Owen, and she did, and he listened.

Claire told him about being a mother, about how it was amazing, more amazing than anything else she had ever done; how remarkable it was to watch this child grow and see your reflection in his eyes and know that you made him. She talked about the comfort of marriage, about knowing each day that Charlie would be there, that when she rolled over at night it was he who stopped her from rolling off the bed and how there was something to be said for this. And she talked about how all she had ever wanted to do from the moment she set foot in a commercial kitchen was to cook, to create, to work with raw materials and fire and come out with food, great, beautiful food, food that made people happy. It was nothing world-changing, this work, but making people happy was more than a small thing, something that at the end of the day you took with you into sleep and it warmed you.

Claire talked because she needed to, because she wanted to hear her own voice in the warm summer night and because Owen was there to listen. She was captivating herself with what she had to say, as if she had suddenly discovered that she was full of convictions, opinions, ideas and all of them needed to rush out her mouth and into the air. It felt good to talk, to be listened to, and even Owen's hand lightly playing with her hair felt all right, it felt like part of it, part of the night, part of the wine, part of her words. Everything was blending into one and when suddenly she stood, he was in front of her, and before she knew it she was kissing him and his lips were on her neck and his arms were pulling her to him.

'Come inside with me,' he whispered.

'I can't,' said Claire, 'I can't.'

'Come,' he said, and his arms were around her, and his lips brushed across the hairs on the back of her neck and his voice was low and pleading as he said, 'Please, Claire, come inside.'

Together they stumbled into the trailer. A candle was still lit and this was the only light and it shot long fingers of shadow up the walls and on to the ceiling. They did not close the door and outside the starlight filled the driveway. She was against the table and he was moving into her and she turned her head away and looked out the door, out toward the blackness that was Eden. She felt him against her and he was hard already and this sobered her, and she said, 'No, Owen, I can't, I'm serious.'

He looked at her then, and their eyes locked, and he held her by the shoulders. She saw the recognition come into his eyes, the arrival of sentience, and this strong, beautiful man in front of her suddenly went slack. His arms fell to his sides and his whole body showed a resignation she had never seen in a man before.

'Jesus,' he said, and as he said it his fist came to his face and he punched himself, a blow to the side of his ear. Claire grabbed his arm.

'Don't,' she said, 'don't. It's okay, really.'

Owen's hands went to his face and he ran them up and through his hair and then down and over his eyes and his cheeks and when they fell again to his sides they were balled as fists and Claire's eyes went to his hands and then up to his eyes and she saw that he was crying, tears starting to slide down his face.

'I'm sorry,' he said, and then he said it again. His words came out muffled as he was crying harder now, and his crying was so real, from the middle of him, all of him stripped away for her now, that Claire cried too, cried for him and for whatever it was he held within him. She moved closer and forced his limp arms around her, wrapped her own arms around his waist.

'It's okay,' she whispered.

'I'm drunk,' he said.

'I know.'

They stayed like this for a while, locked together in the candlelit trailer, and Owen cried and Claire held him. After a time, without speaking, they moved to the bed and Owen lay flat on his back and Claire lay on her stomach and placed her head on his chest and through his T-shirt she listened to the beating of his heart.

Soon she heard him snoring and she shifted her weight and turned and looked up at him. She reached her hand up and brushed the wisps of long blond hair away from his face. She began to rise, half kneeling on the bed next to him, and from this position she started to take off his shirt, pulling it up from his stomach, and Owen stirred as she did so and helped her take it off. When it was off, he lay back down and she stood and took off her own shirt and her pants until she was just in her bra and her panties and then she lay back down, her head back on his chest, her mouth next to the small tattoo of the umbrella. They slept.

18

The morning came fast. Owen slept little and what sleep he got was uneven, spent half leaning against the wall, his brother's wife sprawled across his legs, her long black hair splayed across his thighs. Outside the sun was strong and the day clear and he could hear the songbirds in the trees. He moved slightly and this woke Claire and she slowly turned over and he could see all of her in her underwear and he looked away so as not to be aroused by it.

'What time is it?' she said.

Owen looked at the alarm clock on the nightstand. 'A little after eight,' he said.

Claire looked up at him, rubbed her eyes. 'Ah, my head,' she said.

'I know it.'

'I need to go.'

'Okay,' said Owen.

'Do we need to talk?' she asked, her eyes searching, wondering.

'No,' he said. 'There is nothing to say.'

'Yes,' said Claire. 'There is nothing to say.'

She rose then, suddenly trying to be modest, pulling a blanket up with her as she stood, covering her breasts. She really was a beautiful woman, he thought. Her tumble of hair, those rich, dark eyes, the smooth expanse of white skin that was her back as she walked away from him. He watched her dress and he loved to watch a woman dress more than he loved to watch a woman undress. He watched her wiggle into her jeans, pull her T-shirt over her head and slip into her sandals. When she was finished she stopped and looked back at him, shook her hair out. Her face was so expressive, sad almost, and he thought that maybe he was wrong, there was more to say than he could put words to, but he could not think of anything and he gave her a weak smile instead.

'Okay,' said Claire. 'I'm going.'

'Claire, wait — '

She stopped. 'Yes.'

'Thank you.'

'You're welcome.'

Owen nodded. 'I mean it. You helped. You did.'

'I know,' said Claire.

Owen watched as she opened the screen door and stepped out into the bright daylight. He leaned back and sighed. He lighted a cigarette and listened to her car starting up and he felt the haze of the hangover and the light hurt his eyes but he inhaled and he wondered if only certain men were allowed to truly love.

★   ★   ★

Claire returned home that morning and Jonah ran to see her when her car pulled in, and when he hugged her fiercely, for he was still at that age when he did that, she thought the tears were going to come but she was able to keep them at bay by gritting her teeth. Althea followed the boy and the older woman mistook the dark circles

266

under Claire's eyes for a difficult night spent in the hospital and she said, 'You go take a bath, get some sleep.'

'I can't, Althea, you've been too good.'

'Just go on,' she said. 'Do it.'

She knew she did not deserve it, did not deserve this self-indulgence but she was happy to have it, for the hot, soapy water in which she lay, and from the window she could see Jonah intently working on something in the yard below, though she could not see what. He got that from his father, that ability to relentlessly focus, to block out everything else except the task at hand. Claire wished she had the same ability, especially now, when later in the day she would need to visit her husband in the hospital, look him in the eye, go through the conversational motions that were the heart of a shared life, all the while pretending she had not spent the night in his brother's bed. And she would do this, and tomorrow she would return to Charlotte's, and cook for the first time next to Owen, and they would pretend that they were the same as they had always been, that in the dark of night she had not almost given herself up to him, and that after, he had not sobbed like a small boy, tears running like water down the gutters of his cheeks.

* * *

Owen dreamt of her. She was in his thoughts before he fell asleep, as he lay with his head on his pillow and looked out the dark window. He knew he would see her in the morning and he knew it would be awkward but he did not care. He was excited to see her. Claire. He said her name out loud. He kept imagining her as she was when he woke in the dead of night and saw her with her head on his bare chest, the white skin of her back, the rise of her buttocks beneath the cotton of her panties. The great mass of hair as it fell behind her. God, she was something. Lying there with the black window in front of him, he ached for her. He did not want to fall asleep. He wanted control of his thoughts. He wanted to dwell on her, on seeing her getting dressed, pulling the jeans up over her thighs. He wanted to replay it over and over and he did not want to sleep.

And then he was gone and the dreams came like visions. They were vivid and real. In the dreams she was his and his alone and they swam together in a mountain crater, and after, they toweled each other off and made love on soft green grass and she was on top of him and her hair swung down as she moved up and down, and they locked eyes and the lovemaking was both sweet and fast and he thought: this can never end and as soon as he thought it she mouthed the words — as if she could see inside his mind — 'It won't'. There is nothing to worry about, she said, and as she said it, she ran her hand through her long thick hair and looked down at him and he believed her.

When he woke, it was almost dawn and a gray, diffused light came through the windows. He could hear birds. He was covered in sweat. He shifted the blankets and flipped his pillow over. He tried to fall back asleep, to get back to where he had left off.

★ ★ ★

Claire arrived at Charlotte's a little after nine that morning, getting there earlier than she normally would, leaving the house as soon as the sitter showed up to watch Jonah. She went right to work, taking onions and garlic out of the cooler and beginning the slow process of dicing and slicing them to prepare for the *mise en place*. As she worked, she had a sickening feeling in her stomach that she knew was the nerves though she was unused to it, for a man had never made her nervous before. Charlie had never made her nervous. Not even when they were first together. Of course, there had been nothing complicated about the two of them, other than the small fact that he was her boss and it was a job she wanted to keep. But it was not like this, not like thinking about your brother-in-law while your husband was in the hospital. Not like knowing you could never do what you wanted to do more than anything. Not like being unable to dismiss it even though you knew that was the right thing to do. All the while knowing that you were not dismissing it because you didn't want to and wondering what this said about you.

While she thought these things, Claire watched the clock above the swinging doors. It seemed not to move. Owen would be here at ten and part of her hoped ten would never come at

269

the same time as she wanted it to be ten now.

Claire peeled onions and laid them flat and worked through them, filling the white porcelain bowls with neat slices. She watched the clock. She looked out the window to the sunny day and she listened for the sound of truck tires on the gravel. She tried to calm the butterflies in her stomach and she wondered if when he walked through the swinging doors her heart would rise into her throat.

As it turned out, however, ten came and went and there was no sign of Owen. Claire was marinating fish and by ten thirty it occurred to her that maybe he was not coming at all, that he had gotten cold feet about working at the restaurant, or that maybe what had happened between them had unnerved him so much that he had left Eden. No, she said to herself, don't be absurd, don't think that. And she shook her head at the thought of it and as she did the door swung open and there he was, tall, handsome Owen, his hair pulled back and out of his face, wearing jeans and a long-sleeved T-shirt.

'Hey,' he said.

'Hi,' said Claire, trying to sound bright and normal, as if nothing was on her mind, as if looking at him did not affect her the way it did.

Owen turned his head and looked at the clock. 'I'm sorry, I'm late,' he said.

Claire looked away from him, at the onions in front of her. 'Don't be silly,' she said. 'No one punches a clock here.'

Owen smiled at her. 'You're going to have to show me what to do,' he said. 'It's been a while.'

They had the work and sometimes the work is all you need. They stood side by side and they prepped and it was as Claire had hoped it would be. Outside the bright sun shone and inside its golden light spread across the kitchen. There were five entrées and an equal number of appetisers they needed to prepare for, and Claire had forgotten how much she enjoyed this part of the day, and it relaxed her, and in no time the two of them were laughing and joking and she felt the wall between them pull away and they were no different than she and Charlie had once been, years ago, when she first walked through those doors and into the kitchen of Charlotte's.

During the afternoon they had time for a break and they sat outside on the porch so Owen could smoke. The floodplain in front of them was the brightest of greens and beyond they could hear the low rush of the river. Owen smoked and Claire sat next to him and leaned forward with her arms on her knees and at first they did not talk and it felt suddenly intimate, different from the kitchen with the noise of the prep, and Claire was thinking about this when Owen said, 'I almost didn't come this morning.'

Claire looked at him and then away again. 'No?'

'No. I'll be honest with you, I was scared.'

Claire said, 'It's not hard. You got right back into it. It's really no different from the other cooking you've done, when you get down to it.'

Owen said, 'I'm not talking about the cooking.'

Claire fidgeted with her hands. 'Oh,' she finally said and she knew what he was going to say and she did not want him to say it for she knew there were times when you should not give words to some things and she wanted this to be one of them. She wished they could pretend that there was nothing between them, that they were not moving toward something that would be difficult to step back from.

'I was scared to see you,' said Owen. 'I almost left. Went back to New York. Renewed my card. See if I could catch a ship.'

Claire reached out now and put one hand on his thigh, felt the muscle underneath his jeans. 'It's okay,' she said.

'I know. I'm glad I didn't go, I am.'

'It's going to be okay,' Claire said again.

'I think I love you,' said Owen.

Claire refused to look at him. She could not. 'Don't say that,' she said.

'I can't help it,' Owen said. 'I think I love you.'

'Please don't say it,' said Claire.

'I have to say it. Some stuff you can't pretend isn't true. I have to say it.'

Claire nodded but she still did not look at him. She focused on one of the slender birch trees on the riverbank. A tall, white pole of a tree, its branches spare near its base, skeletal as it went up, spindly arms shooting off it, its leaves full and green. Claire did not look at him, for if she did she thought what he said would become real and that she might cry from the truth of it all. Finally she said, 'I'm glad you didn't leave.'

And when she said it, she heard him chuckle and she turned to see his wide smile, boyish dimples around his mouth. 'What?' said Claire.

'That's a start,' Owen said. 'I'll take it.'

Claire couldn't help but smile. 'Let's go,' she said. 'Only an hour till service.'

⋆　⋆　⋆

The restaurant was busy and this made Claire happy, for in the bustle of the kitchen she could work from muscle memory, flipping fish and meat on the grill, shaking pan sauces, all the while hearing his words: *I think I love you.* She heard them over and over in her mind and how he had said them, the inflection on the 'you'. And as they moved around each other in the kitchen — not bothering to get fully out of each other's way, Owen brushing against the back of Claire as she stood at the grill — she knew that this what she had wanted to hear. She knew she wanted him to love her. That she wanted to be loved. And not in the way that Charlie loved her, the goodness, the surety of marriage. No, she wanted what she thought Owen could give her: a more elemental kind of love, passionate and crazy and not at all interested in consequences or practical concerns. A love that did not care about the future. A love that swallowed the moment, ate it up, that filled her and satisfied her completely. A love so indulgent and irresponsible that it could not possibly belong to her, Claire Apple, wife, mother, chef. Reliable, steady

273

Claire, Midwestern Claire, Claire who had come east to Vermont and still had only seen the ocean once.

And so it was that Claire first crossed the divide. That she first understood what she was about to do and knew she could do it, that she had it in her. That she could step outside her life and into another man's arms, and somehow put aside the fact that this man just happened to be her husband's brother.

19

That night, as she knew she would, Claire went to him. They had closed the restaurant and they did not talk about the conversation they had had earlier, or say much of anything, really, other than awkward goodbyes under the thin light from the crescent moon as they stood in the dark parking lot. Claire saw on his face that he wanted her to say something, that he had said all he could and now it was her turn. But the words did not come, and as she drove back to the old farmhouse on Signal Ridge she hated herself for her cowardice, for her inability to say what she felt, what she decided she could not walk away from.

Then, arriving at the house, it occurred to her there was something she could do. The babysitter, a local girl named Susan, had dozed off on the couch and when Claire woke her she asked her if she would mind spending the night.

'Are you going to the hospital?' asked Susan.

'Yes,' Claire said.

'Sure, Mrs Bender, I can do that.'

'I might actually need you a lot this week. More overnights.'

Susan nodded, rubbed her eyes. She was a good girl, you could count on her. She was solid with Jonah. 'No problem,' said Susan.

Upstairs Claire opened Jonah's door and she stealthily moved across the hardwood floor to his bed. He stirred slightly when she reached him but he did not wake. He was like his father this way and could sleep through anything. His face was pressed into his pillow and his chest moved slowly up and down with the rhythm of sleep. Claire ran her hand through his soft hair, looked at his closed eyes, the long eyelashes any woman would covet. Then she went back out the way she'd come, gently closing the door behind her.

She showered under red-hot water, washing the smells of the kitchen, of the day, off her. As she did, she leaned into the water, letting it run off her long hair, looking to where it fell to her feet, and she thought of Owen. She thought of his hands, his long-limbed body, of his eyes when he told her he thought he loved her. She saw the way he said it, how much he meant it, the dimples that spread out from his mouth when he laughed. An image of him behind her in the kitchen, his hands on her waist, taking her down to the wooden table floated into her mind and she resisted the urge she had. Instead, Claire turned off the water, dried herself off, put on a simple sundress and within twenty minutes she was driving back down the dirt roads, as if going to Charlotte's, though she knew the car was leading her somewhere completely different.

The night was warm and she drove with the windows down and her hair was still wet and the breeze as it dried it felt good. Above her, the crescent moon had now risen high in the sky, and everything was a deep blue, even the black forest on both sides of the road rippled with traces of moonlight as she drove through it.

Soon Claire was on the Hunger Mountain Road and she slowed down as the car bumped over the washboards and as she climbed up the steep incline. When she reached the cut in the trees that was Owen's driveway, she turned off the lights on her Subaru and took the left turn slowly, moving into the trees and trying to be as quiet as possible. She wanted to surprise him.

She pulled in front of the trailer and her heart sank as she saw all the lights were out. It had never occurred to her that he would be asleep. His truck was here so she knew he was home.

Then, getting out of the car, she looked toward the door and she saw now the glow of his cigarette and then she heard his voice.

'I had hoped you were coming,' he said, and she stopped in her tracks.

'You scared me,' she said.

'Who was sneaking up on who?' he said and her eyes had now adjusted to the darkness and she could see his silhouette where he sat on the steps though his face was shielded in darkness, in shadow.

'I wanted to surprise you,' said Claire.

'Come here,' Owen said.

Claire began to walk across the dirt driveway. A breeze blew through the opening in the trees and it was warm and she felt it on her bare legs. She walked slowly, deliberately, and when she got closer, she could make out his face, his eyes, and they were locked firmly on her own face. When she was a foot away, he took one last pull on his cigarette and tossed it out on to the dirt and she saw the smoke spill out of his mouth and then his arms were out and around her waist and he pulled her to him. He did not stand and she stood in front of him and they did not speak. She saw that he wore jeans and was barefoot. His hands went from around her waist to underneath the back of her dress and his hands were warm and Claire closed her eyes. Her body arched toward him as she felt his strong hands moving across her buttocks, up her back and then back down again. His face pressed into her stomach and she let out a slight moan, and then he was rising to stand next to her, and she thought: I will do whatever he wants.

Owen's hand lifted her chin to his face and his other hand was on the back of her head and then gripping a mass of her hair as he kissed her. She kissed him back and he tasted of tobacco but she surprised herself by liking the nutty, pungent taste, and she could not get enough of him.

Claire slung her arms around his neck and they kissed and she felt him pulling her up, and he was so tall, so strong, and she lifted her legs and wrapped them around him, her sandals falling to the wooden steps below.

Owen turned his body and without taking his lips off hers he walked into the dark trailer, half carrying her, his arms holding her up, and he brought her to the small table and sat her on it.

In the dark he lifted her dress over her head and soon her clothes were off and out the still-open door she could see the blue moonlight in the small yard and she did not need to get ready for him and he seemed to know this. He slid her toward him on the table and oh she

278

wanted to feel him and there he was, and when they moved together Claire was grateful for the black night and the lightless room for she was able to give herself up completely, to let go and to focus only on the feel of him, and with his arms gripping her shoulders she knew it was coming, circles of water turning and turning, at its center a great giant pulse, and soon she was falling into him and she felt her body go limp in his arms.

Afterward, Owen carried her to the bed and all she wanted was his arms and sleep. He laid her down and she rolled until her head was in the crook of his arm and then resting on his chest. Against her cheek sweat dried on him. They held each other. Warm summer night air moved through the small trailer. Claire did not want the morning to come. She wanted to stay like this, just like this, for as long as she could.

★　★　★

Owen watched her sleep. He wanted a cigarette but he dared not move lest he wake her. She looked so beautiful, her face pressed into the pillow, the cheek he could see rosy, her hair falling behind her, her lips slightly open with the breath of sleep. Her long naked torso, the side of one breast visible where she met the bed. She is something, he thought. He had made love to many women but none of them felt like she did. None of them gave him the sense of urgency she did; an urgency that bordered on hunger, a feeling so strong that when she first came to him and he sat on the steps with his face buried in her belly, it took all his effort not to sink his teeth into her. He wanted to be patient. He wanted to taste her, wanted to feel the salt of her skin against his tongue. But his need was greater than that, and he saw hers was too, and he made love to her with the urgency that he knew they both, silently, demanded.

Now, lying in the blue of the night with her naked in his bed, Owen was too excited to sleep. He did not want to shut down. He wanted her, all of her, and he did not want to waste a minute. He wanted her next to him and he did not want her to leave. He never wanted to see her go out that door again and he knew that was not possible but he thought it anyway.

Sometime later, as the sky turned from blue to dull gray and Eden slowly lightened, Owen decided he could not wait any longer and he woke her. He slid down next to Claire and he kissed the back of her neck and when she rolled over he climbed on top of her and she smiled and ran her hands across his chest and moments later he slid inside her. He made love to her slowly this time, and they finished with her on top of him, like in his dreams, and her hair moved in front of his face and outside he could hear the birds and everything waking and none of it mattered to him. He now knew what love was: it was this, this woman, this night, this world.

★ ★ ★

There is a space that new lovers sometimes find, a kind of cocoon, a place where no one but each other is allowed to enter. And when they are there together, nothing else matters beyond the immediate, beyond each other. There can be no guilt or remorse or concern of any kind. There is only each of you and day bleeds into night and night into day and you go on like this until something shocks you out of it.

Even Claire, who returned home to check on the babysitter, and to call the hospital and talk to Charlie, offer to come down knowing that he would say no, was able to stay in this space, was able to block it all out. There were moments, sure, when she was back home and with Jonah, or after she hung up from Charlie, that the guilt began to creep into her mind, that she was sick with it, but then she would find a way to return to Owen and it would disappear as fast as smoke.

When they were together, at the restaurant and more definitively during those endless nights at his trailer halfway up the mountain, she cared about nothing except for the presence of him, except for the feel of him, the taste of him, the smell of him.

They made love so much and slept so little she was constantly sore and should have been exhausted except that nothing could tire her out. Claire had never been made love to like this, so completely, so maddeningly, so intensely that she craved it like a drug. Once, when Owen slowed inside her, she pushed him with all her might, and when he smiled lazily at her, she struck him,

281

slapping him hard in the chest with her open palms. This time he laughed at her.

'What?' Owen said.

'Faster,' she said.

And he did what Claire wanted, he always did what she wanted.

There were times, too, of remarkable gentleness. Times when they lay together in the hot post-coital quiet and she would sling one leg over his thigh and they would hold their faces inches away from one another and whisper silly things, words of love and nonsense, and sometimes it was enough to make her cry and when she wept he licked her tears away and she loved him for this as it made her laugh and it also showed her that it was okay to cry, that he did not mind, that it did not scare him, that he could handle her and whatever welled up from inside her.

Other times, they laughed and tickled one another like teenage lovers or they wrestled and Owen inevitably got the better of her, and his strong arms and the manner in which he took her down almost always turned her on, and they were back where they started, joined as one, alone together.

One night they stayed late at Charlotte's and they drank wine and while a soft summer rain fell from the night sky they made love sitting on the bench on the back porch. After, they sat side by side with a blanket wrapped around their naked bodies and they looked out toward the woods, toward the river. There was the sound of the rain and the warmth of their bodies under the blanket. There was the good wine and the delicious fatigue of the day's work and the lovemaking. All of it lovely and warm and there was nothing else on the entire earth that they wanted, nothing they were missing.

At one point, Owen leaned into Claire and said, 'I don't want this to ever end.'

Claire shook out her hair, pushed her thigh into his. 'Me neither,' she said softly.

'It doesn't have to, you know.'

Claire looked over at him. 'Let's not talk about it, okay?'

'We have to talk about it sometime.'

'But not tonight,' Claire said. 'It's too beautiful. The rain. The night. I don't want to think about things.'

'Not tonight then,' said Owen.

'No, not tonight, let's forget about all of that. Let's forget all of it.'

'Okay,' said Owen, and he looked out at the floodplain, and he looked over at Claire, and when he did she smiled and kissed him on the cheek, and then she rose from where she sat, dropped the blanket on him and she stood naked and laughed and he said, 'What?'

'Watch me,' she said and there she went, off the porch and on to the soft, wet grass of the floodplain, spinning and dancing in the dark and in the rain, her pale skin luminous in the thin light. Her hair was matted to her head and her large breasts moved up and away from her as she spun and she was beautiful and it made Owen tremendously happy to see her.

'You're crazy,' he said.

283

'Come get me,' she shouted back at him, and she twirled with her hands over her head, mimicking ballet, the rain falling steadily, and Owen shook his head at her and stood up himself, dropping the blanket to the porch, and he stepped out into the warm summer rain himself, and it felt good on his naked skin, not at all cold, like bathwater from the sky, and he ran to Claire, skipping like a child as he did, and she saw him coming and shrieked and tried to escape, but he caught her, wrapped his arms around her. The two of them naked on the floodplain together and they did not care. He did not let go.

★ ★ ★

Late that night, neither of them wanted to sleep and they lay in his bed and listened to the steady thrumming of the rain on the metal roof of the trailer and Owen told her about the ocean. He told her about the beautiful sunsets he had seen over the Pacific, when that great globe falls suddenly over the lip of the earth and fills you with awe.

He told her about the magnificent storms, how they humbled you, how there were nights when he sat in his tiny bunk and listened to the creak of the big boat, felt it listing back and forth and heard the wind and the water whipping against its flanks and thought about what it would be like to die out here, to die surrounded by black water and among men he could never say he truly knew. He told her about the days of endless, beating, brutal sunshine. About the oppressive heat of the tiny galley kitchen.

'But you loved it,' Claire said.

'Loved it?'

'The ocean.'

'No,' said Owen. 'I don't love the ocean. I respect it. And I loved the ports. Harbors. Places where the water meets the land. Working harbors. I love those. And you need an ocean to get to them.'

'What a life.'

'It was something,' said Owen. 'Really was.'

'Will you go back? Do you miss it?'

'I don't miss the work. But I miss the water. I miss being next to it, seeing it first thing in the morning and last thing before I go to bed. I miss that.'

'That sounds nice. A little house on the ocean. Somewhere warm.'

'There are places like that, Claire.'

'I know it,' she said.

'We could go. You could come with me. We could have that. All that and more.'

Claire rolled her head away from him and looked at the wall. He had said it, broken the spell, talked about something beyond the place they had fallen into together. She felt suddenly fragile, like she was made of glass, and when she rolled back toward him her eyes were full of tears.

'I want to,' she said.

'We can. Really. We can.'

The tears escaped her eyes and she did not wipe at them. She looked at Owen. 'I want to,' she said again. 'But who are we kidding? Who are we fucking kidding?'

Owen reached out and touched her face, with the flat of his thumb stopped one of her tears. He took her head in his large hand, massaged the back of it with his fingers. 'I don't want anything but you,' he said. 'I don't care about anything but you.'

Claire looked at him and the tears fell freely now. 'Just hold me, okay?' she said.

'Sure,' said Owen, and he moved closer to her, took her in his arms and he let her sob away the night while he lay and listened to the rain and thought of a small bungalow next to the water, on the gulf or somewhere where the living was cheap, a place of their own, a fresh start, no history, just the two of them, new and loose on to the world. It would be the life he had always wanted but had not known how to find, and while he knew much stood in his way, it was finally tangible to him now, out there somewhere, waiting for him to grab it.

20

Claire was aware of herself all the time now. Aware of her body beneath her clothes, the way her skin felt against different fabrics. Her breasts were sensitive as they had been after giving birth and she could barely move without thinking about him and the slightest of things aroused her and she worried that it showed. That everyone she saw in town or at the restaurant knew the kind of woman she was, the kind of woman who could run around with her husband's brother, the kind of woman who spent her nights locked in love in a trailer on the side of a mountain.

Part of her enjoyed this feeling. She saw the way other men looked at her and she knew they desired her and it had been a long time since she had noticed men looking at her, and sometimes she thought they probably always had but other times she realised that it was what she gave off to them now. That she wanted to be desired. What woman did not? And Owen desired her, no question. He could not get enough of her. But he also loved her and Claire knew this was where it got difficult, for she was falling in love with him too, and she was smart enough to know that falling in love with him was a luxury she did not have.

At the same time she thought: love is not something one can control. You cannot turn it off like a faucet. You cannot pretend it is not there.

Like little else in life, it is an absolute. There is no room for ambiguity.

And when she thought this, she grew sad. For Claire knew that in time all of it would need to be addressed and such things seldom came to a good end. And for this reason, she tried to put it out her mind and, in general, she succeeded. When she was at Charlotte's there was the work and there was Owen. At night, it was just her and Owen and in his embrace she went to the place she wanted to be, where her mind emptied and all that mattered was what they did in this particular sliver of time: they had no future, no past, only a limitless present.

Sometimes, though, she'd return home in the morning to see her son, the boy she and Charlie had made, Jonah, sitting at the table eating his breakfast and she'd see in him his father and it was like a blow to her gut. He was so young and perfect and tied them together as nothing else could, as nothing that she had with Owen would. And then, of course, there were the conversations she had with Charlie, where they talked about the restaurant, about his healing, and often about Owen, and she had never lied to him before and it bothered her to do so, though she knew that regardless of what happened, he could never know about her, he could never know about Owen, about the two of them. She did not know what he would do if he found out though she knew enough about men — and, now, about brothers — to know that this was one thing that would change everything for ever. There was no returning from this.

While he was in the hospital, she talked to Charlie twice a day. She set the schedule and she counted on it, for this way he could not find out where she was spending her nights. She called him both times from Charlotte's, in the morning when she arrived before Owen, and again at night after service and while Owen was out on the porch smoking. She amazed herself with how easy it all seemed, that this was her life; how good she was at the deception. If she thought about it completely, it might have even changed her opinion of herself.

And then one morning Charlie told her what she was blocking out, what she was afraid to hear. He told her they said he could go home.

'When?' asked Claire, trying to sound enthusiastic.

'Two days. I can't wait, Claire. It'll be so good to be home.'

'Ah, Charlie,' she said. 'That's great. We've all missed you so much.'

'Of course it'll be a while before I can work again. But one thing at a time. It'll just be nice to be back in Eden. Back with you. And to see my boy.'

After she hung up the phone, Claire slumped into one of the chairs in the dining room. Outside it was a lovely day, sunny with a mottled sky of white, puffy clouds. She ran her hand through her hair and suddenly she could hear her heart beating in her ears, in her throat as well, until it seemed all she could be was heart, throbbing, beating heart. She tried to catch her breath but it was hard. It came in ragged gasps and she was scared, really scared, more scared than she had ever been. She gripped her face in her hands and she wanted to be away, somewhere else, far from here, a place where she had no such problems, where her world was uncomplicated, unfettered.

Claire sat in the chair and looked around the small dining room, the dining room with its tangerine walls and its square tables and in time she heard the sound of Owen's truck tires on the driveway. She rose and went to the kitchen, to the work, determined to pretend for now that nothing had changed. She would try to buy herself some time, see if she could figure things out.

★ ★ ★

All that day she kept the news of Charlie's imminent return to herself. The news of it swirled around in her mind, though if it showed outwardly, Owen did not say anything to her as they worked together. It was a slow night and they were able to close a little early, and Claire drove home to the house on Signal Ridge and checked on Susan, the babysitter, and on her sleeping son and then she took a shower. An hour later she found herself back at Owen's trailer and while they sat outside on the lawn chairs and looked at the night sky, the Big Dipper like a white cage in the blue over the hills, she told him about Charlie's release.

When she mentioned it, Owen sprang out of his chair and loomed over her. A cigarette dangled from his mouth and he took his beer bottle and in a moment of pure rage hurled it with his right hand across the driveway where Claire heard it shatter on the woodpile.

'Fuck,' he said.

Claire looked straight ahead and she did not say anything. She sat still and she could feel his rage all around her, electric and coming off him in waves. She sensed him moving around, back and forth, pacing slightly, and she finally said, 'How do you think I feel?'

'I know,' he said.

'This should hardly be a surprise, Owen. I mean, what did you think, that they were going to keep him there for a year?'

'I know. I know. I — just. I guess I'm not ready for it, that's all.'

Claire sighed. 'It's so sad,' she said. 'It's so sad.'

'It doesn't have to be,' said Owen.

'How?' said Claire and she said it like she meant it, like he had the power to stop sadness, to make it disappear.

Owen got down in front of her in the dark. He stubbed out his cigarette on the ground and he kneeled facing her, supporting himself with his hands on the arms of her chair. He looked at her, looked at her with those green eyes she could barely make out in the dim light.

'We could go,' he said. 'Me and you. We could go. Leave here. Start something together. Build a life.'

'Oh, Owen,' said Claire.

'We could. We really could. I mean, I'm not

291

fucking around with this, you know? I love
you, Claire, I do. And that means more than
anything. With that, nothing can stop us, don't
you see? We just have to think differently.
That's all.'

Claire shook her head and looked away from
him. She looked toward the woods across the
road to her left, a different shade of blackness in
the night. 'It's so simple, isn't it?' she said, her
voice betraying her sarcasm.

'It could be,' Owen said brightly. 'Listen: do
you love me? Answer me that.'

Claire turned back to him, her sarcasm gone
now, and she looked at him, at his handsome
face. She did not hesitate and her words
surprised even her with how easily they came to
her. She said to him, 'Yes. Yes, I do.'

'Then what can stop us? It seems to me that
this is the only thing we can do. And I tell you
one thing: I won't sit here and watch you
pretend to love my brother when you should be
with me.'

'Jesus,' Claire said. 'What does that mean?'

Owen stood up. 'I don't know,' he said and
Claire could sense his anger again and she had
never seen him like this and it frightened her.
But then it was as if he grew aware of her fear
and he knew enough to mediate it. She felt him
calming down before he spoke.

'It doesn't mean anything,' he finally said. 'I
just don't know what to do, Claire. I've never felt
like this before, you have to understand that. I
need you.'

His voice was softer now and Claire said, 'This

is hard for me. I have a son. A husband. Jonah. Charlie.'

Owen kneeled back down. 'I know, baby.'

'I don't know what to do. How can I leave them? What would that say?'

'You know I can't help you with that. All I can say is that I love you.'

Claire shook her head again. 'I don't know what to do,' she repeated.

'Think about it, okay? Just think about it.'

Claire reached out and tousled his hair. 'Okay,' she said and she meant it.

They barely slept that night. Neither of them wanting to give in to sleep as if they sensed that each moment together could be their last. They made love with a fury they had not seen before and when they were finished they lay entwined in wet sheets and rested until the need between them rose again and they moved together once more.

Eventually they lay side by side and Owen wrapped his arms around Claire and she leaned into him and they did not speak, for both of them had heavy thoughts about what was to come. Outside the windows the first growing light of the summer dawn was lifting the darkness. The pre-morning was cool and Owen pulled a blanket over the two of them and in the cold of the breeze that came through the window Claire sensed the first taste of autumn and the winter to follow and she thought then of a small house on the ocean, of the life that Owen had said could be theirs. She thought about what it would be like to spend every night in his arms, to make love to him every morning. To not worry about what others thought for it was their life and nobody else's. She thought about sunsets over the endless ocean and the two of them growing old together but never losing the passion that fueled them on nights like this. She wondered if that was possible or if at some point everyone lost passion and they were too new together to imagine that. She thought about the anonymity that would come from a new place, how they could be anything they wanted; how they could define themselves for themselves; how they could live the life they wanted.

And as Claire thought this, as she lay in the crook of his arm and watched the gray of morning begin to come through the narrow windows, as she watched the languid, diffused light, she decided that maybe it was possible after all, that in this life you could step into the void if you wanted, that you could risk it all for love, that maybe, if given the opportunity, you had to risk it all for love. That sometimes you had to give up a tremendous amount to find what was truly important. Nothing good comes cheap, as her father used to say, though admittedly when he said such things it was never love he was talking about. In this case, the price for love was enormous, maybe unthinkable, but in the end, did she really have a choice? Could she really turn her back on the strongest feelings she had ever had in all her life? On this man who had opened something within her she had not known she was capable of? A man who

294

had taught her to be herself, to feel, truly feel, what passion was?

No, Claire thought, she could not. And there were those who would hate her for it, who would blame her for it, and she knew behind her she would leave pain that would never go away. Pain that would be incomprehensible in its intensity. But there was nothing she could do about that. Claire could not deny the truth in her heart. It was, she understood, a truth greater than all others.

*   *   *

They were subdued that next day in the restaurant kitchen as they worked. Part of it was the exhaustion, the hour or two of sleep they were able to find after a night they did not want to end. Part of it was the weight of thought that they both now collectively carried, what they had settled on in the first gray of morning. What they had agreed upon when they knew they had to agree upon something.

Owen was surprised when Claire told him she would go with him. In the week or so he had been thinking about it, it had always been more fantasy than something that seemed possible. Oh, he wanted it to be true. He wanted to believe that the two of them could leave together, could walk out of Eden and only look forward. But he also knew they each had their history here. And for Claire, a family that was hers, a child no less, and a life outside of him that could not be denied no matter how he wanted that to happen.

And then there was Charlie, his brother, the man who let Owen back into his life when he probably had not earned that kind of trust. Years of disappearing into the world only to return and fall in love with his brother's wife. Didn't he owe Charlie more than that? Had his heart gone that cold?

Yet when Claire told him she would go, he saw all of it and suddenly the absurd appeared plausible, like a beautiful dream that lay in front of them. His reservations moved into the back of his mind as he saw their future together. As he saw happiness.

Owen could tell how scared she was, though he could also tell that she was equally scared of losing him, of what they now had, and he found comfort in this, and the more they talked about it, the more their words started to bring this idea, this plan such as it was, into being.

It was Owen who had proposed that they leave right away.

'It's the only way,' he told her. 'A clean break. You pick up Charlie tomorrow and then we work and after we leave right from Charlotte's. It will be a long time before anyone knows we are gone. Probably the next morning. Maybe the middle of the night if Charlie wakes up. But by that time, we'll be halfway to Florida.'

'I don't think that will work,' said Claire.

'Why not?'

'He'll stay up for me. It's his first night back. I think he would get suspicious.'

Charlie scratched his chin. 'The next morning

then. Here at Charlotte's. We'll just not open that day.'

'It's crazy,' Claire said. 'It's so crazy.'

'We just have to get through the next two days. Then it gets easy. It will be so good. It will. I need you to trust me, though, Claire. Can you do that? Can you trust me?'

'Yes,' Claire said, 'I can trust you, Owen.'

'Good,' he said. 'This can work.'

And then, working in the kitchen, Owen watched Claire and he knew the sobriety of daylight was taking its toll on her. It was also taking its toll on him but he refused to acknowledge it. He did not want to dwell on what they were going to do: he simply wanted to do it. He had faith in how he felt for her. It was, he sometimes thought, the only truly genuine thing that had ever happened to him. And every time he thought of Charlie, or of Jonah, or of Charlotte's, it was what he reminded himself of. Love is not something you can walk away from, he said. It is too important, and too rare, and it makes decisions for you, not you for it. As long as you know this, you know all there is to know and everything will be as it should.

That night, their last together before Charlie returned to Eden, they slept the bone-tired sleep of the exhausted, and even if they had wanted to make love they could not. They rolled into each other and though it was a cold night they left the windows open in the trailer. Cool air ripped through the slat windows and a July drizzle fell without ceremony. They rubbed their bodies together under the heavy blankets and they

297

ignored the rain and the cold and what stood in front of them. Everything was about to change as clearly as the summer was about to become fall, and as the fall would soon become winter. No one knew how it would turn out. All they could do was keep warm, keep each other warm, welcome the sleep when it came, listen to the rain, and hope for the best.

21

In the morning the rain had stopped and a dense fog hung in the green valleys of Vermont as Claire drove to Dartmouth to pick up Charlie. There were few cars on the highway at this time and as she drove she looked at the fog-filled valleys, sometimes getting a glimpse of hills and small towns in the distance, the occasional white steeple of a church rising up below the highway. Behind the wheel of the car she felt suddenly alone in the world, steering up and over these long hills, and she was nervous about seeing her husband. She knew this was silly, it was Charlie she was talking about, but now that she was close, she wondered how obvious it was, her and Owen. She wondered if she smelled like him, like his cigarettes, if she wore his scent on her clothes. She wondered if her betrayal showed in her face, if Charlie would see it in her eyes and know right away what she had done, and what she was about to do.

At the hospital, she met him outside his third-floor room and he was all ready for her, sitting in a wheelchair, talking to one of the nurses. He looked the same as he always had and his arm was bandaged and she felt a shiver run through her when she bent down and kissed him.

'Charlie,' she said.

'Can you believe I got a hurt arm and I have

to be wheeled out of here?' he said with a playful shrug. 'It makes no sense.'

'Those are the rules,' said the nurse and she smiled at Claire as she said it, as if letting her in on a secret.

Claire wheeled her husband out and into the day, which was slowly clearing, though the sky was still a leaden gray. As soon as he reached the pavement, he stood and said, 'That's better. Damn, it's good to be free.'

Charlie put his good arm around her and Claire moved into him for a moment before they separated and headed into the parking lot to find the car.

The whole ride back, Charlie wanted to talk. He was full of questions, one after another. Questions about Jonah, about the restaurant, about deliveries and suppliers, about money and menus, and, yes, about Owen. Claire felt like each word she spoke was a betrayal, and especially when she spoke of Owen. He wanted to know how Owen was adapting in the kitchen and Claire told him he was better each passing day, and she surprised herself with the ease of her words, as if she were talking about someone they had hired, not his brother, her lover, the man she was about to leave him for.

The trip took almost an hour and a half, and by the time they reached the house on Signal Ridge, Claire was exhausted. As they pulled into the driveway, Claire saw that Jonah was outside and she looked at Charlie and saw his face brighten and when he looked this way she suddenly felt a twinge of deep love and regret, and she saw him in that moment as she used to see him, long ago, when they were first together, the strong, capable Charlie, the Charlie who loved her so easily, the Charlie who had brought her into his kitchen, his life. Claire parked the car and Jonah ran to his father and Charlie said, 'Whoa, easy, buddy, bad arm,' and then picked him up anyway with his one good arm, swung the boy around and Claire fought off tears and looked away toward the woods.

An hour later she was at Charlotte's and she was grateful to be here, away from her guilt. She arrived before Owen and when he walked in the door she went to him, wrapped her arms around him and he whispered to her, 'It'll be okay.'

They had much work to do but she needed him that morning and they made love in the pantry, and it was cramped and awkward but she wanted to feel him and she wanted to move and to sweat and to not think. She wanted to come and she surprised herself when she was able to, when she was able to focus enough to crest, and when it spilled over she knew she would weep and she did, clutching Owen tightly, her face mashed against his chest, feeling him dwindle within her, feeling him fall out of her while she fell further into his arms.

They worked in silence most of that day and that night the restaurant was busier than usual and they turned out entrée after entrée, working side by side, efficiently, yet talking little, for they both knew that tonight they would separate, they would sleep away from one another, and in the morning they would leave Eden behind, Claire for the first time, Owen for the last.

Despite the frantic pace in the kitchen, the night seemed to drag on endlessly. Claire tried to think only about the work but she knew she wore her thoughts on her face and she kept having to remind herself to do things that normally came naturally: smile at the waitresses, banter with Joe Collins, pretend Owen was just another cook, someone she worked with.

When they were finally finished, Claire turned down the lights and locked the doors before meeting Owen out in the driveway where he had gone to smoke. Outside it was growing cool and the sky above was overcast, a three-quarters moon appearing now and again as thick clouds moved in front of it. Owen stood by his truck and as Claire walked toward him she could see the glow of his cigarette. She folded her arms over her chest against the cold and when she reached him, they did not speak right away and Owen smoked and she looked past him up the road and listened to the sounds of the night-river cutting through the trees.

Finally Owen tossed his cigarette out into the grass and Claire said, 'Hug me,' and he did, moving into her and taking her into his arms. They stayed like this for what seemed a long time, not moving, a light cool breeze blowing on her hair. Eventually Claire pulled away first, leaned up and kissed him on the lips, tasting his tobacco.

She said, 'It's going to be hard tonight. Being away from you.'

'I know it,' said Owen.

'Tomorrow then?'

'Tomorrow,' he said.

Claire nodded at him. 'I love you,' she said, shrugging her shoulders for she did not know what else to do.

'I love you too,' said Owen.

Claire nodded again, stuffed her hands into the front pockets of her jeans and got into her car, drove back to her family, to the life she was about to depart.

★ ★ ★

Owen had the whiskey and he had his cigarettes and the dark in front of him as he sat on the steps of the trailer and wished the night away. Tomorrow was going to come quick and he found it easiest if he tried not to think about it, though he could not help it. The leaving haunted him. He thought about Claire, how she made him feel, how she opened him up, so that he did not feel guarded around her: for the first time in his life he felt like he could be himself, that in front of him lay a future where he would know what it meant to be happy, truly happy, as he sometimes naively imagined most of the people he knew were.

But in the dark, cloud-filled night, he also thought of Charlie, his brother, once his best friend, and it made him angry that he could not think of Charlie without also now thinking of Claire and her relationship to him. Why hadn't Owen met her first? How easy would that have been? Maybe he could have had both, his brother's friendship and Claire's love. For deep down, was that not what he wanted?

Owen sat and drank and ignored the gathering cold. At one point a great breeze came down across the ridgeline and the trees in front of him bent under its strain, the clouds opening up above and the moon appearing, the forest blue-black in its temporal light. It was the time of year when the wind blew like this and he did not think much of it. The summer was short. Fall was coming. Fall was almost here. He drank the amber whiskey and he steadied himself for sleep. He did not want to dream. Not tonight. He did not want to dream.

★　★　★

Back at the old farmhouse, Claire turned off the remaining lights and closed the open windows in the living room and climbed the stairs. She stopped first at Jonah's room, opened the door slowly and saw that he had fallen asleep with his light on. She went and turned it off and then sat on the bed next to him for a moment. He stirred and she ran her hand through his hair and he smiled slightly, aware of her touch, and she wondered how much he knew about her absence the last few weeks. Claire bent down and kissed him on the cheek, pulled his blankets up a little and left him in the dark.

In the bedroom she shared with Charlie, the lights were already off and she could hear him snoring softly. She stepped gingerly to her closet and took off the kitchen clothes, put on pajamas.

It was strange to wear pajamas suddenly. She had grown so used to wearing nothing to sleep in in such a short amount of time. Lovers didn't wear clothes to bed, she thought, while pajamas were the uniform of the married.

As quietly as she could, Claire lifted the blankets on her side of the bed and climbed under the covers with Charlie. His snoring changed rhythm for a moment but then he was back at it again. She rolled over away from him and she wished she had some kind of sleeping pill or something since she knew rest would probably elude her this night. Through the open window she could just make out where the earth became sky over the hills of Eden. She wondered what Owen was doing and if he was thinking of her the way she thought of him. Behind her, Charlie stopped snoring and Claire froze for some reason, as if he were a stranger, as if she had suddenly realised someone else was in the room. And in a moment he moved into her from behind and she knew he was awake and it was suddenly the familiar feel of him, her husband, and in that moment she knew that the love had not left them completely, that it stood unaltered, the quiet love of the married, a love that paled in intensity to what she had with Owen.

'Hey,' he whispered to her. 'When did you get here?'

'A half-hour ago.'

'Ah, you were quiet.'

Charlie slung his one good arm over her and said, 'It's good to feel you.'

Claire did not say anything. She looked toward

the window and his hands on her, the hands that had always been on her, were not strange hands but she did not want them. Not tonight. She needed time to think. She needed the clarity that sex would not bring. She lied to him.

She said, 'I have my period.' She felt him go still behind her.

'Bad timing,' he said lightly.

'I know,' Claire whispered.

She felt his lips on her neck and he said, 'I love you.'

'Yes,' said Claire and she knew it was not what she was expected to say but she also knew he would not catch it and he did not, and in a short time she heard his snores again, the steady rise and fall of his sleep.

Claire watched the dark outside the window. She listened to the harsh early autumn wind rattle the old twelve-pane windows. She listened to Charlie snoring and suddenly the last three weeks felt like a dream, some kind of strange dream. Her husband was behind her, her child in the other room, a child they had made, a child she was responsible for, and this house, this house that had once belonged to her husband's parents, was hers now, had been hers. This was how it had been for a long time. Together it was a life, and it might not be a perfect life, but she had built it and she thought: I cannot do this. What kind of woman could? What kind of woman could leave a perfectly good man and a beautiful, growing child for the incandescence of new love? All love eventually flamed out, didn't it? Was anything permanent? Wouldn't someday she find herself lying next to Owen and feel the same way she felt about Charlie? Oh yes, she thought, what she had with Charlie might not be exciting, but there was something to be said for the quiet love of two people who had been together for ever, the ease they shared, where she did not ever worry about him, where she took him for granted, not as that sounded, but in a positive sense, in the way you come to rely on the snow of winter and the heat of summer, on the solid warmth of a great meal. He would always be here for her, and did he deserve this, what she was about to do?

But then she thought of Owen and she remembered the feel of his hands on her, the way he looked at her in the deep of night when they lay together on their backs and did not talk and were damp with love and she felt like she had finally become the woman she had given up on long ago, a woman who knew what it felt like to be desired, who knew what it was to be alive, palpably alive, the very touch of her own fingers electric against her skin.

Lying there that night with Charlie behind her, Claire hoped for sleep but she knew it would not come, not with her mind hopping from thought to thought, from fragment of image to fragment of image. She tried to find one to hang on to, one that would carry her through, give her the smallest semblance of peace she thought she needed to move forward, to do what she thought her heart ached for her to do. It came in the form of a vision, more than an image, for it cohered in her mind and for a brief moment it allowed her to forget that she had decisions to make. She saw the house she and Owen had spoken of, a small place where a river met the sea, a simple cape, with a wide porch that looked out on to the bright, sun-splashed ocean. It was just the two of them and the water and the salt spray on days when the wind blew vigorously. All of it was light and beautiful and as possible as Owen had said it was. He was right: there was pain between here and there but she knew she could make it. In her mind she said this to herself. And in time she fell asleep and she drifted in and out of dreams. It was fitful and not good but it was all she could expect.

★   ★   ★

Without sleep there can be no dreams. Sleep was as elusive as the drunkenness he pursued with abandon and would not come the way he wanted it to. There was the dark sky above the trailer and the mountain that he could not see but that he knew loomed behind him, like some giant watching his every move, privy to his every thought. A mountain named Hunger, the most elemental of needs. And there were the memories that were unloosed upon him, memories that flowed as quick as water. He could not run from his past any more than he could run from this mountain. Some things were immutable and that night he saw all of it. He saw himself and Charlie, and he saw his beautiful, gracious mother and he saw the specter of his father. He saw the boy he was and the man he had tried to become. He saw the pain and the sorrow and he saw how he had fled from it, only to return to the place that had spawned it. He saw Claire, wonderful Claire, soulful-eyed Claire, the one who had allowed him to make the decision he was about to make and for the right reasons. And he knew he stood on the cusp of a new life, one he could choose for himself, choose for the first time, for long ago he was too young to understand the true nature of choice. Time had passed and they had all changed — the world had changed around them — and he knew that whichever direction he went in when the sun rose would determine what would become of all of them. He had that power. He wanted to choose right. He wanted to choose love.

Owen did not remember going to sleep but when he woke there was bright sunlight coming through the high windows of the trailer. His mouth was dry and he paused for a moment to gauge the hangover. He had drunk almost a fifth of whiskey and he had got his wish: there were no dreams, though now his head throbbed and it took a second to remember what it was this day meant, and as soon as he did he rose out of the bed and tried to pull himself together. He went through the motions of the morning, grinding beans and making coffee, taking a long piss, checking the weather out the door while he smoked a cigarette. The coffee helped, as did a long shower that he took with the water as hot as he could stand it. When he had finished he placed a towel soaked in cold water around his forehead and when he dressed he felt more like himself, more like he was up to the challenges that the next hours would bring.

As it turned out, it was a perfect day, a perfect Vermont day. Warm but without humidity, sun moving through high clouds. The fog and rain and gray skies of the last several days were nowhere to be found. It was the kind of day that reminded him why he loved Eden, with its deep woods and beautiful green valleys, its rivers and its lakes. Houses set into the landscape as if they had always been there, natural as rock outcroppings.

Owen forced down some stale toast after his coffee and he packed one duffel bag and left everything else in the trailer. He did not care what happened to it. He owned it, yes, but this morning he did not care about owning things.

By the time Owen climbed into his truck he figured he was running late, but when he looked at the clock he realised it was not even ten. He was early and that was okay too, for he wanted to wait for Claire, and not the other way around.

He drove under the bright blue sky down the dirt mountain road and out on to the Old County Road. To his left were the mountains and above them a bank of heavy white clouds stood still. To his right was the Dog River, meandering through the woods, in places right next to the road, in other places out of sight. He drove and he smoked and he thought. He was aware of his heart now, as if it were all he was, the steady beating of it, blood flowing through him, his limbs leaden with weight he could not explain.

As he rounded the bend and the road opened

310

up in front of him, he saw Charlotte's now, saw it on the side of the road, in front of the floodplain, and it occurred to him that this might be the last time he would ever see it. Even when he was in other parts of the world, he had always known he would come back here. Now Owen figured that opportunity was no longer his. He pulled into the parking lot. He stopped the truck and stepped out.

Owen stood next to his truck and he looked down the long narrow valley that led to Hunger Mountain. The sun was still low in the sky but was warm on his face, on his arms.

He turned and looked at the small schoolhouse, the red door, the chimney, and behind it the floodplain and the river. It was a beautiful spot and he saw it this morning as others might see it, as his father saw it many years ago on a hunting trip from New York, a trip when he had decided he had to have it. It made sense here, it all fitted together. The schoolhouse on the river, the valley, the mountain looming over all of it. It had been his father's and his mother's and now it was Charlie's. It was never going to be Owen's and he knew that now. And that was okay, he thought, for some things were more important than restaurants, regardless of what his father might have thought. Claire had taught him that, and feeling the sun warming his skin, he was grateful for knowing it.

And then there was the waiting, the waiting for her to arrive. All of him hurt and he knew it was not about to get easier. He had done difficult things in his life, though they had been things he

311

had done for himself and himself only. This was different and he knew that but it did nothing to soften what he was about to do. He braced himself.

Owen turned back toward the road and he heard her before he saw her, the distinct sound of car tires on the hardened dirt road. Her Subaru came around the bend and she pulled into the parking lot and came to a stop. He saw her through the glass and she smiled at him and he was too far away to see how clenched her smile was, though he suspected that she was feeling this as much as he was, probably more.

Owen watched as Claire got out of the car, opened the back door and took out a duffel bag not unlike his own. Her hair was down and she wore a white T-shirt and jeans, the men's work-boots she wore when she cooked. The sun caught her face just right, her hair and her eyes, and he felt something give within himself as he looked at her. Owen smiled at her as she walked toward him and she smiled back and he saw now that she had been crying and before he could say anything she said, 'It's all going to be okay, right? Tell me it's all going to be okay.'

Owen watched her come to him. When she was a foot away, he said, 'It's all going to be okay.'

Claire dropped her bag on the ground and she stood in front of him and there were lines on her forehead, crow's feet and lines that shot out from under her eyes, and in the bright sunlight he saw the first strands of silver in her hair and he had never noticed them before. She was more remarkable than she had ever been and he looked at her and he knew she was about to hug him and he needed to say what he needed to say before she did. He needed to tell her what he had decided and the words when they came were distant to him, as if being uttered by someone else.

Owen said, 'You're not coming.'

Claire looked puzzled for a moment, her eyes widening, and then Owen saw her face go slack and he expected the anger to come then. He expected her to hit him, as she had sometimes during sex, though he knew that came from a different place. Instead, her body suggested resignation and she looked away and he heard her sobs then, and the slight choking in her throat when one cries too hard and when she spoke it was almost a whisper, her voice low and husky. She said, 'I know.'

'You brought a bag,' said Owen.

'I didn't know until I got here.'

Owen nodded. 'It was a long night.'

'Me too,' said Claire, and she looked back at him now and the tears filled her big dark eyes and he wanted her tears to go away but he knew that sometimes you had to cry for things if they were important, and this was important.

'You belong here,' Owen said. 'You do. You know it as much as I do.'

'But so do you,' she said. 'Why are you different?'

'You know I can't stay.'

Owen stepped toward her. He placed his hands on the outsides of her arms and she was sobbing hard now and she felt as fragile as a bird to him, as if she might collapse under his touch. 'It's okay,' he said. 'I was part of this place once but no longer. And sometimes it's hard to figure things out. I don't belong here, Claire, I don't. I don't know where I'm supposed to go. Maybe the ocean, maybe not. But I know now that it's not here and that I cannot take you with me. Charlie loves you. He deserves you. And as much as it hurts me to know this, I know you love him too. I've seen it. I saw it the first time I saw you together. The way you looked at him.'

Claire looked up at him and she wiped hard at her eyes. 'I love you,' she said and her arms fell to her side and as she rocked slightly Owen put his arms around her and pulled her to him, and he saw that she was biting her lip, but still the tears would not stop. He held her as hard as he could, as tightly as he could. She shook in his arms. He was happy to hold her for it allowed him to ignore the fact that he felt like he might crack himself. He could take care of her and pretend that he did not hurt as bad as he did, as bad as he ever had, and by so doing he kept himself from completely falling apart.

'What's going to happen to us?' Claire asked into his chest.

'We're going to be fine,' Owen said. 'We're all going to be fine.'

He held her tighter, his face pressed against the top of her head, his own tears leaving his eyes for the curls of her hair.

★ ★ ★

In the end, Owen knew it was the only thing to do. The night before he had not had to worry about dreams for the sleep would not come and he sat haunted by his thoughts, by his memories. He stayed up most of the night and as he imagined and wished for a life with Claire, he saw the lives left behind, he saw Charlie and he saw Jonah and he knew Charlie had done nothing to him that could equal what he was about to do. Yes, Charlie had got the restaurant, but you could not possibly compare a building, a business, with the love of any woman, let alone a woman like Claire. No, thought Owen, he had done nothing to deserve her, to deserve her grace and her beauty and as much as he wanted her, he knew he could not have her. Her life was here with Charlie, with her son, their family, and maybe Charlotte's had already taken one family apart, maybe this was what that business did, but Owen, looking out into the blackness and drinking his whiskey, was not ready to see it take another. He owed his brother more than that and it had taken him a long time to realise this. He owed Claire more than this as well. She had taught him so much and while it was probably not a gift that was his to give, he knew on some level that he could not take her away from her child, from her future.

Instead, he had decided he would leave again and like the first time he would leave alone. Though he also was wise enough to understand that this was where the similarities between his youth and now ended.

The first time he had left he was just a boy

and he knew nothing of the world and he set out because he hurt and because of the pain and he chose the life he did because he wanted to keep moving, as if in the constant motion he did not need to be open to anything, he could stay closed to all but those things right in front of him: the ocean, the expanse of ship, the galley kitchen, smoking under the great arch of stars at night. Days followed days and there was no meaning and no purpose and in this he found solace for he did not have to love anyone and he did not have to lose anyone. He did not have to care and when you think this way you can never have pain beyond the physical though you can never feel joy either.

Now he would leave and he would leave with an open heart, a heart opened by Claire, and when your heart is open you cannot only think for yourself. You see the web of things, see them for yourself. You see where one person ends and another begins. You see what ties us not only to the land and to the water but to each other. And when you have this sight, you learn to love as well as to see, and when you learn to love, you learn that love carries with it responsibility and an obligation to do your best.

This was what Owen realised that night as he looked at the high-clouded sky above him and he listened to the wind rifling through the treetops. Suddenly his choices were clear. And while he wanted to be sad because he was about to leave Claire, he knew he was gaining something far more important. His brother would now be his brother; Eden would be Eden; and freedom and truth and a life unburdened by the past beckoned. He wanted to explain all this to Claire but he knew she would not understand. Not yet anyway. She needed time as they all did. He only hoped that some day she would understand what she had done for him, how she had freed him to be himself, in a way that no one else had ever done.

In the parking lot that morning, Owen did not leave Claire until he was certain she would be okay. He did not leave until he was certain she would not do anything drastic. He held her as long as he could. It took everything he had to hold it together and he knew he could not last for long. When he finally got into his truck and drove out of the parking lot he told himself not to look back, just don't look back, he thought, but it was not that easy. There was so much behind him and he needed to look. It was only human. And so he looked and he saw Claire standing next to her car, and he saw Charlotte's behind her, and he saw the trees and a ribbon of the river and it was all he needed to see. Above him the sun shone brightly and on the hills in front of him he could see the first sign of color, a touch of red here and there. It spoke of things to come, the change that this time of year always brought. He drove fast, pushing the truck around the corner and out of sight, following the Dog River as it ran away from the mountains, as it ran out of Eden.

Epilogue

They came with regularity, every six months or so, though they were in envelopes now, and he took the time to tell them about his house, how he had had it built on stilts so that the tide could roll right under it. He told them about the fish he caught in the brackish water that ran through the tidal river here and he told them about how he prepared them, simply, lemon and oil, salt and pepper and a hot grill. He told them about the sunrise, how he never got tired of watching it rise up over the water, its golden light on the flowing reeds at the mouth of the river.

For their part, it was Charlie who wrote back. Charlie who wrote Owen and told him to get a phone like a normal person so they could talk more regularly, not only when they had time to write letters. It was Charlie who told him to come back to Eden.

But both of them knew he would probably not take them up on the offer, though Charlie held out hope. Claire fully expected never to see him again.

The summer after Jonah turned sixteen he began to work at the restaurant. He was a tall, gawky kid, with his mother's eyes and his father's build, though he had not filled out yet. Charlie and Claire told him he did not have to be in the restaurant if he did not want to, but Jonah insisted it was what he wanted to do and at night lying in bed Charlie and Claire would talk about it, and when Charlie suggested it would be better if he worked somewhere else, if he had a chance at a different life before he committed to the one they knew, Claire said, 'We shouldn't choose for him. It's what he wants.'

And so they taught him, as they had been taught. Every morning that summer, Claire gave her son blind baskets and she saw that he had the gift, the intuitive gift that his father had, and that she had been told his grandfather had as well. He saw the dishes in front of him as soon as she lifted the towel off the basket, and when Claire watched him cook, watched him follow with great logic the movement from raw ingredients to finished food on the plate, she was humbled by it.

And in her son she saw herself as she had been many years ago, when she first walked through the doors of this old schoolhouse and fell in love first with a restaurant and second with a man. She remembered how everything had felt back then, how it felt to wake every morning and want to be in this warm room with its view of the river, the light streaming through the windows on to the old wideboard floors. She remembered how it felt to get better each day, to learn from Charlie. She remembered how much she loved the heat of the stove, the agile play of cooking so many dishes at once, her personal high-wire act. And she remembered how tired she was at night, the beautiful kind of tired where you knew you had worked hard, where you knew you had earned the tiredness and the day passed was a day you were proud of. By watching her son, by overseeing his tutelage, she realised she could feel all this again, feel it through his eyes.

And she knew she had Owen to thank for this. He had come to her at a time when she had fallen asleep and he had woken her. There were times when she missed his touch, the beauty of his love-making, but that was mostly long ago, when he first left and there were nights that she lay in bed and remembered what it was like to be beneath him. Where she closed her eyes and imagined him moving over her. Nights when she wondered about him, where he was. This was the time before the letters started, letters that when they came she stole from Charlie and read over and over again in the tub.

In time this all became clear to her. It seemed sudden, but in fact it was the accrual of knowledge that comes with the passing of the years. She could see his true gift to her. He had allowed her to be at peace, to know what she had. He had taught her to see again. He had showed her how to love. Claire understood that she had helped him too, that in her arms he had found what he needed to move on, to forget the past. What they had shared belonged to a particular time and place and she knew this now and she did not want for anything. She had a good husband, a good house, a good restaurant, a good son, a good life. She had made mistakes but it was time to forget them. Charlie needed her. Jonah needed her. Charlotte's needed her. Eden was her home.

Everything was right here.

Author's Note

With deep gratitude I would like to thank Kate Elton and Georgina Hawtrey-Woore at Arrow Books for their patience, understanding and editorial wisdom. Without their support, this novel would not have come so fully to life.

I also want to thank Nick Ellison, my agent, for being my patron, my friend and helping my work find an audience.

I want to acknowledge John McPhee's excellent book, *Looking for a Ship*, which was my source for all things related to the Merchant Marines.

Finally, I want to say that while *After the Rain* is set in Eden, Vermont, it is not meant to accurately reflect the actual geography of that quite real northern Vermont town. Instead I have used real landmarks, invented landmarks, and places I see every day to create the terrain of my imagination and to tell the story of Charlie, Claire and Owen.

Thomas Christopher Greene
Montpelier, Vermont
May 7, 2004

We do hope that you have enjoyed reading this large print book.

Did you know that all of our titles are available for purchase?

We publish a wide range of high quality large print books including:
**Romances, Mysteries, Classics
General Fiction
Non Fiction and Westerns**

Special interest titles available in large print are:
**The Little Oxford Dictionary
Music Book
Song Book
Hymn Book
Service Book**

Also available from us courtesy of Oxford University Press:
**Young Readers' Dictionary
(large print edition)
Young Readers' Thesaurus
(large print edition)**

For further information or a free brochure, please contact us at:
**Ulverscroft Large Print Books Ltd.,
The Green, Bradgate Road, Anstey,
Leicester, LE7 7FU, England.
Tel:** (00 44) 0116 236 4325
Fax: (00 44) 0116 234 0205

Other titles published by
The House of Ulverscroft:

MIRROR LAKE

Thomas Christopher Greene

Nathan Carter is a young man in love with falling in love. A serial monogamist, he flits from woman to woman until, as yet another relationship disintegrates, he leaves his busy Boston lifestyle behind him and drives north to the small town of Eden, Vermont. There he meets Wallace Fiske, a man at the end of his life, a man with a story to tell. And as Wallace starts to tell Nathan the story of Nora, the woman he loved from the moment he first set eyes on her, the two men become friends. It's a friendship — and a story — that will change Nathan forever . . .

ITALIAN FEVER

Valerie Martin

Thirtysomething New Yorker Lucy Stark leads a quiet, solitary life working for a bestselling — but remarkably untalented — writer. When he dies at a villa in Tuscany, Lucy flies to Italy to settle his affairs. What begins as a grim chore soon threatens her self-reliance and her very sense of reality. The villa harbours secrets: a missing manuscript, neighbours whose Byzantine arrogance veils a dark past, a phantom whose nocturnal visits tear a gaping hole in Lucy's well-honed scepticism. And to complicate matters: Massimo, a married man whose tender attentions render Lucy breathless.